Lightning Strike

OTHER FIVE STAR WESTERN TITLES BY LAURAN PAINE:

Tears of the Heart (1995); *Lockwood* (1996); *The White Bird* (1997); *The Grand Ones of San Ildefonso* (1997); *Cache Cañon* (1998); *The Killer Gun* (1998); *The Mustangers* (1999); *The Running Iron* (2000); *The Dark Trail* (2001); *Guns in the Desert* (2002); *Gathering Storm* (2003); *Night of the Comancheros* (2003); *Rain Valley* (2004); *Guns in Oregon* (2004); *Holding the Ace Card* (2005); *Feud on the Mesa* (2005); *Gunman* (2006); *The Plains of Laramie* (2006); *Halfmoon Ranch* (2007); *Man from Durango* (2007); *The Quiet Gun* (2008); *Patterson* (2008); *Hurd's Crossing* (2008); *Rangers of El Paso* (2009); *Sheriff of Hangtown* (2009); *Gunman's Moon* (2009); *Promise of Revenge* (2010); *Kansas Kid* (2010); *Guns of Thunder* (2010); *Iron Marshal* (2011); *Prairie Town* (2011); *The Last Gun* (2011); *Man Behind the Gun* (2012)

Lightning Strike

A Western Duo

Lauran Paine

FIVE STAR
A part of Gale, Cengage Learning

W

GALE
CENGAGE Learning

Detroit • New York • San Francisco • New Haven, Conn • Waterville, Maine • London

GALE
CENGAGE Learning

Set in 11 pt. Plantin.

LIBRARY OF CONGRESS CATALOGING-IN-PUBLICATION DATA

Paine, Lauran.
Lightning Strike : a western duo / by Lauran Paine. — 1st ed.
p. cm.
ISBN 978-1-4328-2565-2 (hardcover) — ISBN 1-4328-2565-8 (hardcover)
I. Paine, Lauran. Dawn rider. II. Title.
PS3566.A34L53 2012
813'.54—dc23 2011051013

First Edition. First Printing: June 2012.
Published in 2012 in conjunction with Golden West Literary Agency.

Printed in Mexico
1 2 3 4 5 6 7 16 15 14 13 12

CONTENTS

★ ★ ★ ★ ★

The Dawn Rider

★ ★ ★ ★ ★

I

The light came slowly, as it usually did in late springtime, spectacular only if a person stood perfectly still and watched it arrive, cool, clean, subtly shading through an entire spectrum of pastels, bringing back form and depth and substance to a world lost in night, to the lift of ancient mountains and to the run of tawny plain. There was no time of day—or life, for that matter—to compare with first awakening, even though it went largely ignored, even though it brought unending promise of better things, and, when each day was ruined and stained and dishonored by man, day in and day out, that same unendingly patient promise returned at first light the very next morning. It was a time of day for people to appreciate only if they understood its deeper symbolism. It wasn't just the coolest time of day in summer or the advent of daylight in winter; it was God's promise to Man that something, whatever Man chose to call it, really was everlasting.

That was how the dawn rider's father had explained it to him back in Missouri a couple of years before the Jayhawker attack when Kansas Abolitionists torched the soddy's roof, then shot everyone who ran out by the light of the flames. A lot of things a man's father tells him aren't really appreciated or really understood, until he examines them quietly and lengthily in retrospect. Since that day, some years back, the dawn rider had made it a point to ride through the cathedral hush and soft-toned brilliance at dawn, until he understood exactly.

There was another good reason for riding right at first light. Few people were abroad then and a man could move almost invisibly even across open country. There was still that matter of the stalking and killing of those three Kansas Jayhawkers. All had been shot fairly, but the last one to die did not do so for several hours. He was the one who had named and described his killer, and in Kansas it made no difference that each man had been called out fairly and squarely because no damned Secession sympathizer could legally take the life of an Abolitionist, not anywhere north of the Mason-Dixon Line, not even now, long after the Civil War had been fought down to the last bitter skirmish, because the Abolitionists had won, which gave them the right to carry their vengeance as far and wide, and for as long, as they wished to.

All that had, of course, been long ago. The dawn rider had been barely sixteen years old when he had killed the last of his victims, and now he was about thirty. But, although his conscience was clear—it had never really bothered him—the Kansas authorities still had him on their law books and he knew for a fact that somewhere up ahead in his life, one of those old Wanted flyers would turn up, even this much later. There had been an awful lot of them mailed out. Twice, in Texas, he had been presented with copies, both times by sympathetic Secesh Texans who had been amused at the fierce wording of the flyers. They said: *Wanted For Murder In Kansas, John Lee Tipton. One Thousand Dollars Reward Dead Or Alive. Dangerous. Approach With Caution.* What had amused those Texan range men had been the fact that, when he had hired on with them to drive cattle, he had been eighteen years old, and they had all been veterans of the War Between the States, men at that time no less than thirty-five, with several a bit older. It had amused them that Kansans as old as they were, and who'd presumably been through as much fire and shot and shell, would consider an eighteen-year-old that dangerous. Then there had been the gunfight at Tanque Verde near the Mexican border when John Lee Tipton had outdrawn and had outshot the big, pock-marked Mexican *rurale* officer who had been notorious on both sides of the line as one of the fastest and deadliest men alive.

When he quit to head on west two weeks later, the cow-camp *cocinero,* a grizzled old man named Ellis Franklyn, originally a Tennessean, had taken him aside and had lectured him, hard.

"Now, boy, you listen to me. I'm an old man and I've seen just about all of it, and I can tell you right now that maybe one man out of a thousand is borned with the kind of co-ordination you got, to draw faster 'n' shoot straighter than most folks. Now, boy, maybe you think it's a great gift, and, bein' young and all, you'll let your spurs out a notch like a banty rooster. But you listen, now. That ain't a gift, it's a curse. The best thing you can ever do is try as hard as you can to forget you got it. It's no good. Not even was you to serve the law, it wouldn't be no good. Killin' folks isn't anything to be proud of . . . ever. Not even in a damned war. For you, with that silly damned Wanted flyer followin' you around, it's a lot worse. You go off, now, and you change your name, and you don't let your spurs out a notch, and you step wide every time there's trouble . . . or son, as sure as you're a foot tall, you're goin' to end up like a lot of other pretty good young bucks who got marked through no fault of their own by a stinkin' political war. Like the James boys and a lot of others. . . . Son, I'm not a prayin' man, but I'll say one for you tonight. Good bye, and good luck."

Not many tall, lean, sun-browned top hands without a tie in this world were ever completely without some kind of a grudge. Neither was John Lee Tipton. But there was something else young bucks learned in the cow camps and cow towns and corral lots where everything and everyone was dominated by masculinity: respect. The old cow-camp cook, Ellis Franklyn, menial though his vocation was, had the respect of a lot of very good men, which was good enough for John Lee Tipton, so he remembered, and he obeyed. By the time he entered western Arizona he had become John Randolph.

Randolph had been his mother's family name. She had originally come from the Carolinas, which was about all he knew of her antecedents, except that one time she had told him there were a lot of Randolphs around the Carolina coastlands all the way from Charleston up to Wilmington.

He had been John Randolph now for a long time. He had never returned to Texas, although he'd considered it a time or two, and he had never returned to Missouri, which he had never considered. Missouri was next door to Kansas, and maybe all the intervening years had changed things—they undoubtedly had—but whether he had committed murder or not, as long as the law said he had, then his name would still be there, along with the reward, which was a lot of money. Enough, for a fact, to inspire someone to try and collect it.

He had changed considerably, but the thing still hung there, above his head. He probably wouldn't be recognized, nor even remembered very well for that matter, back in either Missouri or Kansas, but as he had often told his saddle horse, what was the point in running the risk when there was absolutely no reason for doing it? There wasn't a damned thing back in Missouri he wanted to see. In fact, Missouri was about the only place he'd ever been that held things he never wanted to see again.

He had worked ranges from the Canadian line southward, but he hadn't been back in northwestern Arizona in quite a few years. In fact, not since he'd headed west out of Texas as a rawboned, lanky youngster. But it hadn't changed much.

He sat his saddle atop a little bald hill looking out over a huge run of southward grass country that he dimly remembered from his first trip, with a very faint splash of pre-dawn softness brightening the still countryside. There was a set of buildings below and out a couple of miles. There were some horses to the northwest, and on southward, slightly to the east, were some red, rusty specks that were cattle, but they were even farther off.

That was the Harding Ranch down there, but maybe now, after so many years, old man Harding, who had been grizzled and lined when John Randolph had first hired on over ten years back, would be dead. He'd had a son about John Randolph's age in those earlier days; they had worked together at gathers, on drives, at the branding and marking fires. They had even sneaked away one breathless hot summer night and had ridden southwest to the town of Cottonwood, had bought a bottle, and on the way back had got so drunk together that, as Frank Harding had said afterward, neither one of them had been able to hit the ground with his hat. What Frank hadn't said was that both he and John Randolph had lied up and down the next day, blaming their shakes and sweats and upset stomachs on some bad water they'd drunk on the range.

John laughed to himself, now; they hadn't fooled old man Harding one bit. John knew it now, but back in those earlier days he and Frank had been sure they had fooled Frank's father. One thing John Randolph had learned that night was never drink on an empty stomach, and never drink too much. It had been a good lesson, well learned. He had evolved into a sparing drinker as a result of that episode. In fact, after that, when he had quit to drift north and see what the Wyoming-Montana cow country looked like, he hadn't been able even to smell whiskey for almost two years without getting queasy in the stomach all over again.

Well, Frank was probably running the outfit now. John Randolph eased his powerful bay horse ahead and downward, remembering a lot of other incidents from those earlier days. It was a little like growing young all over again.

By the time he reached the wide, deep grasslands, he was recalling some of the elaborate tricks the older range men had played on both him and Frank. It was the custom for riders to teach young buckaroos humility and respect in this manner. Sometimes the lessons were pretty damned painful, but that only made them harder to forget. Well, those old riders, too, would be gone now. He'd encountered a few of them elsewhere over the years, but not lately. It was a strange thing how old cowboys just seemed to fade out. A man heard of them, old friends and acquaintances, over the years, then he began to hear less and less about them, and finally, one day, he might be riding along and suddenly think of someone he'd liked at some ranch bunkhouse or some cow camp, and it would hit him hard that he hadn't heard a word about that old boy in a couple of years. And he would never hear of him again, either.

II

Whatever caused them, and no one seemed to know, not even the sage of the Cottonwood Basin cow country, Dr. Jennings, freckles seemed about as equally divided between the young boys and the young girls. The boys weren't concerned, and some of the girls weren't, either, at first, but as soon as the girls got to be about twelve or thirteen years old, they had a way of driving their mothers to the verge of fits sending off for freckle cures, asking everyone if they knew if calamine lotion or *Doctor Kendall's Indian-Root Remedy* would dissolve them, and sometimes they even created concoctions of their own, like Connie Harding was doing, very secretly of course, at the creek-bank, when she looked up and froze, because directly across from her stood a large, dark-skinned, smoke-eyed range rider she had never seen before. She'd been too occupied or she probably would have heard him approaching because he had spurs on his boots, and was leading a powerfully muscled bay horse behind him. Then she saw his gaze drop to her mixing bowl, to the unappetizing, sticky mess she'd made from creek-bank clay, pounded willow roots, and water, and got as red as a beet.

Connie was thirteen with reddish-auburn hair like her mother, and cornflower-blue eyes, plus freckles. She was tall and long-legged, and up until about a year back she could have been mistaken for a boy very easily. Now, that was changing—a little anyway.

She looked down at her mixing bowl and said—"Howdy."—to the man across the creek. He studied her a long while before answering.

"Howdy, young lady."

She looked up. "It's not mud pies. I'm much too old to be making mud pies."

The large man said—"Oh."—and loosened his stance, hooked thumbs in his gun belt, and continued to regard the grayish concoction in the mixing bowl. "Maybe I hadn't ought to ask what it is," he murmured.

Connie's color still burned red, only now she also got very uncomfortable, too. "Well!" she exclaimed, then let the word hang by itself a moment or two. "Well . . . it's a freckle cure."

Again the large, solemn man said: "Oh." But this time he raised his eyes to her face, where the freckles were. "Does it work?"

"I haven't tried it yet," she murmured, rearing back on her haunches a little to shoot him a look. He hadn't laughed at her, and, as near as she could tell right now, he didn't look like he was going to laugh at her. Nothing under the sun cut as deeply or pained as long as ridicule, when a person was thirteen, and budding.

The man dropped his gaze to the bowl again. "What all is in it?"

Connie squirmed. "Creek clay. That's to dry 'em. And willow root. That's to draw 'em out where the clay can dry 'em. And branch water. That's all."

The man said: "Sounds workable." He looked at her face again. "What's your name?"

"Connie Harding."

"Connie, tell me something. What's wrong with freckles?"

She looked a little flintily at him. She'd been asked that before, and of course it was always asked by older people who did not *have* freckles. "I don't like 'em," she replied. "If folks like 'em, why then they're welcome to 'em. Only, I don't like 'em."

The big cowboy again said—"Oh."—and seemed quite willing to accept Connie's explanation. He raised his head to gaze beyond the creek willows over to the buildings. "Folks home, Connie?"

"My mother's home." Connie leaned to let creek water wash the mud from her hands. "Mister, are you going over there? Well, if you do, will you do me a favor?"

He was willing. "Sure. Be right proud to."

"Well, please don't tell my mother what I was doing down here at the creek."

The man pondered that briefly, then turned back to his horse as he said: "I won't. Don't worry about it." But after he'd stepped up over leather, he sat a moment, gazing down at her, then he said: "I'll tell you something, Connie. I *like* freckles." Then he reined away down toward the log bridge, clumped across it, and rode on over into the ranch yard. Connie watched his progress all the way to the tie rack out front of the main house. When he dismounted, and mounted the three wide steps to the verandah, her mother came out. The cowboy was an easy head taller than her mother. He was, in fact, as tall as Connie's father had been.

Connie turned back and glumly considered her bowl full of thick mud. He wouldn't tell her mother, but maybe even if he *did* tell her, nothing would be said. Not very much anyway. Lately, her mother had been busy with a lot of things that ordinarily didn't come up this time of year. As Earl Buscomb, their hired rider, had said a week earlier, ordinarily cattle ranching is nothing more than doing the same things, the *right* things over and over again, year in and year out, in a kind of natural sequence that went with the weather. In the winter the cattle were held on good feed; in the springtime they were driven to the early feed; in late spring, when all the calves were on the ground, there was the branding and marking bee; in late summer the critters were pushed to the uplands where there was both browse and still some green graze, and that was also culling and readying time. One thing followed another, by seasons. A man didn't have to be real smart to be a successful cowman, he just had to remember the sequence, and do it *right.*

But that was exactly the trouble. Beverly Harding was not a man. She pointed toward the squared-off place where the paling fence was when John Randolph asked about Frank. "Over there," she said quietly, "beside his father," and dropped her arm.

John looked a long while. He hadn't expected the old man still to be around, but it had never for one instant crossed his mind Frank wouldn't still be around. When the shock passed, he said: "How long ago, ma'am?"

"Almost five years, Mister Randolph."

Her tan-tawny eyes lingered on his face as though something had suddenly come out of a very dim past. "Mister Randolph, by any chance are you the man my husband got drunk with for the first time when he was eighteen?"

John turned slowly back. "Yes'm." He didn't smile because right then it would have been hard to do. He considered the hat in his gloved hands. "Well, Missus Harding, I was just passing by. . . ."

She kept looking at him, hard. "Mister Randolph, I need a rider. I was going to have Earl, the only rider who still works here, hitch the top buggy for me, then I was going to Cottonwood a little later in the morning and see if there were any unemployed riders around. There usually are, this time of year. . . . If you'd be interested . . . ?"

He'd had that in mind, as a matter of fact, when he'd come down off that northward hillock an hour or so earlier. He'd changed his mind the moment he'd discovered that the Harding Ranch was now being ramrodded by a woman. There were some things range riders simply did not do, and working for a she boss was one of them.

He said: "I appreciate the offer." He dropped the hat upon the back of his head with an air of finality.

Her tan-tawny eyes showed bleak irony. "I understand, Mister Randolph."

He went back down into the dust at the foot of the steps. "You shouldn't have any trouble in town. Like you said, this time of year there are usually plenty of men looking for riding jobs."

She kept looking squarely at him. "Yes, of course. And I'm sorry you arrived five years too late. Frank told me some of the things you and he did. He always thought you might drift back someday."

John Randolph settled across the saddle, touched his hat brim to her, and without a word turned to re-trace his steps to the creek and on across the logs again to the far side. He was upon the far side, out perhaps a hundred yards from the yard when he heard the grunts and groans and fierce, hard bursts of expelled breath upstream a short distance. It sounded like a fight was in progress up there where the young girl had been. He reined toward those sounds and pushed through the willows.

It was a fight. A tousle-headed blond boy and Connie Harding were locked in what must have seemed to them like a life-and-death struggle. They were evenly matched for height and probably years, but the boy was stringier, more sinewy, and fast. John Randolph swung down, plowed across the creek, grabbed the boy by the belt and shirt, and lifted him two feet in the air. The lad was so astonished he hung up there like a skewered mantis, twisting around to see who had him. Then he suddenly started fighting again. John Randolph turned and pitched him into the creek. He bleated once, then the water closed over him, and until he surfaced twenty feet downstream he couldn't bleat again.

Connie was breathing hard. She probably should have been quaking and sobbing. Instead, she stood up, muddy and scratched and fighting mad. When the boy surfaced, she hurled an epithet at him as he made a water-logged exit into the far willows. "Damn you, Howard Tandy, the next time I'll chew both your ears off!"

John Randolph blinked, then looked around. There was a fishing pole made of creek willow lying nearby, and upon the opposite bank farther upstream a sorrel horse stood in speckled tree shade, watching everything with frank interest.

The boy did not shout back, but, when Connie picked up his fishing pole and hurled it like a javelin across the creek, he darted from the covert to retrieve it, then he slipped swiftly up to the sorrel horse, clambered aboard, and loped away.

Connie looked at herself. She had mud from the knees up, one pigtail was loose, the blue ribbon gone, and her mixing bowl was visible at the bottom of the clear water. She glared upward, still rigid with fury. "I've told him never to come over here to fish."

John Randolph continued to gaze downward. "Did he hurt you?"

She snorted. "Him! He couldn't hurt a fly! He said he could fish anywhere he pleased, so I dared him to come over on this side. He came over, and I caught him a good one just as he was stepping up out of the water. Right in the mouth."

"You hit him first, Connie?"

"Well of course. You didn't expect me to wait around until he hit me, did you?"

The willows parted and Beverly Harding appeared, looking anxious. She saw her disheveled daughter, saw John Randolph, and stopped dead still. "What happened? Connie . . . look at you!"

John Randolph shoved back his hat. "I thought I was saving her from a boy named Howard Tandy. Only it turned out I was saving him. Maybe I was a little rough on him, ma'am. I flung him in the creek when I broke it up." He rolled his eyes around to Connie. "Where did you learn to swear?"

Beverly Harding's tanned, handsome face turned stormy. "Connie! What did you say?"

The girl gave John Randolph a furious look before facing her mother. "All I said was 'damn you' and that's not really swearing. I've heard Earl say it lots of times. Day before yesterday, when his horse stepped on Earl's foot, he said a lot worse."

Beverly Harding raised her eyes to John Randolph and tried an embarrassed smile. "I'm sorry you had to get mixed up in this." She shook her head exasperatedly. "I'm glad I only have this one. Any more and I don't know what I'd do."

John stood hip-shot and thoughtful for a moment, then he said: "I'd like to ask a question, ma'am. Does Earl run the outfit, or do you?"

She must have guessed at least part of what was behind the

question because she looked him squarely in the eye when she said: "I do." Then, unexpectedly, her tough, almost defiant look weakened and she said: "But you can, Mister Randolph."

Connie's mouth dropped open. She looked very slowly from her mother to the big range man with the smoky eyes, then back to her mother again. They had a pact; they had made it when Connie had been very young and her father had died. No matter what, she and her mother would keep the ranch, and they would operate it. A lot of times since, when they'd both gone with Earl to gather cattle, they had reiterated it between them.

John Randolph smiled for the first time. "All right. I'll ride back and set up in the bunkhouse."

Connie stared at her mother and did not utter a sound.

III

Earl Buscomb had been on the Harding Ranch for seven years, almost eight years by this springtime. He was a thick, powerful, graying man, about forty years old, six feet tall, and about two hundred pounds in heft. When he shook John Randolph's hand inside the bunkhouse, he looked both a little skeptical and pleased. "There've been others, over the years," he told John as he shed his gun and belt, draped his black hat upon the horn rack, then went to stir life into the firebox of the stove and make a fresh pot of coffee. "They come and go. It's not the work. There's plenty of that, though, to keep three, four fellers humping. Mostly I just do what can't stand going undone too long. But you're lucky. We put the cattle on spring feed last week. Me and the missus and Connie. So now, I reckon, except for keeping an eye on 'em down there, you and me can do some of the jobs that've been piling up all winter."

Earl was a likeable, pleasant, tolerable man. Maybe, years back, he'd been different, but when the gray sprouts, if a man is still chousing cows, he's learned that the things that anger younger men just aren't really worth fretting about any more. The sun still comes, the seasons still change, calves drop, the wolves get a few head; the cycle keeps right on moving along.

John had taken an empty bunk near the door. Earl had the bunk that usually signified seniority—next to the stove. Getting acquainted was not hard; it seldom was on a cow outfit. They wrestled up some fried potatoes and stringy beef and sat to talk over coffee, when darkness settled down.

Earl had been hired by Frank. He had, he said, stayed on mainly because he was getting a little long in the tooth to be competing each springtime with the younger riders. Then he lit a cigarette, looked steadily across the table, and said: "And, hell, no one else stays long on an outfit run by a woman." He seemed to be asking a question, so John answered it.

"I worked for Frank's father years back. Frank and I team-roped at marking time one year. We got sick as dogs together one time on a pony of rotgut whiskey. It's been a long while. I just figured I'd drop back and shoot a little bull with him. I had no idea he'd be dead."

Earl exhaled blue smoke. "Yeah. Must be close to five years back by now."

"What happened?"

"Doc Jennings said it was something in Frank's guts. Doc had a name for it, but I never could say it very good, you know. Well, whatever it was really don't matter very much. Once a feller dies, it don't matter too much what took him off anyway, does it? Unless, of course, it's a bullet. Anyway, Frank left, and you know this was about the sorriest place on earth for a few months. I'd have quit fifty times. . . ." Earl considered his lumpy cigarette.

John Randolph understood and said: "Yeah. Well, she's lucky you stayed."

Earl ignored that, probably because it made him uncomfortable. "I'm sure glad you come along, John. I got four big orry-eyed colts to start on this spring. I'm not agey, you understand, but being the only rider and all, if I got my back throwed out or something. . . . We'll look at them colts tomorrow, if you'd like."

John never did tell Earl Buscomb that Beverly Harding had told him he would be the ramrod. What the hell, when there were only two men, what difference did it make? Especially when they were both seasoned stockmen; both of them knew what had to be done, when it had to be done, and how to do it. In a two-man bunkhouse a boss was about as necessary as teats on a man. John Randolph bedded down that night, and for a long while, as he lay in the starlit gloom, he saw the faces of men he had known on this same ranch many years ago. That morning he had felt young all over again, but tonight he felt as old as the hills.

In the morning he and Earl went down early, right at first light, to pitch some feed to the corralled using horses, and, while they were down there, Earl showed him the four colts. One was a filly but the other three were young stallions, and John shook his head about that.

"Time to alter them," he said.

Earl was agreeable. "Any time you want." He looked over his shoulder like a conspirator, then looked back, and at the same time lowered his voice. "I've been sweating bullets about this, to tell you the truth. I didn't even want to bring it up with Miz Harding. How in hell do you tell a lady her stud colts ought to be castrated?"

John laughed quietly. "You don't," he said, and they strolled back to the big log barn. "What's wrong with doing it today . . . this morning?"

Earl looked relieved. "Suits me right down to the ground. And tomorrow, when most of the fight's still out of them, we can commence the saddling and riding out. Can't let 'em stand around afterward and get all stocked up anyway." Earl stopped suddenly, near the wide, doorless front opening of the barn. He was staring straight ahead. Suddenly he said: "All right, John, here's your first problem. Yonder comes Connie. She'll dog you and shadow you, and ask questions, and be under and over everything while you're working on it." Earl beamed. "You figure some way to get her and her maw off the ranch this morning so's we can cut those damned stud colts." Earl started toward the bunkhouse. "I'll go commence frying us up some breakfast."

John watched Earl stride away. He heard Connie pipe a greeting and heard Earl return it as they passed, in the vicinity of the bunkhouse, then Connie came bearing down upon John Randolph, her jaw tough-set, her blue eyes unwaveringly upon him. He thought she was angry with him for mentioning in front of her mother, yesterday beside the creek, that she had cursed at the Tandy boy.

But that wasn't it at all. She marched up and said: "Good morning, Mister Randolph. Anything you want to know about things on the ranch, you can ask me. Well, if my mother isn't around, you can ask me."

John smiled. "All right. I'll do that. First off, then, maybe you could tell me how often folks from here ride to town and fetch back the mail."

Connie stood, erect and lean in the golden morning. "We don't get much mail. But sometimes when we go in with the wagon for supplies, we stop by and see if there is any for the ranch." The cornflower-blue eyes became thoughtful. "Are you expecting a letter?"

John looked past in the direction of the main house. If he said yes, then Connie was going to volunteer to ride to Cottonwood, which would be just fine—except that Connie's mother would still be here. He swiveled around the question by asking a question of his own. "How often do you go to town for supplies?"

Connie answered that quickly. "Whenever we're low on things. We went last week. That was the first time in maybe a month."

John let out a big sigh, softly, and looked toward the bunkhouse. Earl Buscomb was a gray fox of a man, damn him.

Connie suddenly dropped her head a little to one side. "Mister Randolph, you aren't one of those riders who's always looking for an excuse to head for Cottonwood, are you?"

John stared, then he laughed. "You know, for thirteen or whatever you are, Connie, you're a smart ki- . . . person. No, I'm not a man who likes to go to town any oftener than he has to." He decided this was never going to come out right, if they stood there for a month, so he said: "Is your mother handy, up at the house?"

Connie nodded. "Yes." Then she stepped around him, heading into the barn. "I'm going to hunt eggs in the mangers, so if she asks if you've seen me, you could tell her."

John nodded absently about that, and continued to gaze over at the main house. Earl was perfectly right. No man wanted to discuss castrating colts with a woman, not even when he was related to her, maybe even married to her, but letting something go too long was sometimes a lot worse than doing what was distasteful.

He walked on over, walked up the steps, and, when he raised his hand to knock, the door opened. Evidently the hollow sound boot steps made over those three long steps carried inside the house. She'd appeared this suddenly the previous day.

He pulled off his hat as she stepped out onto the verandah. He hadn't thought in advance what he'd say but he tried being tactful. "Maybe if you and Connie wanted to drive over to Cottonwood this morning, ma'am, it'd be a very nice day for it.

I'd be glad to hitch up the buggy for you."

Her gold-flecked eyes searched his face a moment. "You and Earl don't want us around, Mister Randolph?"

He looked down. "Yes'm, that's about the size of it."

She did not argue and she did not ask a single awkward question. She simply glanced down toward the corrals where the horse colts were, and said: "That would be very nice, if you'd hitch up the top buggy, Mister Randolph. I've been meaning to drive in and visit."

John got the impression that she was on the verge of laughing at him, but that was probably incorrect. He impassively nodded, and turned to walk in the direction of the bunkhouse. She hesitated a moment in the doorway behind him, then she went inside.

Earl was not a good cook. Very few range riders were, for that matter, but on the other hand very few range men were particular eaters, either, so when Earl slid the greasy eggs upon a tin plate, poured the embalming-fluid coffee, and tossed the fried spuds into a big bowl, he had actually acquitted himself very well, by cow-camp and bunkhouse standards. As he straddled the bench, he said: "You get rid of them?"

John nodded. "They'll go visiting over in town. I've got to hitch the buggy up directly. You can show me which horse goes into the shafts."

Earl was relieved. "Fine. You know, if a damned stud colt had the good sense a bull calf's got, he wouldn't scream when he gets altered. But no, they got to holler, and bring every female within a dozen miles on the run to accuse fellers of being cruel. And what can you say?"

Earl heaped potatoes atop his egg. "Nothing. You can't say a thing." He looked up. "You're a fair cook, Earl."

That made Buscomb's day. That, and the fact that finally he had another man to talk to. It had been very difficult, these past months since their former rider had quit to head for Texas, to mind his language because Connie or her mother were forever within hearing distance, even on the cattle drives. This, he told John Randolph, was like having a gag taken off his mouth. All John said was: "Well, I'm sure you've been careful, Earl."

"Careful!" exclaimed Buscomb, rearing up, coffee cup in hand. "Careful ain't the word for it. I've damned near choked to death a hunnert times to keep from saying something."

John did not look up. "Yesterday I pulled Connie and some shackle-headed string bean of a bid named Howard Tandy apart alongside the creek, and, when the boy was leaving, she said . . . 'Damn you, next time I'll chew both your ears off.' " John looked up mildly. "She said she'd heard you say worse than that."

Earl put his cup down very gently, and considered its murky contents for a moment before speaking. "The hell of it is, John, I try. Few days back a god-damned stupid horse like to broke all the bones in my foot, stepping on me . . . but I *try.*"

John went on eating. He knew nothing at all about young girls, and he knew a lot less than nothing at all about raising children, either sex, but, as he sat there eating, he got to thinking back, and it gradually came to him, now that he pondered it, that all the ranch women and girls he'd ever been around must certainly have heard a lot of rough talk they weren't supposed to have heard. But he couldn't recall a single one of them ever *using* that kind of talk, especially around menfolk, so maybe, he thought, the problem wasn't in Connie's knowing, maybe it was in her using what she'd heard.

He and Earl left the bunkhouse, hats in hand, and went down to hitch up the top buggy, and, when that was done and they had got shed of the womenfolk, to get along with that other little chore. If there was one worthless thing on a cow ranch, it was a biting, kicking, fighting, squealing stud colt.

IV

Most colts, especially when they were in a ranch corral, could be assumed to have been taught something. Maybe they'd only been halter-broke, or taught to lead, but they knew something. The moment John and Earl slid between the stringers, lariats in hand, the four colts exploded and Earl looked embarrassed. "I just haven't had the time," he explained, and built a loop. "I know it's a damned shame, but you can't winter feed, do the chores, do this and do that . . . an' still have time to break colts."

John did not say a word. He picked out the least of the three stud colts to warm up on, roped its forelegs, took dallies at the snubbing post, and upended the colt. Earl was on its head with all his weight and John went to work with Earl's lariat to secure the animal's legs. It was dangerous business; each hind leg had to be tied hard and fast to a rope-yoke made around the lower neck, then pulled up high, almost to the colt's ears, and tied there. Then the man with the knife and the disinfectant went to work.

It still wasn't very warm even though the sun had been climbing now for more than an hour, but both John and Earl were wringing wet with perspiration by the time they had the first colt altered. It was physically exhausting work when it had to be done this way. Quiet colts or older horses were simply put into a leather harness, jerked down, and no one had to fight them every breath of the way.

When they let the smallest colt up, they killed a little time by driving him and the filly into an adjoining corral, then they went over to the trough, doused water over themselves, drank a little, and rested a bit.

Earl had an idea that there should be a better way. He even mentioned some kind of a chute horses could be driven into, that would squeeze down at the farthest end to immobilize a horse. John nodded and studied their next two stud colts. "Good stock," he observed. "I remember old man Harding was a stickler for quality in his horses."

Earl said: "In everything. Frank caught it from the old man. He used to send all the way down to California for horsebreakers, and all the way over to Missouri and Ohio for his seed bulls."

John felt his muscles beginning to stiffen even though the heat was increasing finally, so he got up off the edge of the stone trough and began flicking out another loop. The pair of remaining stud colts were over against the far side of the corral, as far as they could get from the men, softly snorting and rolling their eyes. The smell of blood over by the snubbing post didn't do much for their peace of mind, either, aside from the smell of the men.

Earl stood up, grimaced, and also shook out another loop. It wasn't hard to rope the horses. The corral was round, so there would be no corners for critters to pile up in. All John had to do was get set and wait until one of the horses raced around in front of him. He caught the second one by the head, dallied, worked on taking up slack as Earl larruped the fighting horse on the rump. Then Earl snaked the rear legs out from under the horse and he went down bawling, striking, and fighting so hard dust rose up thickly. This one was a larger colt. He probably weighed eight hundred and fifty pounds, and he still had three years to grow.

They were very careful this time. More careful than they'd been with the smaller colt. Even so, their fighting, squealing, bawling adversary managed to tear the back out of Earl's shirt. After that, Earl at least stopped trying to be as merciful as men usually were when they were cutting colts whose fury and desperation they secretly sympathized with. The second colt became a gelding in quick time.

The dust hadn't settled by the time they let him up, choused him into the adjoining corral, and limped back to the trough to rest. The sun was fully up, the dust was rank, heat was out there in the corral in full force, and, as Earl said, it was a damned good thing they didn't have four more to work. It took a lot out of a man, doing this kind of work. Even when a man was in top physical shape, fighting eight hundred to a thousand pound horses to a standstill with nothing but lariats and a snubbing post took a man's strength and stamina away, right down to the dregs of his reserves.

John finally said: "One more, then I'm going down to the creek and soak for an hour. Let's get it over with."

They did, moving with a lot less agility than they had had, still taking no chances but nevertheless being vulnerable a time or two simply because their reflexes were sluggish this last time. Finally, when they let the last colt up and opened the gate so that all three colts could have the run of both corrals, it was over.

The dust was thick, rank-smelling, and rank-tasting. John was the first to put his hat aside and dunk his head deep into the cool trough water. While he was shaking free, Earl did the same, but Earl also scooped up handfuls of water and doused his entire upper body. He was doing this and making sounds of equal parts pleasure and exhaustion when John turned to retrieve his hat, and saw the four riders walking into the yard toward the dust cloud at the corrals. He said nothing until the riders angled over closer and he could see their faces. Then he nudged Earl.

"Visitors."

Earl turned, wet and ragged, stared a moment, then said in a quiet tone: "Carl Tandy and his riders." John had no premonition at all, until Earl put a name to the thick, dark-eyed, bronzed man riding the Grulla horse in the lead. The name of the lad he'd pitched into the creek had been Tandy.

Earl put his hat atop his soaked and matted hair, watching the horsemen. "Tandy's land adjoins ours northeast. He's not exactly a feller I'd choose, if I had a choice of neighbors, but at least he don't give us too much trouble."

The riders pulled up across the corral. The thick-bodied, dark-eyed man neither nodded, smiled, nor spoke. He sat his saddle studying the hang-dog colts and the battered, exhausted men across by the trough. Then, eventually, he said: "Which one of you beat up on my boy?"

John stared. "Nobody beat up on your boy. I pulled him off Connie Harding when they were fighting and tossed him in the creek."

Carl Tandy's dark gaze lingered upon John Randolph. He made his judgment, then, without speaking. He dismounted, tied his horse, removed his hat and shell belt, hung them both from his saddle horn, and started through the corral stringers. His three range riders also dismounted and started into the corral, but they didn't shed their guns or hats. Earl's breath exploded outward. Neither he nor John Randolph were wearing guns; as a general rule, unless there was range trouble, working riders seldom worked with all that clumsy, unnecessary, and useless weight around their middles. It wouldn't have made much difference now, anyway.

The odds were too great. John knew exactly what was coming. He'd been here a number of times before, for one reason or another, but as he straightened around, facing Carl Tandy, he probably had never before been caught in quite this situation. He ached all over, had nothing left in the way of endurance, and the man who stopped fifteen feet in front of him was just as large, and probably ten or fifteen pounds heavier. It did not take much study to arrive at a conclusion about Carl Tandy; he was one of those men who only initially tried to reason his way through; he was much better bulling it.

He said: "What's your name, cowboy?"

John answered quietly: "John Randolph."

Tandy ignored Earl. His three armed riders were standing back there, keeping an eye on Buscomb. "You're goin' to get a lesson," said Tandy to John Randolph, "about what folks don't do in this part of the country. They *don't* pick on young kids."

John had no illusions but he said: "I didn't pick on the boy. He and Connie Harding were fighting. Maybe in this part of the country it's all right for boys to hit girls . . . but I don't happen to believe in it."

Tandy slowly shook his head. "If you didn't pick on him, John, tell me how he came to have that busted lip?"

In a momentary flash of perception John saw something. This man's son had been too afraid and humiliated to tell his father a girl had done that to him. While this cleared through his mind, he said nothing, and that, evidently, was an incriminating kind of silence to Carl Tandy. The older man moved ahead a little, shuffling his feet in the churned dust of the corral.

Earl straightened fully around. One of Tandy's cowboys, a swarthy man looking like a half-breed, pointed a gloved hand. "Keep out of it, Earl," he ordered coldly. "It's goin' to be a fair fight."

John saw the older man's shoulders slump and settle, saw his thick arms come up, and John moved away from the stone trough, and tried to move clear of the corral stringers behind him, but evidently part of Carl Tandy's strategy was to hold John Randolph to the corral because he side-stepped very swiftly and cut John off. Then he came in.

John knew exactly how to turn sideways, riding away from the first strike, but his legs were like lead. He only half cleared himself and the ham-like fist with all Tandy's weight behind it swung him part way around. The blow brought up every last ounce of reserve strength John had left. The next time he moved he got clean away, but Tandy came on like a bull, swinging, his head tucked into the curve of a thick shoulder. Clearly Carl Tandy was no novice at this kind of work.

John feinted sideward. When Tandy leaned that way, John straightened back in the opposite direction and fired a left with his body turning in behind it. The blow caught Tandy high in the chest and settled him back, flat-footed. His arms dropped a little and his eyes widened. John knew he had only about one more like that left in him and shuffled ahead. If he'd been faster, he might have ended it then and there, but he had no speed in him. Tandy got away, paused to breathe deeply, then he came on again. This time he was chary. But he had time on his side. He maneuvered John against the corral stringers and rocked him with a hammer blow to the shoulder. Hit him again as he flung back both arms to push off the corral, brought blood to his mouth that time, and, as John felt the numbness setting in, and pawed at his attacker, Tandy sprang in close and beat John's middle with both fists at will. The last thing John Randolph remembered was a hot, acid taste in his throat. Then the numbness engulfed him and he crumpled in the hot dust.

Tandy stepped away, breathing hard. He let his whole body sag while he looked at the filthy, bloody wreck at his feet, then he turned, pushed past Earl Buscomb, and plunged both hands and arms into the cool water of the trough. Without looking around he said: "Earl, you tell that feller to draw his pay and ride on. The next time I catch him, it won't be fists. You hear me?"

Earl nodded, and went over to roll John onto his back. Earl, down on one knee, rocked his head from side to side. He'd seen some beatings in his time, but this one was one of the worst. He turned as Carl Tandy and his men crawled back out of the corral. None of the cowboys had said a word during the battle.

Now, as their boss put his shell belt and hat back on, they mounted up and sat their horses like bronzed carvings, looking past Earl at the torn and bloody human wreckage in the dirt of the hot corral.

When Tandy got astride, he led his men on a long lope back the way they had come. Earl went to the trough, filled his hat with water, and came back to wash John Randolph's face. He felt almost as badly about the fact that Randolph would now ride on, leaving him alone again, as he felt about the beating Randolph had taken.

He didn't consider how things might have ended if John Randolph hadn't already been worn down by their exertions with the stud colts in the corral prior to Tandy's arrival. All Earl thought about was that, just as he was beginning to take heart again, and things were probably going to get better on the ranch, this had to happen. It was enough to make a patient man throw up his hands and quit.

Earl got John Randolph across his shoulder and lugged him to the bunkhouse, which was no small accomplishment, either, and afterward Earl dug out his hidden bottle of whiskey, took two swallows himself, and got one down his beaten companion. Then he took another two for himself.

V

Earl lied because he'd been told to. When Beverly Harding came to the bunkhouse door and looked in where John was sitting, freshly bathed and dressed, and with his badly torn and swollen lip and his other puffy, purple bruises, Earl said: "We had a very bad day of it, ma'am. Them colts were just too big and salty for only two men to handle. We got the job done, but I tell you for a fact it liked to killed us both. Poor John got an awful strike, right square in the face."

Beverly Harding was appalled, but when she would have

come over to make a close inspection, John stood up and motioned her away. Talking made his lips bleed so he said nothing, but she was not one of those no-nonsense women; she seemed to sense that he did not want to be stared at in his present condition, so she called Earl outside, and closed the bunkhouse door. The moment they were both gone, John went to the wall mirror for another look.

He did not remember too much about the fight. He did, however, recall that Carl Tandy could hit very hard. In time the lip would heal. Before that, the swelling would diminish. As for the purple bruises, they would also diminish in time. As for the fight itself, he didn't actually hold much of a grudge against Tandy. What he did resent was Tandy's son lying to his father to precipitate the fight. As for drawing his pay and riding on, as Tandy had ordered, and as Earl had forlornly passed along, John had no such intention at all. He winked at himself in the mirror. He looked terrible and he ached from head to heels—but at least their lie to Beverly Harding had been blessed with a very valid plausibility, those damned stud colts.

He went outside by the rear door and headed for the creek. It was cooler down there, and for a while he'd just as soon not even have to listen to Earl, who was, to be fair, a good hand and a likeable companion, but no man liked people all the time, not even likeable and helpful and solicitous people. He got into the creek willows, and saw something he hadn't noticed before; there were pan-size trout in the water.

The day was spent. There was still sunlight, flying insects by the dozens drifted above the water catching cool little updrafts, and except for a few thin shadows roundabout it could almost have been midafternoon, but it wasn't; it was a springtime early evening, something that would get increasingly long as summer approached. John knelt in matted grass and sluiced cold water over his face. It stung, especially around his mouth, but it also had a way of winnowing fever out of flesh. He was still doing that when someone stepped on a twig and brought him up and around in a lunge that was unthinking.

It was Beverly Harding. She recoiled at his menacing swiftness, then offered a wavering smile and a little opaque jar with a hand towel. "Goose grease and laudanum," she said. "That's what my mother used when I was a little girl. The laudanum stopped the pain, the goose grease helped scabs form, and hastened the healing." She continued to hold them out until he took them. Then she pressed both hands across her flat stomach and gazed steadily at him, her tan-tawny eyes a lot wiser than her years could have made them. "I'm awfully sorry, Mister Randolph. I knew, last autumn, those colts should have been worked, but I just couldn't say anything about it. Earl does so much. . . . This was never a one-man ranch."

He forgot his aches and his raw-meat appearance. Sometimes it was easy to slip inside someone else's personal vortex; he did it now and immediately felt all the trials and dilemmas she had faced, and still had to face. They were not actually defeating to him, but he could understand that, too; he was a man. It made all the difference in the world in a country like this where nothing could be done unless men did it.

He kept his lip moistened as he said: "Nothing to be sorry about, Missus Harding. Jobs have to be done, and sometimes folks get hurt doing them. But generally we live through it, don't we?"

She smiled. "Earl thought you might quit."

He wondered just how far Earl had gone in telling her this, and decided that Earl hadn't gone that far, otherwise she'd know it hadn't been a stud colt that had marked him like this. He smiled downward with just his eyes. "Maybe, for a day or two, I'll slack off a mite. But I don't have quitting in mind."

Her gold-flecked eyes brightened. "I'm very glad of that."

She came closer and stood looking down into the creek. "While we were visiting over in town this morning, I asked around. . . ." She raised her face to him. "Henry Jennings told me all that's left is a few bar riders that none of the other ranches will hire."

John, whose interest in the local people was just beginning, said: "Who is Henry Jennings?"

"Our doctor. He has his home and office over in Cottonwood. He . . . looked after Frank during Frank's final illness. He is a fine man."

Someone riding a horse fast made a fading sound back in the direction of the yard. Beverly turned and so did John, but until he stepped clear of the thick, green tracery of the springtime willows it was impossible to see. The sound was gone by then, and the buildings cut off most of the view of the yonder countryside east and north. "Probably Earl," he said, stepping back, not very concerned.

Beverly Harding scarcely heeded the small interruption. "I'd better get back," she said. "I left Connie putting some things away at the house." She stopped with the pale leaves in the background behind her. "Mister Randolph, if you'd like . . . perhaps for a few days if you ate up at the main house . . . ?"

He shook his head. "No thanks. I'm fine." The idea of being babied did not sit well at all. He hadn't liked anything of that nature even as a youngster, and since then, as a loner in a world of rough men, he'd acquired the masculine view of that kind of treatment.

She left, and he moved up just a little to watch her cross toward the main house. She was a very handsome woman. She was more than that, but he didn't know exactly the words to put that into descriptive thought. Which was probably just as well.

He let shadows fall before returning to the bunkhouse. The moment he walked in and saw Connie sitting there, idly scuffing the floor with her boots, saw the look Earl shot him, he knew something had happened. Earl was frying meat and corn pone at the cook stove, with his hat on; his only concession to being indoors was that he'd rolled up both sleeves and had draped his old vest over the foot of an empty bunk.

Connie gazed steadily at John Randolph, her blue eyes darker than usual, perhaps as a result of the shadows, then she said: "I know, Mister Randolph. I'm not supposed to come in here. Only I wanted to tell you something."

Earl made a gesture of some kind from behind the girl with an upraised wooden spatula, but whatever that was supposed to convey was quite lost on John, who put his hat upon the horn rack, closed the door, and faced Connie.

"Howard Tandy came over, Mister Randolph, and he said he snuck along behind his father and their riders . . . and saw his father whip you in the corral."

John raised his eyes. Earl looked helplessly back, made another gesture with the wooden tool, weaker this time, then Earl shrugged, and turned back to his cooking.

John went over and sat on the bench beside Connie. Now he knew who that had been on the running horse an hour back. He had no idea what he was supposed to say, so he ran a hand through his hair and said nothing.

Connie kept gravely studying his lacerated face. "I'm sorry, Mister Randolph. In a way, I guess, it was my fault. I shouldn't have hit Howard in the mouth, should I?"

John almost smiled, but his lip burned when the muscles pulled back, so he only winked as he said: "Forget it. It wasn't your fault. Maybe I just stood up when I should have shut up." He pointed toward the door. "Your mother thinks you're up at the house, so you'd better get up there."

Connie slid off the bench and stood arrow-straight. She seemed to want to say more, but didn't know what to say. Then she turned and left. The moment the door closed, Earl said: "And now she'll tell her mother." That was something that hadn't crossed John's mind until this minute. "And her mother's going to think I'm a damned liar. And you, too."

John saw the bottle of whiskey on the plank table near the stove and went to pour two tin cups three fingers full. As he handed Earl one cup, he said: "Don't worry about her mother, and don't worry about her. And don't worry about me. Just get that damned supper fixed. I'm hungry as a bitch wolf." He winked, downed his whiskey, then swore because the liquor got into the split in his lip.

Earl waited until that blue-air lifted, then said: "You going to quit?"

John, eyes watering, shook his head. "Hell no. Why should I? Because some misguided bastard thinks I should?"

"No," responded Buscomb soberly. "But it might be something to mull over, since that misguided bastard happens to be Carl Tandy . . . and he's mean an' tough, an' no one just walks away when he tells 'em something."

John went to trickle water from the drinking dipper over his stinging lip and paid no more attention to Earl until, later, when they were sitting down to eat, he looked up and saw Earl sitting across from him with his hat on.

"You folks have some odd customs in this part of Arizona," he drawled. "Only down in Mexico have I seen men eat dinner wearing their hats."

Earl looked up, then swept the hat off, and sent it sailing unerringly across to his bunk, where it settled neatly dead center. "That isn't the only odd custom we got," he said, and went to work on his meal without elaborating. But when they had finished and Earl was comfortably rolling a smoke and spilling the residue into his plate, he said: "Who *did* hit Tandy's kid, if you didn't?"

"Connie," replied John, pursing his lip so that, when he drank coffee, he wouldn't sting himself again.

Earl twisted off the end of the cigarette and popped it between his lips. "In the mouth?" he said.

"Yup. Right square in the mouth. It drew blood, too. Not like his father's punch drew blood on me, but then she's only eleven or twelve years old."

"Thirteen," corrected Earl, and dragged a match across the taut cloth of his trouser leg to light up. "You know, that isn't lady-like, hitting fellers in the mouth."

"And cussing them out, too," agreed John, putting down his cup and grinning with his eyes. "I think her mother's got just about all she can handle around here. Otherwise, maybe I would quit, because my staying around isn't going to make the Tandys friendly toward the Harding Ranch, is it?"

Earl evidently didn't want to answer that; at least he sidled around it rather deftly by saying: "Well, this late in the season there wouldn't be many riding jobs still open, would there? And besides, maybe if you just stay on Harding range, Carl won't get no big bow in his neck."

John looked skeptically across the table. "Earl, you don't believe that."

Buscomb considered the drooping ash on his cigarette. "I reckon I don't. On the other hand, I sure hate the idea of talking to myself again." He smiled. "One thing you can count on. Next time they'll have two plows to clean. Today I had no more idea than the man in the moon what was coming."

John arose. "Let's go down to the corral and see how those colts are making out. Maybe we'd ought to lunge them a little to keep too much swelling from coming in."

Earl went after his hat, and for no real reason he also hooked his shell belt, and buckled it around his middle as they trooped away from the bunkhouse and went ambling along through the quiet, serene, warm night.

Everything that people had done to make this day as troubled and soiled as they made every other day was hidden now beneath a great fall of darkness, and come dawn the clean, soft new promise would be extended again, once more, all over again.

VI

The following morning they rode out early, earlier, in fact, than Earl was accustomed to riding out. He didn't have much to say, either, until they'd cleared something like three or four miles of range and came upon the first Harding cattle, recognizable by the big rib brand, a Rocking H, on the left side, but gradually, as Earl opened up, and as the warmth began to loosen his muscles and hide so that the aches could work loose throughout his carcass, he pointed out landmarks as well as particular groups of cattle. He had been keeping the first-call cows closer to the ranch, which had been Harding custom, and he'd also been salting back a mile or so from the creek so that the cattle wouldn't have far to walk for a drink after licking at the salt logs. Of course he could have put the salt logs closer to the creek, but southward a dozen miles or so there were people who used that water for their cooking and drinking, so the custom was to keep the herds from hanging around close by, for obvious reasons.

John remembered most of it. The cattle were all different, of course, but that wouldn't have made much difference anyway; a thousand or two cows and bulls looked pretty much the same, whatever generation they happened to belong to. It was a pleasant morning, not too hot, which had been John's idea in making their excursion early. They discussed a lot of things as they rode. Here and there they picked up little bands heading away from the open country toward the distant hills—where bears and panthers and wolves lay waiting—and pushed them back. Usually there were timid and overly protective wet cows with young calves at their sides.

This was how riders got acquainted. It was a rather casual thing, which was perhaps the best way for men to get to know one another. Each had his tests for a companion. By noon when they had been in the saddle something like seven hours, they turned back, and, when the ranch was in sight, John said: "Feel like sacking out those colts this afternoon?"

Earl was willing. He did not say whether he felt like it; he only signified that he was willing. Earl wasn't yet on the sundown side of forty, but he was getting there, which meant he didn't bounce back from punishment as he once had. But the spirit was willing, even if the flesh was still a little bruised from the previous day.

When they rode in and swung off to lead their horses into the barn to off-saddle, Connie appeared from the overhead loft, and Earl rolled up his eyes in an expression of purest supplication. Fortunately neither man had been swearing, but since rough language went with a rough occupation, it was simply a small miracle that they hadn't been.

She came down the loft ladder like a lean lizard after a crippled fly, and, when she hit the hard-packed earth, she said: "Mister Randolph, you look a lot better today." Little girls, even ones that weren't that little, even though they acted it, were not always the souls of tact. John gave her a look and an impassive nod.

She stood a moment, watching, then wanted to know where they had been. Earl explained with great patience, then John draped his rig from a wall peg by one stirrup, and, as he hung the bridle from the horn, he said: "Connie, we're going to have to work something out."

She looked up at him, her freckles blending with the golden

tan, her cornflower-blue eyes open and admiring and trusting. John looked at her a moment, then looked at Earl. Lamely he said: "Well, one of these days we'll have to work out some rules, anyway."

She left on some errand of her own and Earl raised up slowly across his mount's sweaty back and leaned. "All right, now you know what I been putting up with. Only with me it's been years instead of days, and when she was littler. . . ." Earl gave his head a woebegone wag. "I never wanted to raise no children. I never even wanted to get married. And look where I ended up . . . playing godfather or something to them both. Well, let's get something to eat, then get to work on them colts."

It was an active early afternoon even though neither of them was in much of a hurry to get to work on the colts, after eating. Nor did it help much that Connie came and perched atop the corral as excited as a cricket and equally as active.

They did not have too much difficulty. None of the new geldings were sufficiently recovered from the crude surgery really to fight, nor did they seem to have much fighting spirit left. In fact, after working the colts from the ground for a couple of hours, John went to saddle his own private mount, which hadn't been ridden in a couple of days, and went back to snub the colts one at a time for Earl.

Only one colt tried to climb into John's saddle with him. The other two set back, and sulked, then tried half-heartedly bogging their heads and lunging, but snubbed close, there really wasn't much they could do, so they settled down, after a bit, to what they could do, which was simply plod along beside the burly bay horse and suffer the ignominy of having a man in the middle of their backs.

It went so well that Connie raced for the main house and eventually returned with her mother. Then the pair of them sat atop the uppermost stringer of the round corral, and watched.

The heat finally built up enough to discourage additional riding, when there really was no point in keeping it up anyway. Over-riding a green colt was far worse than under-riding him. They off-saddled the last colt, and, while John put up his bay horse, Earl went to work trying to lead the big colts from the ground. When a man was knowledgeable about this, he could win a lot of bets, for although an eight-hundred-pound horse was as immovable as stone when a one-hundred-and-sixty-or-seventy-pound man tried to pull him into taking the first forward step, there were several very elemental ways of using all that heavy weight against the horse, and teach him to lead in minutes. By the time John returned to stand in shade over by Connie and Beverly, Earl had the lightest of the colts leading quite well.

As Earl came over and passed the rope to Connie, he said: "Climb down very slowly, now, and don't look back when you lead this pony. Just walk slowly off and give him half a chance to decide he ought to follow you. Don't ever look a horse in the face when you're breaking him to lead, and don't ever make any sudden, fast moves. Now walk off."

Connie did, and, miracle of miracles, the colt followed. John laughed at the girl's sudden look of unbelieving rapture—and his lip split. He said: "God . . . darn it." Beverly laughed. Earl turned away as Connie came hiking along. He didn't want to be caught up in John's embarrassment, so he said: "Slower, Connie, walk slower. Now don't let that slack get so low he'll step over it. It's important to remember you don't want to make even one single small mistake, when you're starting one. You don't want to confuse him or spook him, no matter what. Now just keep walking around."

Beverly offered John a clean, small handkerchief. He almost did not accept it. He had a red bandanna in a hip pocket. But this was the second time she'd wanted to help. He held the little scrap of cloth to his lip and lowered it. It was soaked through with dark blood. He said: "I'm sorry about that."

She raised her hand to his hand and gently pushed his hand, with the cloth in it, back up against the bleeding lip. She was still smiling. "Nothing to be sorry about. It's only a handkerchief." She held his hand up. "Did you use the salve I gave you?"

He hadn't, but he was saved from making this confession as long as she wouldn't allow him to take his hand away from his mouth.

Connie came up bursting with pride. She offered Earl the lead rope. "This one's broke to lead. Let's get one of the others."

Earl took the shank and rolled his eyes. "You got any idea how many folks I've seen get hurt because they was too confident? All right, we'll get another one. But you'll clamber back atop the stringers until I've led him around a time or two."

Connie looked archly at Earl. She was about to say something. Without warning John reached, one-handed, lifted her bodily, and put her upon the topmost stringer. He did it all without removing the soggy little ridiculous excuse for a handkerchief from his mouth. They all looked stunned, perhaps more that he had done it, than that he had done it with just one hand. Of course Connie wasn't a very heavy girl, but still. . . .

Earl crowed: "You see? Now you stay up there!" He led the smallest colt away, toward the far corral, and after some muttering and furious cursing—in a whisper—got the halter and shank on the next colt.

Beverly, leaning to examine John's split lip, acted the least irritated by what had happened to her daughter. Connie was too astonished to react, until she saw Earl leading the second colt forward, a foot at a time. This struggle between the man and the horse absorbed her to the point that she forgot the humiliation of being hoisted to the top of the corral.

This second colt was not as tractable as the other one had been. He bolted past Earl twice, nearly snapping the head off Earl's neck, and the last time he did that John winced. He saw the words coming as Earl set his heels down hard and swung the colt. They came, in spite of Earl's best intentions. John looked at Beverly. She looked straight back—and winked—the dust flew, the colt lunged, Earl reached the snubbing post, took dallies, then used his hat to teach this big, brawny young horse respect for a rope.

Finally, then, Earl started out again. This time the colt got the idea. He wasn't dumb; he was just ready and willing to fight again, that was all. As Earl finally got him untracked, he looked over and said: "Connie, you aren't going to lead this one for a spell."

Beverly turned and smiled up at her daughter. Connie saw only the big colt. She ignored both her mother and John Randolph, and, as far as John was concerned, he'd had enough dust and sweat and strain for one day, so he handed Beverly back her soggy handkerchief and headed for the gate. Without hesitating, Beverly went along with him. As they passed out of the corral, she said: "John, I want you to know that I'm grateful that you didn't quit." Her tawny eyes were fully upon his face as she spoke, tough and tender at the same time. "Connie told me what really happened yesterday while she and I were gone." She closed the gate, latched it, and turned to walk slowly along with him toward the shade of the barn front. "I really hate the thought of you leaving."

He stopped. "I told you I wasn't going to quit."

She looked up, smiling. "No, you're not quitting. You're being fired."

He stared.

"I'm not going to be a party to what will happen the next

time Carl Tandy meets you. It's not fair to you. The only backing you'll get from this ranch is from a woman, a young girl, and an aging cowboy. That's not enough against the Tandy outfit."

John raised a hand to see whether or not his lip had stopped bleeding. Evidently it had because, when he lowered the hand, there was no blood showing. He stood a moment gazing at Beverly Harding, then shook his head.

"No good," he growled. "This is no good the way it's coming out." He loosened a little and kept gazing down at her. Finally he said: "All right, I'm fired. But it'll take me a day or two to get my things together." He turned on his heel and went to the bunkhouse, entered, and closed the door, leaving her looking after him, puzzled and not really able either to understand him or to accept the fact that he had allowed her to fire him. Something was not quite right. She had no idea what it was, but a moment ago he hadn't acted exactly like a man who would be leaving. No rider who appeared with one horse, a set of saddlebags, and a bedroll needed two days to gather his things together before leaving. She'd seen enough of them come and go; the most they'd ever needed was a couple of hours.

She turned back toward the corral to talk to Earl, but when she got down there, her daughter and Earl were too engrossed with the colts to heed her presence, so she turned back again. She probably couldn't have got anything out of Earl anyway.

VII

On the ride to Cottonwood, John thought he was pushing things a little. He wasn't in the best condition he'd ever been in. On the other hand, Beverly Harding hadn't left him much in the way of choices. Then, too, there was something else. Carl Tandy hadn't beaten him fairly and squarely, and that also rankled.

He rode through the late afternoon heat, thinking that he was picking up an old banner for two men he had liked years ago, Frank Harding and his father, but that actually he did not owe either of the dead men any favors. But that wasn't what set him on this present course, exactly, and he knew that as well. Beverly and her daughter were one reason, and the other reason was strictly personal. He owed Carl Tandy.

Maybe it wasn't a foolproof set of reasons for what he intended to do now, but as he reflected, about the same time he saw the roof tops and the back lots up ahead in the dancing heat, men did not always function according to foolproof reasons obviously, or a hell of a lot of things never would have been allowed to happen in this world. Cottonwood, as he recalled it, had been a kind of sleepy village even at the peak of the riding season when the ranches for a hundred miles around had full riding crews. It did not look very different now, as he angled in off the range, heading for the north end of town.

Of course, during the hot time of day, folks didn't do much more than they had to do. As John Randolph reached the dusty main thoroughfare and started down it, only two horsemen, and one buggy shared the thoroughfare with him. The saloon, which had a tree-shaded side lot on the south side where there was a long tie rack, had six or eight horses drowsing in the shade, and down in front of the general store there was a parked buckboard with two hundredweight sacks of flour in the back.

Where a public trough stood at the edge of the westerly plank walk, beneath a large, unkempt old tree, three elderly men sat upon a bench, also in shade, idly talking. They were the only people in Cottonwood who paid the slightest attention to John Randolph, and even they weren't too interested. This time of year mounted strangers passed through almost every day. People paid more heed to the horses men rode than to the men; good saddle animals were always a pleasure to see, but men, aside from always being something of an unknown quotient, were a dime a dozen.

John turned in at the livery barn, paid for an inside stall, graining and haying and currying of his animal, then he struck dust from his trousers with his hat, and walked over across the roadway and northward up to the saloon. There were three places in a cow town where men congregated—the livery barn, the saddle and harness shop, and the saloon. Since there was no one at the livery barn excepting the day man, and, since it was hot enough for range men to want beer when they reached town, John passed by the harness works and entered the saloon, which was a weathered, plank building with a warped wooden awning out over its stretch of plank walk.

It was like a hundred other saloons John Randolph had been in, even to the gamy smell, when he pushed past the spindle doors, which was a compound of tobacco, liquor, and horse sweat. The bartender was a bull-necked man who wore his jet-black hair parted straight down the middle and greased down on both sides. He also wore sleeve garters and a very prestigious gold watch chain from one vest pocket to the other vest pocket. He was older than John Randolph, and, although he smiled, there was a knowing and calculating look in his brown eyes as he made a perfunctory sweep of the bar top in front of John, then said: "Beer?"

John nodded, shoved back his hat, and pushed a sleeve across his forehead. "Hot out there," he growled, and the barman, whose pale skin indicated that he did not leave his cool saloon very often, nodded absently, then went after the beer.

The saloon had some range men down at the north end of the bar. Three of them were grizzled, gray men, indicating that they were probably ranch owners. The others were slightly younger men, riders, probably, or perhaps range bosses. John leaned and studied the men until his beer arrived, deciding in his mind that they were having some kind of meeting, which was commonplace. There were few better places for livestock men to meet than a saloon.

The bull-necked barkeeper returned, set up the glass, and picked up the 5¢ piece John put down. Undoubtedly because he had no other customers at the moment, the barman leaned and looked past into the shimmering roadway and said: "Better rain soon or we're going to be in for a bad time on the grasslands." He jerked a thumb. "That's what those fellers are cussing about." The dark eyes drifted back to John's face. "If you rode in looking for work, it's pretty late in the season. But at least you picked a right good time to walk in for a beer. Them's the men who own almost all the range east, north, and south from Cottonwood for one hell of a long reach."

John tasted the beer. It had a pleasing bite to it. He gazed up where the cowmen were soberly and quietly talking, and hooked a boot over the brass rail. He wasn't looking for a job, but the barman's conversation sowed a seed of thought in his mind.

"Is that all the owners north and east?" he asked.

The barman answered carelessly. "Naw. There's a couple others. Feller named Garrison due east, and a feller named Tandy to the northeast. But they ain't arrived yet."

Someone farther along, where those cattlemen leaned, struck the bar top with an empty glass, and the bull-necked man heaved backward and turned to walk down there.

John drank his beer slowly, looked at a clock on the backbar wall, then decided, since he might have quite a wait, to do it sitting down, and took his beer glass over to an empty table near the front window.

He had no plan at all. For what he had in mind there was very little reason to evolve a plan. If Carl Tandy walked through those roadway doors, he would see, and no doubt recognize, John Randolph. After that it would be up to him, so, beyond knowing exactly what he wanted from Tandy, how he got it, or even whether he got it, would be up to Carl Tandy. He did not dwell much upon the possibility of Tandy striding in with his riders, because that wouldn't make a whole lot of difference. Not here, in this saloon and in this town. It was one thing for a cowman to use his men arbitrarily upon the range against one or two unsuspecting other men, or even to ride into someone's ranch yard and do what Tandy had done, using his men to back up his play, but that sort of thing wouldn't be allowed here. When John Randolph called Carl Tandy this time, it would be strictly according to the custom of the cow country, which meant man to man. Maybe those cowmen up along the bar wouldn't approve of a stranger waiting in the saloon expressly to force a fight, but they would not make an attempt to stop it as long as it was fair and square.

A lawman might want to stop it. There was a jail house down the road, with a marshal's office in front. It had been there years ago, too, and, although it was possible even the same lawman patrolled Cottonwood, John thought it more probable it wouldn't be the same man, it would be a younger one. But he didn't expect trouble from this quarter simply because, as long as the town marshal didn't just happen in out of the heat for a beer while John was calling Carl Tandy out, the whole thing should be over and finished before the local lawman even learned that it had come about.

The barman brought over a fresh glass of beer and picked up John's empty glass. He looked around as two more cowmen walked in. Neither of them was Carl Tandy, or any of the three men he'd been riding with yesterday, so John hardly spared more than a glance at the newcomers, but the barman smiled and called a greeting, then went back over to the bar and drew off a couple more beers, and took them down where the cattlemen's meeting was taking place.

It was comfortable in the saloon. It was also noticeably cooler inside than it was outside. John relaxed and allowed the beer to work its small miracle by easing all his lingering aches.

He had been there about two hours and the cowmen's conference was beginning to break up, when a tall, rather raw-boned older man with a shock of almost pure white hair entered. He had a darkly tanned face that contrasted with the white hair. He was a striking man, one of those people who, even in a room full of people, attracted notice. He looked directly at John and nodded. It could, of course, have been simply a common courtesy, since their eyes had met briefly, or it could have been something else. As John watched this older man step to the bar, almost everyone in the room either called a greeting to him, or smiled in his direction, but when the barman went fumbling beneath his bar and came up saying: "Doc, I got something special off the morning stage. That bottle of sherry wine I sent out to San Francisco for."

The newcomer, then, had to be the Dr. Jennings Beverly had mentioned. John smiled to himself; he'd have to be someone pretty damned special to get that much attention from a cow-town bartender, and he also had to be special to dare sip a glass of sherry in a cow-town saloon.

John was idly studying the medical man when the spindle door quivered inward and a thick, familiar body hung in the opening a moment, then turned without a nod to anyone, and walked over to John Randolph's table. It was Earl Buscomb and he looked unhappy as he pulled out a chair to straddle it, then leaned both arms upon the table as he said: "I figured you might have lit out for town, when Miz Harding told me what she done." Earl thumbed back his hat and gazed disgustedly at John. "You know, I never did really believe the good Lord gave women sense enough to come in out of the rain."

The bartender came over with a foamy glass of beer, winked amiably at Earl, an old customer, and departed with his 5¢

piece in one big hand. Earl half drained his glass and John smiled at the look on Earl's face. This smile encouraged the older rider to say: "You're not really going to let her fire you, are you, John?"

That kind of a remark made John's grin widen. "It's her cow outfit," he said.

Earl put his glass down, empty. "Oh for Christ's sake," he grumbled, "she was being noble was all. She told me what she said to you, about not wanting you to be at the mercy of Carl Tandy, or some such damn' fool thing to say to a grown man." Earl's shrewd eyes made a long, close study of John, then with forced and palpably false camaraderie he said: "Let's head back. The sun's about set now. It'll be cool riding back."

John gazed dispassionately at Earl. Obviously Buscomb had no inkling why John was sitting in the saloon. He thought John was just loafing, perhaps brooding or sulking after being fired. There was nothing wrong with this. John did not want Earl involved when Carl Tandy arrived in town. He did not want anyone at all involved, least of all anyone from the Harding Ranch. Tandy was patently a vengeful man. John Randolph no longer worked for the Harding Ranch. Whatever he and Carl Tandy did, now, was personal. It had nothing at all to do with John's former employer. At least that was how John's thoughts ran as he said: "Go on back, Earl. Maybe I'll be along later. Maybe not."

Buscomb's face clouded again. He stared for a moment, then, evidently deciding further argument would be useless, he shoved back his chair and stood up. "I got to roll my blankets," he growled. "I've been in one place too long anyway. Furthermore, a man is hired to ride, not to wet-nurse a widow woman and a stripling kid."

John sat there, comfortably regarding Earl Buscomb as he said: "You know better, Earl. They'll bury you out there fifteen, twenty years from now. Go on back. Maybe I'll see you tomorrow."

That ended it. Earl left without another word, and without so much as glancing up where the cattlemen's meeting was continuing. Earl was disgusted enough to chew cannonballs and spit bullets.

VIII

John gave up, eventually, and went in search of a place to eat. At best his direct approach had been devoid of guarantees, but he had, whether by accident or not, happened along, as that bull-necked barman had implied, at a very opportune moment. The trouble was, of course, that Carl Tandy had not arrived, and that could have happened if they'd had an iron-clad agreement to meet today.

He found the hole-in-the-wall café, took his choice of what appeared to be the safer alternative out of the only two selections chalked upon a blackboard across from the counter, and ordered antelope stew, coffee, and apple pie. Antelope stew in northern Arizona was probably antelope stew, but in central or southern Arizona it was much more likely to be made with goat meat.

The café's proprietor was a hard-faced, cold-eyed, rather large woman with hair dyed such an abominable shade of black that it was dead-looking. Even lamplight wouldn't reflect off her hair. She said almost nothing, to which John Randolph did not object, but near the end of his meal that changed. John was lingering over his pie and second cup of coffee, while the black-haired woman was reading an old newspaper down the counter several yards. Someone rode up out front and grunted down. Each sound carried through the opened roadside door—left open to entice some coolness inside as the day died.

John arose, dropped some silver coins atop the counter,

stepped back, and turned—and found himself looking squarely into the black eyes of that swarthy half-breed-looking cowboy who had been with Carl Tandy the previous day at the Harding place. The half-breed had a man with him, but John did not recognize him. As the half-breed stopped suddenly, the man behind him pushed ahead, growling: "Go on, Mike, what'n hell you waiting for?" The second man pushed past and only paused when he saw the large man staring at the half-breed—the large, calm-eyed man with the badly bruised face.

The half-breed let his glance slip. He moved out of the doorway toward the café counter, trying to make the impression that nothing was troubling him. John Randolph let him almost reach the counter, then called him.

"Hey, cowboy, you're a rider for Tandy, aren't you?"

Both men turned. Now, finally, the half-breed knew he was not going to be able to saunter away casually, so he stopped, facing John, hooked his thumbs, and stood flat-footed. "Yeah, what of it? I'm his range boss."

"Did he come to town with you, range boss?"

"No. And you're damned lucky he didn't, after what he told you yesterday about getting out of the country before he sees you again."

Over behind her counter the black-haired woman was taking all this in. Behind the half-breed that other cowboy was doing the same. Whether the woman realized it or not, that second cowboy did—there was going to be a fight damned quick now. The cowboy eased very quietly and very slowly well away from his half-breed companion.

John said: "Sorry he didn't ride in, too." He jerked his head. "Step outside."

The range boss showed interest along with scorn. "You never get enough, do you?" he said, and turned to head for the doorway. As he started through, he shot a look over his shoulder.

"Order for us, Les, this ain't going to take long."

John trooped on out behind the half-breed. He did not really expect the range boss to make any kind of a treacherous move once he was clear of the building, but he stayed up close anyway, and, when the half-breed slowed outside on the plank walk, John reached and shoved him toward the roadway. That physical contact brought the half-breed around with a snarl.

John said: "Toss the gun down." When the angry range boss did not obey, John dropped a hand to his holstered Colt. "Drop it or draw it."

The range boss seemed half willing to do the one, then half willing to do the other. In the end he pulled out the gun and leaned to lay it upon the edge of the plank walk—then he whirled on his upward course and swung a big, looping blow that John turned away from. He then turned back as the half-breed's momentum brought him up straight. While the range boss was completing his initial attack, John settled down hard on his heels, and swung into the half-breed's unprotected middle. The range boss jackknifed, with pain twisting his face. He covered up and backed clear.

John did not go after him. Two men upon the opposite plank walk stood in astonishment, watching this private, silent battle. Then they called out to someone else, and three men hurried over to get a better view in the late dusk.

The range boss did not really recover from that sledging blow in the middle, but he pushed in again, no longer scornful. Now he wanted John Randolph's blood.

More men arrived, their boot steps echoing upon both plank walks as the combatants maneuvered out nearer the center of the road. John, who had never had doubts about this fight, had less doubts now as the half-breed, protecting his sore middle with a forearm, came in again, black eyes as deadly, as unwaveringly savage as the black eyes of a predator.

The half-breed shifted leads, changed course in mid-stride, and, when John switched positions to offset this fresh direction, the half-breed lunged, both arms pumping. One blow landed solidly, but the next two missed John, who was back-pedaling. He dropped his arms as he retreated. The half-breed saw his opportunity and with a ripped-out curse he plunged onward. John waited until the very last moment, then stepped in, settled, and fired his right hand, which had been hauled back and cocked. The half-breed's body wilted as his head snapped violently backward. His knees went rubbery. John fired his left fist. The half-breed went over backward, half twisted by the last impact, so that when he struck the roadway he was on his right side, and rolling.

He did not move. For three or four seconds neither did anyone else. Then a stocky large man with a battered felt hat moved up beside the range boss and said: "Too bad. Carl won't like this." The stocky large man turned almost dispassionately to face John. "What started it, mister?"

John's left-hand set of knuckles pained him, but his opposite hand, the one that had really done the damage, did not hurt at all. He massaged the left hand with the right as he said: "Just a little personal thing. Nothing very big, I'd say. It's settled now."

The blocky large man studied John Randolph a while, as did about a dozen other men who crowded up closer to make out John's face better in the poor light. "Your name?" asked the large man.

"John Randolph."

"Who you riding for, John?"

"No one. Right now I'm not working for anyone." John began taking an interest in this large, blocky man. "Are you by any chance the town marshal?"

The blocky man shook his head. "Nope. The marshal's down with the Mex pocks. Me, I'm only his brother-in-law. I help out a little, now and again." He looked down again. "Mister Randolph, this man is Carl Tandy's range boss. Now then I'd guess you don't really have much call to hang around town, do you? Take my advice, saddle up and get to riding. Carl isn't going to like this at all."

John smiled. "I'll think about your advice," he said, and went over, retrieved the half-breed's Colt, walked back to hand it to the large, blocky man, then he smiled again. "He'll be all right. A mite sore in the middle for a day or two is all."

No one spoke, or moved to interfere as John returned to the plank walk over in front of the restaurant. Back there stood the cowboy with whom the range boss had entered the café. He looked stonily at John Randolph. He was no taller than Beverly Harding, which made him about a head shorter than John. This did not act as a deterrent, though. As John turned southward, this rider said: "Mister, the next time, I kind of doubt that anyone around here's going to let you use your fists."

John paused. The shorter man had his hand already in place upon the butt of his Colt. "I don't think we have a fight going," Randolph commented. "I don't even know you. As for that other . . . well, if you're going to Tandy's place with the range boss this evening, tell him John Randolph will still be waiting around here tomorrow. There were two others with him, along with the range boss. Tell him to fetch them along, too."

John shouldered on past heading in the direction of the livery barn.

The half-breed came around. Someone brought him a glass of water from the café. Someone else hastened up to the saloon for something stouter than water, but the half-breed allowed himself to be helped to the edge of the plank walk, and over there, when the whiskey arrived, he shook his head. His stomach already felt as though a horse had kicked him in the middle; it did not need any other obstacles to try and surmount.

He asked the cowboy who had been inside the café with him to go fetch their horses from the livery barn, and to everyone else in the crowd of men who asked, the half-breed simply turned a snarling expression. He had been hurt, and of course he had also been humiliated, but most of all he had been beaten badly by a man he had seen Carl Tandy whip to a pulp the previous day, and the half-breed knew for a fact he was younger and tougher than Carl was—and yet that same clumsy drifter Carl had bloodied in the Harding corral yesterday had just handed him the worst beating of his life, in the shortest length of time. He did not want to discuss it with anyone.

The man he sent for the horses encountered John there, in the middle of the wide, long runway. John said nothing, but when he turned and their eyes met, the other man felt impelled to speak. Some men were like that; let them get agitated about anything at all, and their first response was to get vocal. The cowboy was stepping briskly deeper into the barn, looking for the night man, when he said: "You're smart, mister, rigging out and riding on. That Tandy outfit eats 'em like you for breakfast every morning."

John laughed. "Are you a Tandy rider?"

The cowboy nodded. "Yeah. I just hired on this morning. Me 'n' the range boss met on the northeast range and he hired me on the spot."

"Well, then," said John, still amused, "you haven't really been working for Tandy long enough yet to know how tough the outfit is, have you?"

The cowboy hurried on deeper into the barn without additional conversation, and that blocky, large man who was the marshal's brother-in-law came ambling on up to John. He did not look tough or mean, or even annoyed. Back there in the center of the road, gazing downward, he'd been equally as calm and seemingly detached as he was now when he said: "So you're leaving."

John leaned upon a stall door. This was the second time that assumption had been made. "No, I'm not leaving," he replied, looking at the blocky man. "I couldn't go now even if I wanted to. I sent word to Carl Tandy I'd be waiting around town for him tomorrow."

The blocky man showed his first different expression. His dark, heavy brows pulled downward and inward. "Are you saying this here personal feud you had with Tandy's range boss includes the whole Tandy outfit?"

"Just two more riders, and Carl Tandy." John turned as a hostler brought forth two horses and went to work saddling them for the nervous cowboy.

The blocky man studied John for a moment before speaking again. "Mister, that just ain't going to happen. Not in this town. Not as long as I'm taking over as lawman for my brother-in-law. Nobody's going to start any big gunfight here in Cottonwood."

John leaned and said nothing, and kept watching the cowboy and the hostler. When the saddling up was finished, the cowboy mounted one horse and, leading the other one, rode past, outward bound. But this time he would not so much as turn his head to look in John's direction.

The blocky man evidently did not like John's silence. He reached and gently tapped John's chest. "Do us all some good, mister. Do yourself some good at the same time. Saddle up tonight and head out."

For a moment that tapping on the chest brought a slight cloud to John's face, but it passed. He turned and moved away, still without speaking. The blocky man seemed to want to intercept him, but in the end he did nothing, and, as John walked back out into the night, the hostler came forth from the depths of the barn and said: "I wouldn't go to pushing that one too much, Will. I've seen them real calm, sort of smiling ones before. That's the kind that'll kill you."

IX

Cottonwood was not a large town, but it could have been twice as large as it was and the news of that bizarre fight out front of the café southward of the saloon would still have made the rounds in record time, because everyone around Cottonwood knew both Mike Farrell, the range boss at the Tandy outfit, and Carl Tandy, the man no one expected to take the beating of his range boss with a smile. Also, there was interest in the man named John Randolph, who had administered that beating. Up at the saloon the bartender told it all again and again, but, unlike the livery barn night man, the bartender offered no personal assessments. All he said when people asked was that John Randolph had appeared to him just like any other cowboy who'd ever loafed away half a day in his saloon. But the bartender did recall one thing. He told Will Sutton who was filling in for his ill brother-in-law, the town marshal, that Earl Buscomb from the Harding place had ridden in earlier, at about midafternoon, and the two of them, Buscomb and Randolph, had sat and talked over a beer or two.

No one approached John, even up at the bar where most of the customers, townsmen and range men both, had this interesting fresh scrap of local information to dissect. They did not bother John because he stood slightly apart, to himself, something that did not invite friendship. Only the bull-necked barman had anything to say, and he offered it from a generous heart.

"Mister, if I was you, I wouldn't spend too much time strutting. You did it fair and square, the town realizes you done it that way, and no one's going to call you for whipping him . . . but the longer you stay around, the worse it'll be for you."

John sipped his drink, listening and thinking. The barman had no reason to dislike John. He seemed to be speaking sincerely. The only acknowledgement he got that John Randolph had even heard was when John said: "Tell me something. How far from town is the headquarters for Tandy's range?"

The barman squinted his eyes a moment, then answered: "Just guessing, I'd say maybe six, seven miles."

John calculated, then said: "The range boss had to ride six, seven miles home, and he wasn't much in shape to make a rush out of it. Then Tandy'd have to get organized and ride back six, seven miles." John upended his whiskey glass, downed the contents, set the glass aside, and bobbed his head at the barman. "See you in the morning. Those fellers would have to waste two-thirds of the night to get back here. I'll look for them in the morning."

The barman's dark gaze turned sardonic. "You'd better look for Doc Jennings in the morning, too. He does all the undertaking work around here. Mister, Carl Tandy won't forget to be here. You're making one hell of a big mistake."

John went across the road to the back alleyway, then he turned southward, and at the lower end of town he entered the livery barn from out back in the darkness, which was the customary way for saddle bums to bed down in someone's hayloft. He wasn't a saddle bum, but he had been one a time or two, and it still rankled to have to spend good money to rent a room with a bed in it for just one night. Haylofts were usually cleaner and better-smelling, anyway.

He made it up the ladder without being discovered. Most liverymen did not take kindly to the custom of itinerant riders using their hay for bedding, but the only time they really raised a ruckus was when some fellow bedded down up there, then had a smoke before going to sleep. Someone else might have had trouble sleeping, but John Randolph simply closed his eyes.

He had no more dread of the morrow than he had had of the day that was now ending.

In the morning he washed out back, shaved at the tonsorial parlor, then breakfasted at the same hole-in-the-wall café where he'd dined the previous evening. The only noticeable difference was that today the hard, cold-eyed woman at the café with the dyed black hair was slightly more pleasant. Not much more pleasant, but a little, and later, when John returned to the livery barn to check on his horse, they were unusually civil down there, too.

He was amused. At the saloon the same barman with the same plastered-down hair and the elegant gold chain across his vest set up a beer glass without being told, and because John was the only one in the place so early, the barman rolled a smoke, leaned comfortably, and became slightly confidential.

"Mike and some others are sweating blood," he told John. "They know Tandy'll come to town today, ready to claw his way through a stone wall to make trouble."

John considered the bull-necked man. "And you don't care?"

The barman raised steady dark eyes. "Why should I? No matter which way it goes, friend, folks'll end up in here drinking. They always do."

John stood watching the other man. "Care to tell me anything about Carl Tandy?"

The barman shook his head. "Only that he'll sure tree you, mister. If you had to go out for trouble, why didn't you pick someone else's range boss. You could have taken Garrison's man out, or Flint's man, or even old Angus McDouglass's range boss . . . but you had to take Mike Farrell. Care for another beer?"

John paid for the one he'd had and strolled outside, strolled over across the road by the public trough, and with three old duffers watching him with great interest he stepped into their tree shade, facing slightly northward in the direction of the upper end of town, and, when the first old man gravely nodded and said—" 'Morning."—John Randolph replied the same way.

" 'Morning. Going to be another hot one from the looks of things."

The three old men exchanged slitted looks. One of them slapped his leg and cackled. "Sure will be, young feller, unless you hitch up and shag your tail out of Cottonwood."

John smiled at this particular old man. "Maybe Carl Tandy is made of iron. What makes you so sure he's going to eat me alive?"

The old man shot a cautious and slightly malevolent glance upward, then jumped his eyes away when he spoke. "Mister, I *know* the Tandys. I've known 'em, father and son and grandson, for an awful lot of years. They've always been right bad people to cross. And mister . . . I don't *know* you. Never seen you before in my life that I can recollect now. So you see, the odds as far as I'm concerned, are sure stacked against you."

One of these three oldsters was leaner and tanner and more fit-looking than his companions. He did not actually seem as old, either, but that was something a cursory glance could never determine, but in any case he meticulously rolled a cigarette and spoke without taking his eyes off his work: "Cowboy, since last night folks around here haven't been talking of much else but you, and generally they think you're either crazy to be challenging the entire Tandy outfit, or that maybe you aren't crazy at all. Maybe you got friends hid out, or something." The old man lit up, blew smoke, snapped his match, then, finally, raised his eyes. "You das'n't be doing this all by yourself. Because even if you could best Carl and any of his men as wanted to take it up for him, you sure as hell couldn't make no headway at all against the whole town." The old man removed his smoke. "They're going to stop it, if they can, cowboy, and, if they can't stop it, they're going to be at a dozen windows around here. You start a bad fight here and you'll get riddled."

John listened to this particular man. He knew the type, had, in fact, lived and worked right alongside of them since he'd had to flee Kansas. This man was not malevolent; he was practical and shrewd and without any particular illusions.

"It'll be fair," John said.

The old man smiled gently. "Naw, it won't. One way or t' other, it won't be fair. Either you're crazy and Carl's going to kill you, cowboy, or you know something the rest of us don't know, and you'll kill Carl Tandy. The minute *that* happens, cowboy, you're not going out of this town standing up."

"Carl Tandy's the local hero?" asked John, and all three of the old men snickered.

The lean, tanned one removed his cigarette, again, to answer. "I don't believe Carl's even a hero to his own family. But that ain't it. If you're a gunfighter, cowboy, and, if you kill Carl, the town's sure as hell's not going to send someone like Will Sutton out in the roadway to take your gun. That's what folks are waiting to see. If you outdraw Carl Tandy, who is a good man with a gun, you're as good as dead."

"And if I don't outdraw him?"

The old man, the one with the malevolence lurking behind his smile, answered up: "If you don't outdraw him, mister you're also dead." The old man laughed and slapped his leg and continued to laugh.

John smiled. He and the youngest and toughest-looking of the old men looked steadily at one another, and, although John looked amused, the tanned man did not. He went back to smoking his cigarette and gazing out into the morning light in the roadway. As far as he was concerned, the conversation was finished.

John left the shade by the trough, but he did not walk far.

The large, blocky man named Will Sutton, who was the town marshal's brother-in-law, came out of a deep doorway and said: "Randolph!"

John turned. The blocky man was wearing a gun and shell belt, something he had not worn the previous evening in the roadway, or later down at the livery barn. He looked bleak and craggy as he faced John.

"Your horse is saddled," he told John, and pointed down in the direction of the tie rack out front of the livery barn. As he dropped his arm, the stand-in town marshal sighed as though he really did not much like this rôle of obdurate law enforcer. "No one wants trouble with you, Mister Randolph, but no one wants a fight in town, either. You'd better mount up and light out."

John sensed, rather than saw, that this was not a one-man action, and perhaps he should have expected it, except that he hadn't really expected the town to care all this much about two men settling a difference. He had, evidently, made one serious mistake. He had underestimated the town, not the man he was waiting for.

Will Sutton said: "Don't touch your holster." He said that sharply, but in the next breath his voice softened again. "Listen to me. You aren't going to be allowed to call Tandy out. That's final. This morning before breakfast we had a meeting of the town council. It was decided that if we had to, we'd disarm you and lock you up ourselves."

John turned slowly. Across the road two men were standing slightly apart in front of the general store. Up in the direction of the saloon, another man was standing, relaxed and easy, in overhang shade. All three of those men were armed.

Sutton, guessing John's thoughts, made a suggestion. "If you want, you can walk down to your horse without no armed escort. Why don't you do that, Randolph? Save us all a lot of embarrassment. We got nothing against you. We just don't want to see no one get killed here today."

John faced him, lifted out his six-gun, and offered it to Sutton. "I'm not leaving until I've seen Tandy."

The blocky man was puzzled. He made no move to accept the proffered weapon. "You can't stay . . . and be unarmed," he finally said.

John continued to hold out the gun. "Sure I can. I don't want to kill him, particularly. That would be up to him. But if I'm unarmed, and, if you boys will see to it that he is also unarmed, and if you'll keep his riders off my back, all I want to do is settle a score with him. No one is going to get killed."

Sutton's broad, low brow furrowed. "You mean . . . just fist fight him?"

"Yes."

Sutton still did not take the gun, but he raised questioning eyes to the men across the road, first, and then he did take the gun. Stepping around John, he went hiking toward those waiting townsmen.

X

Occasionally people wagered on the outcome of gunfights, but not too often. The results of a gunfight were seldom the kind of thing people derived any pleasure from at all. Even when someone got himself killed who had, in the eyes of the community, earned it, and perhaps had even deserved it, no one really derived much of a sense of satisfaction from it. Death was too awfully final. But what in the cow country was commonly called a dog fight, meaning a brawling fistfight, was something else. It was not actually considered the kind of thing grown men ought to get involved with, but that did not keep them from getting involved, as participants, as spectators, or as wagerers.

The way the barman explained it to Rhett Carver, the saddle

maker, John Randolph did not stand a chance, and those who for some silly reason based on principle—or whatever—did not put good money on this fight deserved to lose out on what was surely the best bet to appear in Cottonwood in a blue moon. Even when Will Sutton met with those armed members of the Cottonwood town council, carrying Randolph's weapon as proof of what he said, he was of the strong opinion that, since Randolph only wanted to dog fight with Tandy, the town council hadn't ought to interfere, and, as for himself, he was going up to the saloon and see what kind of odds he could get.

"Odds on who?" one of the town councilmen asked.

"Randolph," Sutton replied, and immediately there were three loud snorts of derision, three outcries, and before the marshal's brother-in-law could get away to head for the saloon, he had already made three bets of two-to-one favoring Tandy and against John Randolph. At the saloon Sutton got a look either of skeptical suspicion or of abject pity. Only when he solemnized a wager with the barkeep did Will Sutton began to have a terrible feeling in the pit of his stomach. It was not possible for him to be right against so many men around town, most of whom could have bought and sold Will Sutton. But it was done. Will bought a beer and took it to a roadside window, then sat there, feeling more and more disconsolate. Not until John Randolph walked in an hour later, sighted Sutton by the front window, and went over to inquire amiably how he had made out with the town council, did Will Sutton's spirits rise even a little.

He leaned upon the table and said: "How come you to figure you can whip Carl Tandy?"

John got comfortable before replying. "Because I've fought him before."

Sutton's entire face brightened. "And you won!"

"No," stated John, "I lost." Sutton's face fell. John got no opportunity to explain because the barman brought a beer and stood with his fat palm extended for the 5¢ piece. He smiled indulgently at John Randolph, then departed, and, as John watched his retreat, he had an impression that he had just faced one of those who would wager against him.

Sutton said: "You should have told me this before."

John's brows lifted. "Why should I have? What's it to you whether Tandy and I've met before?"

Will Sutton, the blocky, large man with the resolute expression, looked dolorous. "Because I got three hundred and fifty dollars bet on you, and it's taken me three years to save all that money . . . and, if I lose it. . . ." Sutton shuddered and rolled up his eyes, and John Randolph laughed at him.

"I thought you people weren't going to allow a fight?" Randolph said.

"This is different. This isn't a gunfight." The substitute marshal leaned and dropped his voice. "Tell me . . . what do you figure your chances are of winning?"

John drained half his glass before replying. With a sardonic twinkle in his eyes he said: "About seventy-thirty." He drained the beer glass, arose, nodded, and started toward the bar, leaving Will Sutton to puzzle out whether John Randolph thought he had a seventy percent better chance to win than Carl Tandy had, or whether he thought it might be the other way around.

Someone out in the roadway called out, the way it was customary to do when a stage had been sighted up the roadway. John ambled to a window and looked northward. Others crowded over, also. A small band of riders was swinging down through morning's golden brilliance, scuffing dust and pressing along. They looked to be perhaps a long mile upcountry, but no one who saw those horsemen had any doubt at all about who they were.

John turned to where Will Sutton was standing and said:

"Are you going to disarm Tandy and his crew?"

Sutton looked back from the window. "Nothing was said about that."

With a motion hardly anyone saw, John leaned and swooped the gun from Sutton's hip holster and dropped it into his own empty holster. As Sutton stepped away and put his right hand to the empty place, John said: "I told you I wasn't here to make bad trouble. And now I'll tell you something else. I'm not here for anyone to toss to the wolves. You want this gun back? Then disarm Tandy and his crew and I'll give it back to you."

John stepped rearward around a card table and went over to the doors. He growled and the men who were crowding up over there dissolved on both sides, allowing John to walk outside under the wooden overhang. From there, he had a much better view of the oncoming horsemen, and, by turning his head, he had an excellent view of the southward roadway. Cottonwood's main roadway was just about deserted. There was no pedestrian traffic, either, on the opposing plank walks. John turned as someone shouldered out of the saloon behind him. It was Sutton. John did not smile but he made a facetious remark. "It's like Christmas morning out here in the road."

Sutton, with a dogged expression, said: "Give me back the gun."

Instead of answering, John stepped down off the plank walk into the dust and barely more than glanced northward as he struck out in the direction of the big tree by the public watering trough.

Sutton did not follow. He turned and hastened back inside, evidently to confer with others. Now Will Sutton had more to worry about than losing his $350.

The town of Cottonwood had survived dilemmas before, many of them, and in terms of numbers of people involved, it had lived through many that were infinitely more baffling than this current one. As word trickled around in the saloon, that John Randolph was armed again, and that what everyone had wagered money on as a dog fight might now turn into a gunfight, the townspeople reverted to their earlier disapproval. No one, it seemed, wanted a killing in the morning roadway. A little punching was all right, but no guns.

The problem, though, with Tandy riding steadily toward town from a mile or less out, was how to disarm Randolph. No one, it turned out, wished to leave the saloon at this late stage of developments, go across and try to take the gun away from Tandy's enemy. When the suggestion was made, several onlookers inside the saloon demurred on the grounds that they did not like the heat in the roadway and would therefore prefer to remain where it was cool, inside the saloon. Another passable excuse, no worse at least than the first one, was that, while someone might get across the road to where Randolph was waiting, down by the public trough, there was precious little chance of them getting back again. Carl Tandy was bound to be fighting mad, and for some innocent man to get caught over there beside Randolph was just plain foolish.

Nothing happened, of course. Nothing could have happened even if the townsmen had had some unanimity of opinion. It was, as the oldsters in the saloon opined, just plain too late.

As far as John Randolph was concerned, he was probably the least disturbed man among all the people in town watching those riders swing closer to the north end of town. He had expected there to be about five men with Carl Tandy, but evidently someone was missing. It wasn't hard to guess who had stayed behind, unable, and perhaps also unwilling, to make this ride, having already made it once the previous evening. Still those were formidable odds. Four-to-one. Carl Tandy and those three cowboys loping along with him, against one man down by the public trough, leaning upon that raffish old unkempt tree down there.

By the time it had been decided among the town fathers that a posse was to be made up, someone at the doors of the saloon turned and sang out: "It's Tandy all right! Him and his riders just reached the north end of town. Now, they're slowin' down to a walk."

There was reason for Tandy to slacken speed. He and his men could look all the way out through the lower end of town and see only quiet storefronts, empty roadway, and dazzling sunshine. It was like riding into an empty or an abandoned town. It was probable neither Tandy nor his range riders had ever before experienced anything like this in the Cottonwood country, and for men bent on trouble, every change, everything that was even slightly different than it should have been, stood out clearer, sharper, more menacing.

John leaned upon the tree in deep shade, watching. Carl Tandy looked the same as he had three days earlier. What people around town had either told John, or had implied to him, was abundantly clear. Carl Tandy was a bad man to cross. As he rode slightly in the lead of his men, dark eyes narrowed beneath the tipped-down rim of his hat, Tandy's eyes probed and searched. He did not see John while he was still north of the saloon, but eventually he would see him. John could very simply have stepped out of Tandy's line of vision by moving around the big tree, but he chose to remain where he was.

Over at the general store a large, paunchy man wearing a white apron walked forth upon the plank walk, stood a moment looking up where those riders were moving southward, then he turned and without haste went back inside.

At the livery barn the day man was leaning upon a manure fork in the doorway, as still as stone. He had an even better view; because the day man was on the same side of the road as John Randolph was, he could see John more clearly than he could see Tandy. It must have suddenly crossed the day man's mind that being behind and southward of John Randolph was not the best place to be. He lifted his fork and went scuttling back down deeper into the barn.

Carl Tandy swung in toward the side-lot tie rack next to the saloon, swung down, looped his reins, then tipped back his hat and stood, thumbs hooked above his shell-belt buckle, waiting for his riders to tie up, also. While he stood like that, he made a yard by yard examination of the yonder roadway—and saw John Randolph, leaning there behind the stone trough.

John did not move. This would be Tandy's first opportunity. They were sufficiently distant from one another to make it an interesting gun duel. Except for the men in the side lot, no one was moving out in the roadway. John remained motionless. Finally, when his riders came forward, Carl Tandy turned without a word and headed for the saloon.

John loosened a little in his pleasant shade. The first crisis had come and gone. He smiled slightly over that. Tandy had made his first mistake. Facing someone was harder each time a man had a chance and turned his back on it.

At the saloon, the hush that had prevailed earlier was shattered the moment Tandy and his riders walked in. John could hear it all the way over where he was waiting. Men's voices, unrecognizable even though they were raised loudly, were warning Tandy. They were also encouraging him. No one, it seemed, was actually neutral. Maybe no one in Cottonwood had ever actually been neutral, and this, to John Randolph, had been his secret weapon. He had not mentioned it, even to Earl Buscomb, but he knew from years of experience that men who were known as bullies had enemies. He was gambling on this now.

While he waited, John examined the Colt he had taken from Will Sutton. It had good balance and was loaded with six shells, instead of the five-shot-spread some men used. He dropped it back and drew it forth, twice. It was a good, dependable weapon. The last time he eased it gently into the holster.

Tandy would have to come out sometime. What John was curious about was whether the townsmen over there with all their opposition to a gunfight would allow Tandy to leave the saloon armed. John was privately betting that they would not, but just in case—he let his right hand lie lightly upon the handle of Will Sutton's six- gun.

XI

It was still early, only a little past 10:00. The heat was increasing. It seemed to arrive more quickly in town than it did out on the range. Where John stood, waiting, though, it was very pleasant. No doubt that was why those old gaffers had selected the area around the public trough for their daily meetings. Today, they did not appear. Not for a long while did anyone at all approach the place. Then it was that paunchy individual from across the road. He was the proprietor of the general store and his name was Burt Stebbins, but John only guessed his occupation by the white apron and otherwise knew nothing about him at all.

He had a look of granite-like determination on his face as he marched across the empty roadway and halted on the near side of the stone trough. "Mister Randolph," he said in a harsh tone of voice, "there's been a meeting held at the saloon."

John gazed at the paunchy man coolly. "Is that a fact?"

"Yes, it's a fact. Carl Tandy has agreed to come out into the roadway unarmed. None of his men will come out with him."

John nodded. "The no-gun faction won out, didn't they? How did you know about this?"

The merchant replied in a less harsh tone: "Some of the boys up there come down the back alley and told me. I was to walk over here and ask if you'd do the same . . . hand over your gun and walk out into the center of the road."

John did not hesitate. "Sure. The minute I see Tandy up there in the center of the road, alone and with an empty holster, I'll put this gun on the trough." John smiled. "How are you betting, storekeeper?"

The paunchy man did not smile back. "I'm not a wagering man." He paused, studying John. "I have your word?"

"You have it. No one is to be in the roadway until Tandy and I've settled things. No one!"

The paunchy man bobbed his head briskly. "I'll tell them," he said, and turned to march back to his store.

John looked southward. The town was still and quiet in that direction. He thought he caught the faint sound of a rig, or perhaps a wagon, somewhere southwest of town, but up in front of the saloon someone made a kind of muffled call that brought John's attention back northward.

Carl Tandy came forth under the saloon overhang without his hat and without his shell belt. He looked disdainfully toward the public trough and seemed not to raise his voice when he said: "All right, cowboy, put the gun on the trough." As he spoke, Tandy stepped out into the roadway, moving slowly, almost nonchalantly. He was obviously very confident. He had reason to be.

Several men followed out as far as the edge of the plank walk. One of them was the bull-necked bartender; another was Will Sutton. It was Sutton who reached when a third man would have stepped off the plank walk and hauled him back with a growl. Evidently John Randolph's terms were going to be followed. Across the road the paunchy man in the storekeeper's apron came out just beyond his doorway and nodded toward John without opening his mouth. He was, evidently, acting in some kind of capacity for John Randolph.

For John, the private gamble had paid off. He moved without

haste around to the front of the trough, unbuckled his shell belt and draped it upon the edge of the trough. He did not remove his hat, as Tandy had done. He did not expect to wear it for long, but at least it offered shelter from the sunlight until he had walked over to where Carl Tandy was waiting, standing with all his weight on one leg, looking contemptuous. Tandy had been riding through the sunlight and was accustomed to its glare. John needed a minute or two for his eyes to become accustomed to the glare. Everything seemed clearer, sharper, almost painfully distinct to John Randolph as he went forward. Even the tough-set lines around the dark man's mouth were visible to him, and the drawn-out narrow expression around Tandy's eyes. The cowman was making his appraisal now, making his judgment, and deciding upon his course. John knew it and purposely showed what could have been a faint hint of reluctance. When they were closer, Tandy said: "Cowboy, you can still get your horse and ride out."

John did not respond until they were something like fifteen feet apart. Then, instead of pursuing this topic, he said: "There is something you might want to think about on your ride home this evening, Tandy. Your son lied to you. He probably lied to you because he couldn't make himself admit that Connie Harding split his lip with a punch. If you hadn't been in such a hurry to rough someone up the last time we met, maybe you could have got the truth first."

Tandy's contemptuous expression deepened. "What kind of a man tries to weasel out of a beating by laying the blame on a kid?" Tandy ended the talk at this point by starting to move. He was a powerful man, and, as John already knew, he could hit with the force of a mule kick with either fist. There was nothing tricky or scientific to this kind of a battle. It would be power opposing power from start to finish. Tandy was experienced, too.

John had an edge no one understood. He knew exactly how

this fight was supposed to go. He had been through a lot of these dog fights, and from them all he had learned just one thing—when two men were as nearly matched in size and power as he and Carl Tandy were, then the man who would win would be the one who could grasp the initiative at exactly the right moment, and use it. That was what John was thinking as he let Tandy march straight at him. At the last moment, John feinted to the right, using a tactic he had used upon Tandy's half-breed range boss. When the cowman shifted course to continue advancing, John stepped suddenly to the left and pawed Tandy off balance.

The cowman was angered, but he covered up well and back-pedaled. He also lost a little of that look he'd been wearing, and began to concentrate harder on the younger man out front. John started in, and this time, because he anticipated a furious charge, he moved on light feet. When Tandy made his grunting lunge, John twisted clear, then twisted back and swung.

Tandy went down in a heap, rolled cursing to his feet, and sprang up, his face white. He hadn't been injured; he'd just been caught with one foot off the ground and knocked sideways.

John started forward again. Tandy would not try a second lunge so soon, but John kept up on his toes regardless. They sparred, pawed, sought advantages, and John ducked below a corn-husker's powerhouse, came up under Tandy's guard, and sank a combination left and right into the cowman's unprotected middle. This time, when Tandy gave ground, his legs were sluggish and his mouth was white from the pressure of pain and self-control.

John had not noticed any shouting, up until this moment. Then he noticed it because it suddenly stopped completely, as everyone stared in disbelief. Carl Tandy fought to overcome the pain and to regain his breath. He managed to keep clear as John stalked him. He threw a blow that grated across the bone and sinew of Randolph's upthrown forearm. He tried the left-right feint John had used, but his legs weren't quite up to it. John started moving around Tandy. The cowman had to keep twisting, keep turning, had to keep trying to keep John off while he got set. But he could not get set when he was constantly off balance, twisting around.

John moved more swiftly. Tandy had to do the same. John suddenly halted and swung. Carl Tandy, again off balance, saw the strike coming too late. He dropped his face into the curl of a protective shoulder and took the blow high on the head. His arms dropped. John reached, caught Tandy's shirt front, yanked the cowman to him, then swung from the belt. That time, the blow was muffled. Tandy's shoulders dropped. John gave him a fierce shove backward, then sledge-hammered him under the ear, and, as he was falling, John crossed with a loose-looping left and finished the demolition.

Tandy struck the roadway and dust flew. He reached around on each side with blind, scrabbling fingers trying to hold something, trying to gather himself up. He was functioning now by nothing but pure instinct.

In front of the saloon a man called over in a shrill voice: "That's enough. Randolph, god dammit, he's had enough!"

John hadn't put the boots to the downed man, nor had he reached to haul Tandy half upright so he could end it with a strike to the jaw. Evidently someone over in front of the saloon, though, expected these things to happen. John's left hand pained him. His right knuckles were skinned and raw but otherwise he had suffered very little injury.

A tall, lean, white-headed man came walking forward from nearby the general store. John recognized him as the local doctor. When John stepped clear, he happened to turn and glance southward. There was a top buggy not a hundred feet away in the center of the road. It was motionless. Earl Buscomb had the lines and beside him upon the single seat were Beverly Harding and Connie. The only one who looked engrossed was Connie; she had one small nut-brown hand curled into a fist.

John met Beverly Harding's gaze without smiling. She was pale, her eyes dark with shock. If she had seen the entire fight, then she might well be shocked. It had been a merciless beating right from the start.

Dr. Jennings arose, dusted his knee, and shot a glance at John Randolph. "Are you satisfied?" he asked.

John nodded. "Plumb satisfied. How about him?"

The doctor shrugged. "That's a good question. I wish I could answer for him, but I can't. All I can say, young man, is that he'd be foolish to try it this way again." Dr. Jennings was not friendly. He saw the buggy and turned his back on John to walk down there.

Will Sutton was crowing over on the plank walk in front of the saloon, calling out names and demanding his winnings. It wasn't exactly what a professional lawman might have done, but then Will Sutton wasn't a professional lawman.

Tandy's riders came over, malevolent and menacingly silent as they lifted their employer and took him over to the water trough to sluice him off. Other men approached. John knew some of them, most of them in fact, by sight, but he did not know their names. He went on across the road and into the general store, which was about the only place close where he could find with any luck some privacy, at least a moment or two during which he could catch his breath and flex his hands.

The paunchy storekeeper stood and gravely regarded him. He did not look as though he approved at all, but on the other hand he did not look entirely disapproving. He saw the lacerated hands and wordlessly produced a jar of liniment and some pieces of clean cloth. As John was smearing salve upon his hands, the storekeeper said: "I think what you did was stupid.

One man bucking an entire cow outfit. And the Tandy outfit at that. But you've made your point. Now, if you're wise, young man, you'll put a lot of miles between you and this town."

John finished with the salve and clean rags, dropped a silver coin atop the counter, and hardly more than nodded as he walked back out into the roadway.

Carl Tandy's men had carted him over to the saloon. There were little clutches of talking and gesturing men up and down the roadway on both sides. The Harding Ranch top buggy had been driven out of the center of the roadway, and, as John stepped forth from the store, a man's gravelly voice said: "Why didn't you tell me this was what you was up to, dang it? I'd have stayed in town last night and been around to lend a hand today."

John turned to face Earl. Connie was standing very erect, beside Buscomb, looking up at John with an expression John could not define. He winked at her, then said: "I'll do that next time, Earl. This time I sort of wanted to settle it my way, and alone."

Connie smiled. "You sure settled it."

Earl glared downward. "Go set in the top buggy with your maw."

Connie did not budge until John turned slowly and showed his faintest annoyance with her. Then she left at once and Earl said: "Boy! Miz Harding was surprised right down to her boots when we turned up the road . . . and there you and Carl Tandy was, whacking away at each other. She looked like she'd seen a ghost."

XII

Dr. Jennings was over with Beverly Harding in the shade of the side lot next to the saloon when John walked over. Connie was there, too, big-eyed with hero-worship and as still as a mouse when Dr. Jennings straightened around at John's approach, and gravely inclined his head.

"If I sounded brusque out in the roadway," he said to John Randolph, "it was because I had no idea of the circumstances surrounding your fight with Carl Tandy." Dr. Jennings leaned his head sideways in the direction of the top buggy's occupant. "Beverly has explained."

John was courteous to the doctor, but he really had no interest in him, so he simply smiled and nodded, then moved closer to the interior shade of the buggy. When Beverly Harding looked over, he said: "It's a pretty poor way to settle differences, ma'am, I'll agree with that, but Carl Tandy doesn't think so, which left me without much in the way of an alternative."

She did not discuss the fight. She said: "Are you coming back to the ranch now, Mister Randolph?"

Connie leaned, tensed for his answer. He looked briefly at her, then at Dr. Jennings. "Maybe not, ma'am. As long as I'm not on your payroll, if there is some unpleasantness comes out of this fight . . . and the one last night . . . it would be better all around if you weren't mixed up in it."

Dr. Jennings spoke up. "Mister Randolph, I know this town. No unpleasant aftermath will come from here."

John gazed past Beverly at the medical practitioner, his expression slightly sardonic. "Can you say as much for the Tandy outfit, Doctor?"

Jennings surprised John. "I can, young man. I can tell you right now Carl Tandy will not take this one step further."

Jennings was one of those men that, when he said something, even something as improbable as this statement, it carried a ring of unimpeachable authenticity. John studied the man, remembering what Beverly had said about him. He also remembered the amount of respect the bartender had shown to Dr. Jennings. John smiled. "Miz Harding, when will you be heading back for the ranch?"

She looked enormously relieved about something when she answered: "As soon as Earl gets through over there across the road."

John turned. Buscomb, his hat back, his fingertips thrust into the saddle pockets of his Levi's, was holding forth in a sonorous voice over in front of the stage depot. John walked over, and, when Earl saw him coming, Buscomb came down from his authoritarian perch and raised enquiring eyes. John pointed. "The boss wants to head for home." He smiled, then turned and walked on down to the livery barn.

The day man was already bringing forth the strong bay horse. When John strolled in, the hostler could not quite do enough. He insisted on currying the horse all over, not as livery hostlers ordinarily did, just up where the saddle sat. He even went back to the saddle pole and lugged John's outfit over himself, and, when the bridling was also finished and John reached reluctantly into his pocket for some silver coins, the old man held aloft a work-enlarged hand and with an expression of benignity upon his coarse, seamed features, and said: "I couldn't hardly take nothing for helping you out a mite, Mister Randolph. Come by any time. Around here we're always right proud to see our friends."

John did not see the top buggy when he rode out, but he guessed that by now it would be a mile or so beyond town, heading northwest. He walked his horse until he was beyond the back lots, the town corrals, and the last clutch of residences, then he let the horse out a notch. It was willing to lope along; in fact, after its enforced delay at the livery barn where it had got no exercise, the bay horse was willing to do a lot more than just lope.

John held it down and kept peering ahead. Eventually he saw the top buggy. It was making good time. A lot had happened and the sun was only now reaching the meridian. In fact, as he loped along, watching the buggy, it seemed to John that more had happened in this day, in this half day than had happened in almost any other day within his memory. And there was another thing that rattled round inside his head. When he had ridden away from the Harding Ranch, he hadn't really been sure he would ever ride back again, not today, not five or ten years hence. Maybe, now that it was general knowledge that he had been in the employ of Beverly Harding, and that Carl Tandy had beaten him when he'd been practically unable to prevent it, back in Cottonwood he just might get a little more understanding. He could live without it. He'd never yet been in a town he couldn't live without. But for as long as he was on the Harding place, it would not hurt any to have a few friends in Cottonwood.

He hauled down to a long-legged walk for the last mile in order to give Earl ample time to put up the buggy and off-harness the combination horse. He also did not especially want to have to go through a lengthy explanation to Beverly and Connie; right at this moment he'd had about all the involvement with Carl Tandy he wanted to think about.

The buggy was still out front of the barn, shafts in the dust, and Earl was somewhere inside the barn when John rode up closer, close enough to see Beverly and her daughter almost at the main house. This looked like an opportune moment, so he rode down to the barn, swung off, and led the horse inside where Earl was swearing at the buggy mare for not standing still while he tried to pull the harness off backward, starting up front and walking toward the mare's hocks, bringing everything with him. Earl saw John walk in and said: "You're supposed to go over to the main house after supper this evening." Earl chortled. "You're going to get a chance to lay down a real impression. I never yet seen a woman who didn't look like she smelled something bad when she seen two grown men fighting, then, afterward, wanted it all re-told punch by punch. Mighty perverse animals, females." Earl gave the harness a savage tug and freed it off the mare's long tail. In the process he also pulled out a healthy handful of tail hair and the indignant mare let fly with one hind foot. She missed, but only just barely, and Earl, looking furious and also surprised, said: "You see. You see. Try and be nice to one of them and this is what you get for it. I'm all in favor of the Apache way. They give a man any trouble and he cuts their noses off."

John plucked off his saddle, poled it, then turned back to lead his horse out back by the bridle reins. "That's only for squaws they catch inside another buck's blankets," he told Earl. "Married squaws."

They finished at the barn and went to the bunkhouse. John gathered up his towel, his slab of lye soap, left his gun belt and hat, and trooped down to the creek. The last thing Earl said as John was walking away was: "Mind Connie now."

It was good advice. John knew even from the short period he'd spent at the Harding Ranch that Connie could be anywhere; she could drop from the barn loft or she could be hovering over some magical concoction to make freckles fade. She could also be in the midst of a biting, spitting, kicking, hitting, dog fight.

John laughed to himself as he turned northward up the creek. She wouldn't be as far from home as he would walk, to take his bath, but he would not rule out the entire possibility, either. So, he walked and walked.

It was a long afternoon, as it had been a long day. He was in no hurry in any event. By the time he found the ideal place for his bath, hidden in a maze of pale green creek willows quite a considerable distance northward of the ranch, he was content to lie in the water, which was not actually very cold because the pool was shallow and the overhead sun was hot, and go back in his mind over the events of the past week or so. He hadn't had an inkling any of it might happen when he'd sat upon that little northward knoll, looking a little nostalgically down toward the Harding ranch buildings. He felt his lip, felt the stiffness, felt the fading bruises elsewhere on his face, and decided he had been paid in full.

Later, he toweled off, with the sun well down, and dressed in the speckled shade, then gathered his effects and started back. There was still a good bit of daylight left, even after the sun departed. The walk was pleasant, the air heavy, the light no longer at all intense but still more than ample for good visibility, and a flock of lazy-flying insects of some kind flew along directly above John's head as a sort of winged escort.

When he reached the ranch again, there were lights at the main house and also at the bunkhouse. He entered down at the more functional building, just in time to see Earl starting working at the firebox of their cook stove. Earl usually did this with a good deal of profanity, but he wasn't the only bunkhouse or cook-shack *cocinero* who could not get a meal without profanity. In every cow camp John had ever visited, there had been at least one profane cook.

Earl craned around, then wrinkled his nose: "You didn't go up as far as the lilac bushes, did you?"

John looked. "As the what?"

"The first bathing hole northward has some wild lilacs over across on the yonder bank. The last feller who slept in the front bunk you're using used to come back from his bath up there smelling like a Mexican."

"Yeah, yeah," said John, "I know what he came back smelling like."

Earl turned. "Say, how's come you don't have your six-gun?"

"The town council's got it," replied John, going over to the water bucket which, in a bunkhouse, was never full. As he picked out the dipper and hung it from its peg, he said: "I'll ride in one of these days and get it back." Then he hiked due west to the creek to re-fill the bucket.

Earl rolled a cigarette one-handed, for practice, and spilled tobacco into his stew pot inevitably. When John came back, Earl asked seriously if he was bothered by worms, and, when he got a strange look, Earl said: "Well, it's a fair question. Lots of folks got worms. What I was going to tell you was that I spilled some terbacco into the pot, and, when I was a kid, they used to always say if folks had worms, put terbacco in the food."

John strolled over after parking the bucket, and looked. It was impossible, now, to tell whether Earl had spilled in a lot of tobacco or just a little; his stew was the same color, and in some places it was also of the constituency of flake tobacco.

John went back to the table, tossed his hat across to the door bunk, sat down, and leaned back, gazing out across the yard through the opened door. "I think this has been the longest day of my life," he confided. "It just doesn't seem to want to end."

Earl had his lumpy cigarette lighted. Now he was being careful to avoid dropping ashes into the stew. "It isn't over yet," he said. "The boss is probably going to fire you again . . . or something. I don't know why in hell she has to see you over on the porch after supper."

John looked around. Earl's expression showed candid curiosity. John laughed. "Maybe she's decided you are to teach Connie reading and ciphering and spelling, Earl. She can't let that kid grow up to be a holy terror without some kind of schooling."

Earl was flabbergasted. "Me? Me, teach a kid how to spell and cipher and all that? In case you didn't know, this here is summer vacation from school, and in the autumn she'll start back to school in town." Earl snorted. "Me? Mister, how could

I teach any of that stuff when I can't do any of it myself?" Earl pointed. "There's that bottle of whiskey hidden in the cupboard. If you'd get it out, we could at least have a drink before you go up there and get fired again. . . . Me? Teaching ciphering and spelling . . . ?"

John went after the whiskey and filled two small glasses. As he handed one glass to Earl, he said: "If she fires me again, I think I'll take her over my knee."

Earl drank his whiskey, shrugged off that suggestion, and held out his glass. "You got to go up there stone sober. I don't. How about re-filling my glass . . . and how about not re-filling yours?"

XIII

When John Randolph reached the wide, low steps at the base of the porch and glanced upward, he found that Beverly Harding was already there. She looked as though she might have been out there for some little time, perhaps a half hour. She arose as he started up toward her. She was wearing a white blouse that was sleeveless, and had a pale tan sweater flung around her shoulders. Her skirt was one of those split ones for riding, and she had on boots. She looked to John more as though she were ready to ride the range than to talk to anyone on her verandah.

She smiled at him gravely. "It's such a beautiful night, Mister Randolph."

He hadn't noticed, nor did he take this opportunity to look up and around. Whatever the night over his shoulder might be like, it could not possibly be as beautiful as she was. Starlight reached under the overhang and touched her lifted face, taking it back in years to early girlhood, making her young and sweet and wonderful again.

She returned to her chair, and, instead of taking the one beside her which she offered, John sauntered to the porch railing and eased down there, his back against a log upright. He could see her better from that point of vantage.

When she remained quiet, he said: "You'll want to know about the fight."

Her teeth shone, white and even, as she shook her head. "No, not particularly, Mister Randolph. I don't think you fought him without a valid reason."

He sat, admiring her, wondering what else she could have wanted to see him about. She did not appear in any hurry to bring up the subject, whatever it was. "Did you hear I also had a fight with his range boss last night?"

Beverly nodded. "I heard." That was all she said. John had his opinion about her indifference to these matters reinforced by the tone of voice she used. She sounded very slightly annoyed.

He sank back into silence and waited. Whatever was on her mind, she would have to bring it forth in her own good time. He had done as much as he cared to attempt toward encouraging conversation between them.

She looked at him and said: "Mister Randolph, I have a particular problem. Since Frank died, I really haven't known quite what to do, whether to sell the ranch or whether to build it up again, the way it was when Frank and his father were living. I'm a woman. . . ." She lifted her shoulders and let them fall, as though to indicate she really did not have to elaborate on that last remark. In fact, she did not have to enlarge upon it. John knew exactly what she had meant.

"If I build it back up, perhaps for my daughter to have someday. . . ." She paused again and looked him squarely in the face. "Earl won't be able to ride indefinitely, will he? I've noticed the last two years that he tires more quickly than he did once."

John defended Earl who he liked. "Don't we all tire a little sooner than we once did?"

She studied him, then softly smiled. "I like loyalty, Mister Randolph."

He didn't know about that, but he'd had about all that "Mister Randolph" he could stomach. "My first name is John," he told her. "The only time I expect folks to call me Mister Randolph will be when they pat me in the face with a shovel and some preacher stands up there telling the world what a wonderful feller Mister Randolph was." She was smiling, so he smiled back. "All right, ma'am?"

She was agreeable. "All right, John." She continued to smile as she reverted to her original topic. "You've guessed what I'm leading up to . . . John. Should I sell out and take Connie to a city and put her into a school that will make a lady out of her . . . or should I hang on, build up the place, and stay in the cattle business, which has always been good to the Hardings?"

He said: "Why ask me? I only work here. And sometimes that seems like an off-again, on-again thing."

"Because you'd know the answer, John. And because I'll only hang on and build the ranch up if you'll agree to stay on as range boss." She suddenly leaned forward. "You know a woman cannot possibly do it by herself, and you know why she can't. In fact, you're a very good example of that kind of prejudice. The reason you didn't want to stay in the first place was because, being a lifelong range man, you had a range man's inhibitions against ever working for a woman. Isn't that right?"

It was, but John didn't like the implication, so he simply said: "No one likes to think of themselves as being prejudiced, do they? So why don't we just leave that out of it?"

She remained intent as she said: "We *can't* leave it out, John. If I have a range boss men respect, they'll hire on, won't they? If I try to do the hiring . . . well, look at the situation I'm in now. There just is no point in my building up the ranch, if I have to ramrod it myself. I'd be much better off to sell it and move near some large city."

He swung his leg and gazed at her. The way she was leaning, the way her lovely face was lifted to him, with star shine upon it, made it hard for a healthy man to think of something having to do with ranching. But he looked away, eventually, out over the yard in the direction of the bunkhouse with its little squares of lamplight in the front wall.

She said: "I'll pay you the going rate for a range boss. I'll leave it up to you how to build the herd back up. In return, John, I need your promise that you'll stay. . . . I know how it is with range riders. They become inherent wanderers after a few years."

He looked back at her. "Not all of them, ma'am." He smiled a little. "The first six or eight years, yes, that's about the size of it. But later, a man has seen about all the country and has ridden just about all the trails, and been in most of the towns. There is a time, ma'am, when a range man thinks about something else."

She kept looking directly at him. "Settling down?"

"Yeah."

"Would you settle down here, John?"

He stood up off the railing, and looked down at her. "Yeah. I'd settle down here, ma'am." It was a bold thing to say when a man was thinking the kind of bold thoughts Randolph was thinking.

Beverly Harding was a full woman; she had every intuitive sense all mature women had. She also had something more, something many mature women did *not* possess—a candid understanding of herself, of her needs, and of her wants. She arose and went over beside him at the railing. She offered him her hand, and she knew, even if he did not know, that a handclasp between a woman and a man was not at all the same as a handclasp between two men.

"That's all I wanted you to say," she told him as their hands met. "I could never have done it without you."

They were close, facing one another in the warm, fragrant night. He held her small hand in a light grip. At first, he thought only how pathetically vulnerable she was. The admission that she could not do it without him would have been under different circumstances and with a different man a dangerous, perhaps even a fatal, thing to say.

He raised his free hand to her. She did not waver, did not drop her eyes as she brought up her other hand and laid it upon his palm. An entirely new and haunting aura came into the shadows around them, and, although John Randolph was a man of strong discipline and strong control, he wavered now.

She smiled. "In my lifetime there've only been four men I'd trust with everything I have. You're one of them, John."

He freed her hands and reached for her waist, let his hands rest lightly as he swayed her toward him. She did not resist, except to raise both hands to his chest as she lifted her face. He knew exactly what he was doing, and yet he had a peculiar sensation of being above this scene, looking down upon it as he lowered his head and felt the yielding, warm softness of her lips under his mouth. It was a gentle kiss.

She pushed free and said: "I didn't think it could be just . . . friendship . . . not even that first day you rode in, and then rode out again. I didn't believe you would really leave." She put her cheek against him and finally kept her face averted. "I should be ashamed of myself, John."

He was quiet. The nearest he had ever come to knowing a woman had been down along the border five years earlier, and that hadn't ended well; one morning he had awakened and the girl was gone. He never saw her again, but later he heard that she had married a Texas cowman. He had long since forgiven her and had manufactured a very plausible reason for her disappearance—why would any lovely girl want to throw her life away on a wandering range rider? But tonight, in the hush and wonder, there was much that was very different. Tonight he was a mature man. What he wanted from a woman now was not the same.

He roused himself and said: "Why should you be ashamed, Beverly. There's nothing to be ashamed of . . . unless, come morning. . . ."

"I won't feel differently in the morning, John. I'm not a confused girl in a man's arms for the first time. Do you want to know what I really am?"

The way she said that, in a strong voice, made him flinch from answering. "A beautiful woman," he replied. "A strong, tough, self-reliant woman."

She sighed against him. "I try to be strong and self-reliant, John, but I've never been able to quite make it. I'm a woman who needs a full, rounded existence." She suddenly drew back a little and shot him an upward look. "What are you?"

He looked down, and smiled. "Tell me what you want me to be, Beverly."

She spoke through a widening smile. "Nothing very different from what you are, I suppose." She freed herself, stepped to the railing and leaned upon it, both arms behind her, looking at him. "This . . . this, just happened, tonight. But, John, I think it would have happened anyway, eventually."

He thought she was right. In fact, now that he dared let down the bars within himself, he could have told her he, too, had thought it might happen, had most certainly wanted it to happen, right from that first day when they'd first faced one another on this same porch, in morning sunlight.

Something caught his attention down across the yard. The bunkhouse light had just gone out. Evidently Earl had given up waiting for John's return so that he could find out what Beverly

Harding had wanted with John Randolph.

She caught that change, too, from the corner of her eye, and turned with him to face the yard. She probably guessed his thoughts because she said: "Earl could possibly help you as straw boss, John? He's been so wonderfully loyal and protective." She looked up. "Will he be resentful?"

John doubted that. Earl had been a rider all his life. That was all he aspired to. He had as much as told John that several times. "I'll talk to him the next time we ride out, Beverly."

"Make it as gentle as you can."

He slid an arm round her small waist. "I'll try. There's something else."

She read his mind about that, too. "Connie? She thinks you're the hero of all heroes. Don't worry about Connie."

She turned and leaned against him full length. He knew, the moment he reached for her this second time, that his lips, as well as his pounding heart, were going to betray him. A dozen tangents crossed his mind, all bearing upon this vital, firm, and lovely woman in his arms. In the end his discipline failed him. He seared her lips with his needs and she responded with a fire that he had never encountered in a woman before, but that other time the woman had been a girl, and this time it was very different. She was a woman in every way that counted, in every way that a woman had to be, in order to respond this way to a man.

XIV

It had seemed so simple the night before, but as he and Earl rode out the following morning to look at the cattle, check the first-calf heifers, and make certain the salt logs were still full, John found it very difficult to explain what he and Beverly Harding had discussed the night before. What made it difficult, of course, was his part in what would shortly now become a revitalized Harding Ranch.

Earl did not push it, although over coffee at breakfast he had put out a tactful feeler, just in case John wished to talk about it. John had eased away from the conversation at that moment by saying they ought to get an early start, and by leaving the bunkhouse bound for the barn. But eventually, when they got over where the first salt log stood, and were sitting their saddles, looking out over the distantly grazing cattle, John watched Earl make a cigarette, and told him exactly what had been decided the night before up on the verandah at the main house.

Earl lit up, blew smoke, snapped the match, then leaned with both hands atop his saddle horn, looking far westward toward the watercourse as he said: "I was hoping it might be something like that. To tell you the truth, I been pinning my hopes on you since the day you rode in. And the reason's pretty damned simple. I couldn't ever be a successful ramrod. I like being a top hand. But I'm getting along, and pretty quick now I'll have to step down from my saddle and go looking for a job tooling camp wagons and such-like. I don't mind that, John. We all get there someday, don't we? But the trouble on this place is just that . . . when I can't do it, there won't be no one who can. That's worried me a lot the last couple years. I'd lie awake nights thinking how Frank and the old man would be looking at me if they knew I had to let Beverly down." Earl removed his cigarette and smiled over at John. "I'm right pleased you're going to stay on as range boss. I'm right pleased, John."

They rode on closer to the watercourse and studied a ton bull with little mean eyes that was standing in mud at the side of the creek. "Pretty damned early for that," Earl growled, looking at the bull with an unfriendly expression. What he meant was that it was early in the season for a breeding bull to walk himself tender-footed, snorting up bulling cows, and have to find cool mud to stand in for a few weeks until his hoofs grew out again. The reason range men were not sympathetic was because, as long as a bull stood in mud, he wasn't out there on the job—and next year the calf-crop percentage would show up poorly.

John rode closer. The bull ducked his head and shook his horns, but he had no intention of charging. John turned and joined Earl in riding back in the direction of the salt log. Earl was quietly thoughtful for a while, then he said: "How do you figure to build the place up?"

John looked over. "How many head will it carry, Earl?"

"Thousand more'n we got, for a fact, and I've seen it, when old man Harding was alive, carry two thousand head more. But the old man was one of those cowmen only show up once every couple hundred years."

John grinned. "Maybe, between the two of us, we could work up until we could equal the old man."

Earl did not grin back. "Take one hell of a lot of work, John. Take maybe four, five more men. It'd also take a lot of money to get the herd built up again, but she's got that all right."

John looked searchingly at his companion. He had not asked Beverly about finances last night. In fact, after they'd been out on the porch for a long time, he hadn't mentioned the ranch at all. Now he said: "You sure she can swing it?"

Earl had no doubts at all. "Frank told me the last month before he died, she would have all the money she'd ever need. He told me to watch out so's she didn't get talked into anything."

They rode back toward the home place with a hot sun hovering over John's left shoulder, but with a vagrant low breeze curling along over the tops of the grass to make the range fairly pleasant for men and animals. There was never any such breeze in Cottonwood; if one came along, it got broken up by the clustered buildings.

They saw a horseman far ahead, and slightly southward. Earl was immediately interested. He would have turned off and gone in pursuit, but John said: "What for? He's heading straight for the ranch. All we've got to do is keep along right where we are, and we'll meet him directly."

It was true, but since they did not reach the yard until the sun was nearly down, they only barely got a glimpse as the rider loped out, heading northeast this time. Connie was out front of the barn, hands behind her back, fingers entwined, watching the rider disappear in the bronzed, distant daylight, when John and Earl came riding up to the back of the barn, dismounted, and led their animals inside. She turned at the sounds and walked down where the two men were off-saddling. She alternately looked at the men, at their horses, at the ground, and now and then she'd twist to look back out where that rider had gone.

John thumbed back his hat. "Who was the visitor?" he asked.

Connie's cornflower-blue eyes lifted. "Just a caller, was all."

John smiled. "Yeah, I know it was just a caller. But who?"

Connie's face reddened slightly. "Do you have to know everything!" she exclaimed, and turned to run out of the barn.

John and Earl looked after her, then looked at each other. John looked baffled. "What did I say that made her do that?"

Earl hoisted his saddle and went with it to the pole. "Hell, pardner, I wouldn't know. I tell you, since she was ten or eleven, I quit even trying to figure out what causes her moods."

They turned the horses out and crossed the yard to the ranch shop to make certain there were plenty of blanked-out horseshoes hanging on the pegs near the forge and anvil. Both their horses needed re-shoeing. While they were over there, they saw Beverly leave the main house bound for the bunkhouse. Earl, watching through squinted eyes, said: "Oh, oh. One of us is maybe in trouble. I haven't done nothing, so I reckon she's looking for you." Earl stepped deeper into the rank shadows.

"Go on over and see what she wants."

John grinned, but he went across the yard. He'd have done it if there'd been a dozen savage Mexican bulls between him and her. All the time he was crossing toward her, he was looking at her. She was erect and straight, the way she walked and stood. The late day sun made her coppery hair dance with dark fire. She saw him, then, and stepped up out of the sunlight upon the porch of the bunkhouse, waiting. As he had done, she also did. All the while that he was crossing to her, she watched him.

When he came near, he smiled and said: "Earl and I were just talking to Connie at the barn, and for some reason she took off like a scalded cat."

Beverly nodded. "I know. She didn't want either of you to know because she thought you'd tease her."

He leaned upon the railing. "Know what?"

Beverly's lovely eyes brightened with tender amusement. "That rider who came in from the west was Carl Tandy's son, Howard. He brought Connie a string of trout he'd caught a couple of miles below the ranch. They stood out there in the middle of the yard where it had to be as hot as the inside of an oven, as though it were a cool day, scuffing dust and . . . John, it was the cutest thing you ever saw. I wanted to cry."

He looked at her. "You wanted to cry because it was cute, seeing those two kids together?"

She looked long at him. "John, I think you're going to get quite an education around here within the next four or five years."

He accepted that. "All right." He glanced back over where Earl was staying out of sight, then he said: "There is one thing that got fairly well neglected when I was a boy . . . education. I'm willing." He remembered Connie's acute embarrassment and discomfort, and wagged his head. "I guess that's how it works . . . first she tries to brain him, then she accepts some heat-spoiled fish he brings her. . . ." He turned to look at Beverly. "And . . . ?"

"That's what mothers cry about, and I'm not going to discuss it with you. But I was wondering . . . if you aren't too tired from being in the saddle most of the day, would you care to ride up the north range with me after supper?"

He said: "Beverly, you know I'd do that with you if I had to crawl the whole blessed distance down on all fours."

Her laughter was husky and wonderful in the dying day, and her arch look at him with its warmth and tawny-tan challenge said a whole thick volume that words never really could have said.

"Will you saddle the horses, John?" she asked, and moved down off the bunkhouse porch, to look around. "Where is Earl?"

"Hiding," replied John honestly. "We were over in the shop and saw you heading this way. We figured someone had done something wrong. Earl said I should go over and find out." He smiled at her. "We had a long talk today, while looking at the cattle. Earl's not the least bit resentful. He said he was downright pleased that you're going to keep the ranch and build it back up."

"Did you tell . . . was there anything else you told him?" she asked, probing the bronzed, square-jawed face opposite her.

"Only that we'll build it back up, that I'll be range boss, and that I'll need his help right alongside of me. That's all he has to know."

She nodded. "I'll meet you in the barn after supper."

He watched her departure, thinking that whether she thought much about it or not, since Earl Buscomb was no man's fool, if John and Beverly met like this a few more nights, no one was going to have to tell Earl anything. He could figure it out all by himself. Anyone could figure it out. John winced. Even Connie, in the throes of her own first terrifying infatuation, could figure it out.

As he turned to enter the bunkhouse, John decided that there was nothing he could do about that, unless of course he was willing to stop seeing her, and that he was never going to do, unless she told him to.

He was washing up out back when Earl entered from the front. He poked his head out the rear doorway and said: "Well?"

Without raising his face or sluicing the soap out of his eyes as he spoke, John answered: "She and I are going to ride up onto the north range this evening, after supper."

John purposefully did not want to open his eyes. He could guess the expression on Earl Buscomb's face. At least he thought he could guess about that expression, but then Earl said in a very matter-of-fact tone: "In that case you'd better go back up the creek and take another bath." Then Earl pulled back and went over to stir life into the stove. John rinsed his eyes, looked in, and was completely surprised. Evidently Earl was a lot less dense about some things than John had thought he might be.

Later, when they were working at their last meal of the day, Earl dug out his bottle and set it in front of John. "Pour me four fingers," he said, "and pour yourself two fingers." He put an admonishing glance upon John. "Remember what I told you last night . . . women don't like men smelling of whiskey. The only thing they like even less is men acting like they have had a drink."

John did exactly as he had been told to do. He smiled to himself. Yesterday had been the longest day in his life, and he had been sure only two people in all the world really understood why it had turned out to be, also, the most wonderfully significant day in his life. But evidently he'd been wrong about that. As he handed Earl his tin cup, John raised his own cup without saying a word. Earl did the same. He did not speak, either, not even when their eyes met. Then they both downed the whiskey, and Earl gasped.

"God damn! The next time I go to town I'm going to get a different brand. This stuff will gnaw holes inside a man."

Whatever was in both their minds was obviously not going to find expression. There were some things even earthy range men did not willingly discuss among themselves.

XV

Springtime, even late springtime, was a very special time for all things that lived, even the motionless, rooted things, the trees and bushes. Even ugly clumps of sage and chaparral became softly wonderful, even beautiful in springtime. When the season was well advanced, the nights retained much of the day's long period of warmth. In northwestern Arizona, late springtime was in many ways the kindest time of year; generally everyone's cows were calved-out by then, and for a while longer the feed would remain green and succulent. Cows made more milk, their calves grew into four-legged butterballs, and, if there was a better time of year in other places, there surely was no better time here.

The north range country John and Beverly rode over hadn't had cattle on it since the previous fall; this was the part of Harding range that was kept for wintering the herds. The grass was cannon-bone high already, the creeks were running full, moon shadows touched the grass stands here and there, and once John's bay horse dropped suddenly into a tense squat as five black-tailed deer abruptly sprang out of their early beds and exploded in five different directions in their flinging escape.

John shook his head and Beverly laughed. She thought the husky bay horse was going to buck, but John knew better. He and the bay horse had come to an understanding about bucking a long time ago. Sometimes, when he was running free and feeling so good it hurt, the bay horse would turn on and even bawl in mock rage, but he knew better than even to act like he might buck under saddle.

Beverly sat a horse well, not stiff, not erect; she rode with her animal as though she were part of it. When John complimented her, she looked over at him with a small smile. "Did you know I grew up in Denver and was never on a horse until after I married Frank? In fact I was scared stiff of anything larger than a dog, until I came down here. Even then, I was still afraid of large animals. But you couldn't be that way around the Hardings. I died a thousand times when they'd insist I ride out with them." She shrugged rounded shoulders. "One day I climbed up into my saddle . . . and I wasn't the least bit afraid."

She also looked good atop a horse, but he did not tell her so because she looked good anywhere he had ever seen her. She was a full-bodied woman, firm and durable and muscular. She even looked good simply sitting in a top buggy the way he'd glimpsed her that day in Cottonwood, and it was not a very easy accomplishment for anyone, man or woman, to look good, crowded into a drab top buggy.

She showed him a flat-topped large stone near the meandering creek. There were no other stones anywhere around, not even small ones. He drew rein in the moonlight, studied the flat grasslands left and right, then said: "How did it get here?"

She beckoned, led him around to the creek side, then pointed. Dimly discernible in the pewter glow were some colored hieroglyphics. "No one really knows how it got here, John, but there was an Indian legend Frank's father heard a very long time ago, about some Indian priests rolling it down here for some ritual." She looked at the stone. "Every time I ride up here and see it, I can't help but think how fragile we really are. How frail and unlikely to succeed in being permanent. Maybe we ought to roll a boulder down here, too, so that, when other people ride by this spot in five hundred or maybe a thousand years, they'll at least know we lived."

He looked at her with a smile. "In a thousand years, why should they care, Beverly? In a thousand years why should we care?" He lifted his reins, rode closer to her, and reached forth a gloved hand to rest it upon the swells of her saddle as he leaned. "Yesterday seemed to me to be just about the longest day I ever lived through. Last night was the perfect ending for the longest day."

She put one hand upon his shoulder, her other hand upon the saddle swell where his hand rested, and kissed him. She would have straightened back but he gently shook his head, so she leaned forward again.

They didn't say anything when it was finished, and they turned to continue their ride. A veil-like cloud came from nowhere and sifted across the face of the dusty, high moon; the warmth still rose up from the crumbly earth. Except for the soft song of their spurs and the equally subdued sound of swinging rein chains, they made scarcely no noise at all.

Eventually a sound intruded upon John's thoughts. At first he hardly heeded it since there were always deer in a country like this. They did not have actually to see mounted people; deer would bolt if they simply caught the smell of horse sweat mingled with saddle leather. But the sound persisted. John lifted his rein hand, stopped his horse, listened for a moment, then turned his horse to look back down the opaque night.

Beverly said: "John, that's a rider, that's not a loose horse."

He had already made that judgment, so now he sat looking and waiting, and saying nothing.

The oncoming horseman hauled back down to a slow lope, which probably meant he knew there were two riders ahead of him. It did not once cross John's mind that there was danger coming toward him. He was sure the rider wouldn't be Earl, but beyond that he wasn't concerned.

Beverly, though, frowned as the oncoming horseman dropped down to a lope. "It's almost like he's stalking us, John."

There was an answer to that, but when John was ready to give it, the rider southward from them somewhere suddenly stopped making any sound at all. This finally brought up John's suspicions. He sat a moment, waiting for the sounds to recommence, and, when they didn't, he reached down with his right hand and flicked loose the tie down over the six-gun Earl had insisted on loaning him yesterday, until he went to town and got back his own weapon. He had freed the gun and was leaning to swing loose his right boot for the dismount when the gunshot blew the hushed night apart. John did not see the upward-lancing gush of red-orange; he felt the sudden blow, felt the breath being knocked out of him, felt the unaccountable sudden heat explode deep down inside him somewhere. Then he toppled down the left side and hit the ground like a stone.

There were two more shots, only one of them from the stalking bushwhacker southward in the night. The second shot was from him. The third shot was from John's borrowed six-gun in Beverly Harding's two hands. She was ready to fire again, but the bushwhacker sprang back across leather, whirled, and raced back down the warm, pleasant night.

Beverly got John over onto his back, arms and legs organized. The bullet had been traveling upward on a climbing ascent when it somehow managed to catch John Randolph just forward of his left armpit, rip through flesh, emerge, and plow up alongside his head above and slightly behind the temple. In the moonlight the blood glistened black. Beverly had to fight back her panic, her urge to jump up and race back for Earl. She put down the six-gun, tore John's soggy shirt away from the armpit injury, leaned close to ascertain just how bad this wound was, then she used both hands to part his hair and examine the bloody gouge up alongside his head. She decided, more because she could not believe otherwise, that he would live, and with that thought firmly fixed in mind she went to work, white and with shaking hands, but toughly resolute.

She had no water and no whiskey along. The best she could do, after stopping the bleeding, was make John comfortable by removing the saddle from his horse and propping his upper body in a slightly raised position. She then took the sweaty saddle blanket and draped that over him, full length. Then she stood up and fought a bitter fight with herself. She did not want to leave him even long enough to go back and bring Earl with the wagon, but she had to. There was no chance at all of someone happening by this late at night, upon this particular stretch of range—unless it was that bushwhacker, and she was certain that he was many miles away by now, and still riding.

Finally she mounted, kicked her horse over into a lope, and held him to it much longer than she should have, pulling the tired animal down to cool him out only when she could make out the buildings up ahead. The bunkhouse was dark. She did not want to awaken Earl, but there was nothing else she could do.

As it turned out, Earl Buscomb was a light sleeper. He was already peering out the slitted door when Beverly ran toward the porch. He said: "What is it?"

"John's been shot up on the north range, Earl. I need your help. Please hurry."

Earl slammed the door and reached for his trousers, then his boots, and finally for his shirt and hat. When he emerged from the bunkhouse, he also had a booted Winchester and his gun belt and Colt. Beverly was already at the barn bringing in one of the combination horses. Earl took the animal from her and dragged it swiftly to the harness rack. As he worked, he called out to her: "Who shot him?"

"I don't know. Someone was riding toward us. We heard him coming. Then we couldn't hear anything . . . and he shot John from somewhere south of us, down in the grass."

Earl flung on harness and worked as fast as he could. When Beverly had the second horse inside the barn, Earl motioned for her to bring it over. Then he said: "How bad is he hit?"

She wasn't sure, but she had begun to suspect it was not as bad as it had initially looked. "In the upper chest, and up beside his temple . . . Earl?"

"What?"

"Shouldn't I ride for Doctor Jennings?"

Earl tossed her a line. "Take this one out to the wagon. Doctor Jennings can wait. We got to get him back here first."

She helped hitch the horses to their pole, then she clambered up to the high seat and waited while Earl flung in feed sacks, old horse blankets, some ancient, rotting old Army blankets someone had left in the barn thirty years earlier. Finally Earl grunted up, flicked the lines, and let the team warm-out for a mile before he said—"Take hold, ma'am."—and busted the team across their rumps with the tag-end of his leather lines. The ensuing jolt as the horses sprang ahead could very easily have flung Beverly from the high seat if she hadn't been holding tightly, in anticipation.

They could not talk much as they sped along. It was more important to try and avoid driving into gullies that could pitch the riders off their high perch. There really was very little to say anyway; they had said as much as Earl had to know back at the barn.

All the north range looked like all the other parts of the countryside, even in daylight. In darkness, it took more than a knowledge of the land, it also took an inherent instinct to drive directly to the place where John lay. But Earl did it very expertly, without even thinking about it, with Beverly guiding Earl unerringly.

The bay horse was grazing, reins dragging, and that provided them with something to focus on, but they would have made it to the spot in any case. As Earl hauled the excited team down and compelled them to walk the last few hundred yards to cool them out, to let them overcome their prancing agitation, Beverly pointed. John was right where she had left him—but he was sitting up.

When Earl set the brake and leaped down, neglecting to go around and help Beverly down, John looked over at him. "You didn't happen to bring that whiskey from the bunkhouse, did you?" he asked, and Earl stopped in mid-stride, turned, and looked at Beverly who was just reaching the ground and turning to hurry forward. "We didn't have to risk our necks and half kill them horses," he said, sounding annoyed. "He's sitting up."

She came forward, paid scarcely any attention to Earl, and sank on her knees beside John. Then she started to cry.

John looked at Earl with pain-filled eyes. His head was covered with matted hair and blood. He was in pain, but when Earl leaned down, John smiled shakily.

XVI

Dr. Jennings was subdued and grim-faced. John looked worse but felt better by midmorning of the day following his bushwhacking, and Dr. Jennings had given him a pain-deadener, which made him even more nearly normal, except in appearance. The chest wound was superficial. Jennings had told them all that, in the bunkhouse, while he was dressing the wound. The crease alongside John's head was also superficial, but Dr. Jennings shook his head over that one.

"Just luck, that's all. If you'd been leaning slightly more to the left, or if the assassin had perhaps squeezed his trigger instead of jerking it, you would be dead, Mister Randolph." Then Dr. Jennings got around to what had been in the back of his mind since he'd been summoned from town by Earl. "I feel somewhat responsible, because I told you in town Carl Tandy wouldn't take his fight with you any further. This is humiliating for me, Mister Randolph. Not just because of what happened to you, but also because I've prided myself upon being a good judge of men for many years . . . but evidently I wasn't."

John could see Connie's chalk-white face and immense blue eyes peering from behind the taller adults. He winked at her and held out a hand. She came forward a little hesitantly, and took the hand—and for some reason she blushed crimson. But she would not relinquish her hold. Her mother decided they had all been in the bunkhouse long enough. She asked Dr. Jennings if he didn't think John needed rest, and, upon receiving an affirmative answer, she herded them all outside. The last one to leave was Earl. He craned around to make certain Beverly did not see, then he unbuttoned the rider's coat he hadn't removed since arriving back from town with Jennings, dug out a quart of whiskey, set it quickly upon the small table beside John's bunk, then hastened to follow the others.

John almost laughed. Actually the crease alongside his head, which had been extremely painful most of the night, hardly pained him now at all. In fact it had begun to hurt much less about an hour before the doctor arrived, and, conversely, the wound near his armpit, which was a messier wound and which was more swollen this morning, gave him the most pain. He dared not move his left arm at all.

He didn't open the bottle of whiskey Earl had brought from town. Shortly after the others had left, he fell asleep and did not awaken again until evening, which surprised him very much. He had thought he might have dozed off for an hour or two, but, when he opened his eyes, Earl was over at the stove, wearing his hat as usual, getting supper, and there was a lighted lamp upon the bunkhouse table. He must have slept at least six hours, and, more probably, almost eight hours.

His head no longer ached at all. He couldn't see himself in a mirror or he might have decided he was worse off than he felt. The swelling made his entire face look lop-sided. He raised up very gingerly because the bandaged chest wound, which included a sling to immobilize his left arm, made movement awkward, and he did not want to start the chest wound bleeding again.

As his feet touched the floor, Earl turned, looked disapproving, and said: "Where in hell you think you're going?"

John stood up. He hadn't expected to be so weak. Coils of spiraling dizziness nearly overwhelmed him briefly. "Going to see a man about a horse," he replied, and Earl, poised to intercede, shrugged and went across to open the rear door.

"All right. But take it slow and be darned careful."

When the dizziness diminished, John moved over and looked at himself in the mirror. He was shocked, but Earl, who had grown accustomed to the swelling, said: "I've seen worse. I've seen 'em with no tops in their heads from a shot like that. Now you'd better go out there and do your business and get back to bed. Doc said you shouldn't be allowed up for a couple more days."

John turned. "You haven't been back up there, by any chance, have you?"

"No, been too busy otherwise. Anyway, whoever he was, he's long gone by now. Even if I found his tracks and maybe a shell casing, it wouldn't tell me any more'n I already know. Some son-of-a-bitch shot you, and, if he'd had better light, he'd have killed you." Earl stood a moment in thought. "I did discover one thing though, John. She loves you. I've been around Miz Harding a good many years and only once before did I ever see her go all to pieces like she done last night." Earl paused again, gazing steadily at John, then he turned back to the stove. "And on the way back with my arm around her and her bawling on my shoulder . . . she told me she loved you."

John said nothing. He turned away from the mirror, though, and after a few moments he went carefully out the back door of the bunkhouse.

It was no more than fifteen minutes later that he heard horsemen coming across the range from the direction of town. Earl did not hear them because he was indoors, and had meat sizzling upon the stove, but, when John appeared in the rear doorway, Earl looked around.

"Riders," John said, moving across toward the gun belt looped around a chair near his bunk.

Earl reacted by pushing his fry pan off the burner, then he, too, went for his shell belt, but where John simply lifted the gun from his holster, Earl took the time to buckle his shell belt into place, and he even took time to lash the holster to his leg, and pull loose the safety tie.

John stepped to the table and blew down the chimney mantle, plunging the room into darkness. Then he eased to the door and opened it just a crack. The sound was much stronger now. Whoever was out there was almost into the yard.

Earl hissed. "I'll step around from in back. Don't you open that door no wider. How many does it sound like?"

John listened, then said: "Three. Maybe four, but no more than that. Earl, be careful out there."

The riders suddenly hauled down over across the yard, prompted to caution by the suddenly darkened bunkhouse. A rough, harsh voice sang out: "Hey, you boys at the bunkhouse! This is Carl Tandy with Will Sutton and Doc Jennings! We want to talk! All right?"

John gently pulled back the hammer of his six-gun. "Ride on

over, Tandy, and all three of you keep your hands up in plain sight." John opened the door a couple more inches for better visibility. The three horsemen advanced slowly, then stopped at the tie rack where John could recognize them all, and sat there without moving or making a sound.

Earl stepped around the corner of the bunkhouse, gun up and cocked. "Tandy, you bastard," he said. "You've had this coming for a long time. Get down and step clear of them other fellers."

Before John could intercede, Dr. Jennings spoke out in a flinty tone of voice: "Put that gun down, Earl. Listen to what he has to say. Put it down!"

People usually obeyed Dr. Jennings, Earl included. He let the gun barrel droop a little. Jennings spoke again: "Where is John Randolph?"

The answer came softly from the dark interior of the bunkhouse. "Here. Speak your piece, Tandy . . . and keep your hands in plain sight."

The dark, burly cowman kept watching Earl's gun. "Last night I didn't leave my house. You fellers ought to know why. I couldn't. I was too sick in the guts. There were six people with me, including my riders and my family. Randolph, I had no hand in that bushwhacking. . . . Randolph, you were right. I talked to my son. He didn't want any of us to know a girl had split his lip. I acted like a damned fool when I came over here and jumped you, and I got no complaint coming over what happened in town, either. I've never been an apologizing man, but then I've damned seldom been such a fool as I've been about you. Randolph, I apologize."

John stepped out upon the porch and Earl walked over a little closer. The riders were in front of them, facing the bunkhouse, and for a moment or two no one spoke, then Will Sutton leaned and said: "He's telling the truth. I buttonholed two of his men in town this afternoon. They didn't know you'd been shot. They were with Tandy last night, and they told me they had a hell of a time getting him home after the larruping you give him, and that, after they got him to bed at his house, he couldn't hardly hold his head up, let alone ride five or six miles over here, then ride five or six miles back."

Earl holstered his gun with a look at John. He was about to speak, when, without warning, a Winchester exploded over across the yard, and southward, midway between the workshop and the main house. A great raw chunk of wood tore loose from the door behind John, and the door itself was flung inward so forcefully that, when it struck the wall, one hinge broke.

Those three horses, twelve feet from John and Earl, all reacted the same way to that completely unexpected explosion; they shied violently. Tandy and Will Sutton did not seem to lose balance but Dr. Jennings had to grab two handfuls of mane to keep from being flung from his saddle as the horse whirled and gave a tremendous leap, then lit down, running. Dr. Jennings tried to find his reins but the horse was fleeing back in the direction of town, and within moments Dr. Jennings was lost to sight in the darkness, the hoof falls of his panicked saddle animal steadily diminishing.

John's reaction, the moment that Winchester let fly, was to drop and roll off the porch. He knew about where the bushwhacker had fired from, and he had his gun up and ready, but, before he could pull the trigger, Earl let go with two snapped-off shots over John's head.

Tandy's cursing was monumental. He finally abandoned his horse and stood in the center of the yard, legs spread, systematically spraying shots from his handgun.

Will Sutton did not fire. As he, too, left his agitated mount, gun in hand, he missed his footing and fell.

The bushwhacker opened up with another muzzle blast, this

time aimed in Carl Tandy's direction. How the man missed was a mystery, unless all the gunfire being sent over in his general area had unnerved him, but miss he did, and this time John fired. He had been waiting for this second shot from the Winchester. He bracketed the flame on both sides, then drove his last shot directly to the center of the muzzle flame.

It was over. No gunshot came back. None of the outraged men facing away from the bunkhouse had anything to fire at.

Up at the main house a light came on, then a second light. John heard Earl curse for fear Beverly or her daughter might rush outside. But no one appeared up there.

Carl Tandy, still recklessly furious, stood where he'd been standing, in plain sight, and swore aloud as he reloaded his Colt.

John got to his feet, winced from the pain in his shoulder, and started across the yard. Earl called a sharp warning, but John was sure he had hit the bushwhacker with that last shot.

He had. The man lay on his back, his Winchester three feet away in the starlight. John shoved the six-gun into his waistband, and, as Earl came running up, John toed the dead man over onto his back.

It was Tandy's range boss, Mike Farrell, the man John Randolph had humiliated in their fight in town. When Carl Tandy came up, he stopped dead still, then he said: "I was right. I was going to tell you he wasn't on the ranch last night. One of my men saw him heading over in this direction on horseback right after nightfall. I figured it had to be Mike . . . the damned fool. I tried to tell him. . . ."

Dr. Jennings came riding back, sitting stiff with outrage until he came over and leaned, and saw the dead man. Then the stiffness evaporated as he alighted and stalked over to drop to one knee. The others were not medical men, and they did not have to be. The half-breed range boss had two bullets in him, one in the center of his chest, one through his left shoulder. He couldn't have been any more dead if he'd been born that way.

Tandy stopped John and Earl halfway across the yard. He looked as grim as ever. "This here is my fault, too," he said. "When you whipped him the other night, I told him I'd take care of it, for him to keep out of it. Then I came back last night barely able to stand up, and I knew Mike this well. He figured I hadn't been able to take care of it, and that now he'd have to." Tandy shook his head. "God damn it, I never had anything like this happen before in my life."

John felt sorry for the older man. "Let's get some coffee at the bunkhouse," he said. "Forget it, it's over." He nodded, and Earl led the way the balance of the distance across the yard.

XVII

John's recovery was slow. Not from the gouge up into his hair behind his ear, that swelling went down within a couple of days and he could eventually put his hat on over the small bandage Beverly had made for him, but the chest wound was a lot slower at healing. John fretted about having to wear the sling, but on Dr. Jennings's last ride out, John was told he could throw the sling away, if he wished to, and the wound would tear open, and the entire healing process would have to start all over again. John kept wearing the sling, but it inhibited him greatly. He couldn't even saddle or bridle his own horse. He could, however, throw the light driving harness upon the mare Beverly used between the shafts of her top buggy. He and Connie drove out to look at the cattle a few times like that. He let Connie do the driving. They talked about a lot of things, and once they removed their boots and dangled their feet in the creek, and she reminisced about her father. She also remembered her grandfather, but not as well.

They did not discuss Howard Tandy. As John got to understand Connie better, he decided that she would almost rather die than talk about Howard, even though John had seen Howard ride over a few times, shyly, and had seen how Connie had reacted to his visits. He told her mother, one evening up on the verandah at the main house, that raising a young girl had to be a lot more complicated than breaking a young colt, and Beverly had laughed at his gravity when he made that statement.

"I suppose it's more difficult than raising a young boy," she replied, "but then I've had no experience along that line. Girls . . . well, when girls become Connie's age . . . yes, it's difficult."

A week later, when his head wound had begun to heal over, with the hair growing back, he and Earl saddled up one morning to go check the salt logs, and they hadn't got more than a mile out before they heard someone running a horse behind them. It was Connie, pigtails flying. When she caught them, her whole face was flushed with pleasure. They were glad to have her along, even though it posed certain problems for two men who would be out on the range all day long.

She was effervescent, hardly stopped talking for the full distance over by the creek where the salt logs were, and finally John turned a puzzled look to Earl, and got back a simple, resigned shrug of broad shoulders. Earl could not explain Connie's mood; all he knew was that it came and went.

On the ride back, later in the afternoon with the heat a solid force, Connie was riding between the older men when she said: "Mister Randolph, I'm a good buggy driver, aren't I?"

John nodded. "Pretty good, Connie."

She turned guileless eyes upon Earl and said: "You've taught me how to look after the livestock, haven't you? Ever since I was a little kid, you've been teaching me how not to overheat a horse, and to make sure he's watered and fed and all, haven't you?"

Earl fell into her trap, too. "Sure have, honey, and you're about as handy a youngster with livestock as I've. . . ."

"Then neither one of you would care if I harnessed the mare and drove the top buggy over to the Tandy place, would you?"

Earl still had his mouth open. He blinked at her, then raised a blank look to John. For several yards the three of them rode along. John understood, finally, how neatly they had both been led right up to Connie's private little figurative chopping block. He looked at her. She stared back, with a slow-gathering moisture in her eyes. "Ask your mother," he said gently, because obviously this meant a lot to the girl.

"I did ask her. I asked her this morning as you two were riding out. And she said, if neither one of you objected, why then I could do it. That's why I saddled up in such a hurry and chased after you."

The cornflower-blue eyes were swimming with unshed tears. Connie was holding her mouth firmly compressed. John sighed. "You're good enough to do it," he said, and Connie suddenly wheeled her horse over until it bumped John's horse, then flung both arms around his neck, planted a moist kiss upon his cheek, then grabbed at her reins, and went racing away in the direction of the ranch yard.

Earl lifted his hat, scratched his head, resettled the hat, and, still peering ahead where Connie was growing small, he said: "God damn it." That's all he said, and it sounded bemused, and baffled, and resigned.

That evening after supper John went down to the corrals to look in on the colts they had altered. Someone had turned the filly out, so only those three geldings remained. There was a two-thirds moon in the warm late evening. Summer was nearing, curing grass, and the perfume of cottonwood trees up the creek a mile or so made a fragrance that was endemic to this particular part of the country, which was two-thirds desert and one-third something else; in springtime and early summer, it was one-third paradise.

He leaned there, breathing deeply of the night scent, when someone, approaching softly, brought him half around. Beverly smiled through the soft-layered night. She had her heavy mane of coppery hair caught at the back with a small white ribbon. It made her look only slightly older than her daughter. John eased around, still leaning, and, as she came closer, he said: "I learned something about young girls today."

"What did you learn?" she asked, stopping near him.

"That maybe they're young in years, but they sure aren't young in the head. Connie made Earl and me look like a couple of Siwash Indians." He laughed, then explained, and afterward Beverly went up and also leaned upon the corral.

She faced him, arms down, looking up into his face. "Women don't have many weapons, John. No guns, no big muscles. Do you mind terribly being talked into things by . . . us . . . by Connie and me?"

He didn't mind at all. He couldn't think of anything as he stood gazing down into her moonlit face, except that she was the most wonderful thing that had ever happened to him. He said—"I don't mind."—and raised his arms.

She only had to take a small forward step and slide both arms around him. She burrowed her face against his chest, waiting.

He said: "Do you reckon Connie could . . . well . . . sort of grow accustomed to the idea?"

Beverly answered quietly: "She could. With you, she could I'm sure."

"Well then . . . could you, Beverly?"

She answered the same way, with her face averted, with the words coming up to him muffled. "I could, too, John." She squeezed him, hard, and lifted her face. "Are you asking me to marry you, John?"

"Yes'm."

She smiled. "Then kiss me, to seal the bargain."

He did.

★ ★ ★ ★ ★

Lightning Strike

★ ★ ★ ★ ★

I

The lightning strike was a cattle brand that resembled a serrated, zigzagging, vivid scar down the rib cage of every animal, horned and otherwise, that crossed out of the Cimarron country bound up through the maze of mountains and plateaus that separated New Mexico from Wyoming. Originally there had been three thousand head, but getting an early start in order to put the cattle onto Colorado grass by midsummer meant pulling out of the Cimarron very early in the year. This was not a problem because the Cimarron territory was usually warm, and sometimes downright hot early in the year, but by the time the men had herded on past Raton and were heading up through the high pass, moderate and predictable weather was left behind. They had lost a few head in the first blinding blizzard before they got out of the cañon, and they had lost a few more head just before they left the pass to fan out across the big prairie. That time it had been predators. Not coyotes, they wouldn't even attack a weak critter, but wolves and bears and pumas would, and this was the time of year when those big predators were starving hungry.

Heber Jenks had shot a cougar that had measured eight feet from his nose to the tip of his tail, and he had not budged an inch when Heber had ridden out of the frost-rinded trees to find the big killer tearing at the still warm carcass of his cow kill. The puma had dared Heber, and Heber had accepted. He had shot that big cat through the head from a fair distance and he would have skinned it, too, for a trophy, but the drive boss had come in response to the gunshot, had viewed his dead cow with bleak and bitter eyes, then, when Heber had mentioned dallying a little to skin out his cat, Walt had said: "You're getting paid to ride, not skin. Get on up the trail."

It was probably just as well; they did not have enough salt to roll the hide, and they had nothing to cure or tan it with, so if Heber had brought it along, as soon as it stopped freezing during the days as well as the nights, that thawing green hide would have created such an odor none of them could have lived in the same camp with it.

They had trouble with foot-soreness. There were always a few critters that got caught with the first exposure when they hadn't ought to have, and now they were swelling fast with calves. That was something else no one ever wanted on a cattle drive—baby calves. Hoof rot, calvy cows, terrible weather, short feed, and spindly browse, and Colorado lay just up at the yonder end of the pass. But that was not salvation, either, because when Junior Plunkett made the scout and returned, he told them at the supper fire one night there were drifts of dirty snow up there ahead of them seven to ten feet high in the cañons, and that down on the flats it was three to four feet thick.

"An early start," he concluded, "ain't nothing I ever want to get tied in with again. My feet been so cold so darned long. . . ."

All their feet had been cold a long while, and not just their feet. A frigid saddle seat didn't do much for a man's outlook every blessed morning, either. Walt drank scalding black coffee, stamped in his boots, and did not appear very worried about being turned back by those blockading fields of snow. He had reason not to worry. At the rate they were now traveling, there wouldn't be a trace of snow by the time they reached Colorado, and it was just up at the far end of the very pass they were now cursing and stumbling through.

The cattle lost out. So did some of their saddle animals, but some horses were natural browsers as well as grazing animals; the browsers could hold their own on leaves and bark and brush. The strict grazers found precious little grass even in the sheltered places; every frost inhibited grass growth that much longer, and that in turn meant gaunter and gaunter cows making their foot-sore way up through the rocks and across the black-frosted earth.

Heber said one night that for a plugged *centavo* he would turn back, and the lightning strike cow outfit could take his wages and put them where the sun would never shine on them. All of them excepting Walt Clanton said that, at least once, and Walt looked at times as though he were thinking it, but a trail boss was supposed to encourage, not discourage, his riders, particularly when so many adversities were making the drive as bad as this one had turned out to be. All Walt would say was that within another five or six days the weather and everything else would improve. He was right about as often as he was wrong, which was an exceptional average; most men were more often wrong than right; some were just plain never right at all.

Tomorrow, which never seemed to be capable of arriving through the cold and discomfort, always managed to come along, and for almost a full week it brought no alleviation. Then one morning there was sunshine with warmth, instead of gray dawn with cold air, and occasionally a brilliant sun. From that warm morning onward, as Walt Clanton had predicted, things improved. Not the feed, not right away at any rate, and not the bitterly cold nights when the stars were so close a man could almost reach from his hunkering place close to the fire and touch them, but longer and warmer days arrived, along with fewer causes for accidents and casualties among the livestock, fewer patches of black ice treacherously to snare unsuspecting animals.

They even began finding more dry firewood, for some mysterious reason; there really was no way to explain something like that. The ground was still damp. There were still snowbanks in the sheltered places and deadfall timber still looked darkly wet, but each time they fanned out to fetch in their evening armful, they found dry wood. There was nothing like a roaring fire on a bitterly cold night to heighten morale—a roaring fire and black coffee.

They still had to break trail, and once they passed their highest place there were still big drifts, but not upon the trail so the two riders who pushed ahead opening the way eventually were able to rest their horses often, and in the end, where they could see beyond the pass to the limitless vast plateau beyond, they laughed aloud with relief because the snow was melting fast. There was pale grass beginning to show in abundance, and even the distant leaden skies of Colorado began to have blue edges, and centers that showed a strongly enduring background of something that could have been the azure harbinger of springtime.

The cattle moved slowly. They had suffered the most and their recovery would be the longest, but, as Mike told the others, they weren't running a foot race. As far as he knew, there were no other drives ahead of them, and, if this was the price they had to pay for trailing up the first big drive, they would pay it because at the Wyoming end they would also get the topmost dollar.

Arnie Wheaton, the youngest rider, asked one night why people in those cold places like Wyoming and Montana didn't trail down to the desert during their terrible winters, or maybe even put up hay the way the clodhoppers did, instead of stoking up their roaring fires and sitting around during those black blizzards as snug as bugs, while their cattle died by the dozens, and each ensuing springtime they had to rely upon fresh trail drives to replace their losses? It was a question range riders scoffed at. Who would possibly be able to put up enough winter hay for a full herd of cattle—even if he knew how, had time and equipment—and who in his right mind would trail to the south desert country from up as far as northern Wyoming? Why, hell's bells, it would take all summer just to move a big herd down that far.

Arnie was stubborn. "They could stack hay, then," he averred. "Them homesteaders do it for their mules and milk cows and such."

Heber Jenks gazed with pitying disdain at the lanky, shock-headed youth. "Boy, it'd take a regular damned army of folks, plus a regiment of harness horses, as well as all summer long just to cut the hay to feed critters through the winter. Besides, the way things stand now, the old critters die off, which is right, and the strong ones are around in springtime to start getting fat and raising calves. That's how things is supposed to be."

Walt sat there, smoking his pipe and listening, and as usual being content to say very little and absorb fire warmth and sip black coffee. Some men needed a lot more from life, but Walt, who had seen easier, more affluent days, did not yearn for them back; he was content doing exactly what he was doing. When Arnie said—"It's plumb wasteful the way cowmen operate."—Walt blew a little puff of smoke and agreed. "It's wasteful, Arnie, and so is too much grass in summer, too little grass in winter, too much firewood in July and never enough in December. Son, folks don't conserve . . . why should they when it's all right there for them to take hold of? If the north country stockmen didn't lose a lot and have to buy replacements, what do you suppose you and I would be doing for a living?" Walt smiled. "We'd probably be doing something that's hard and rough and uncomfortable for a living, instead of what we are doing."

They all laughed, even Arnie.

Across the big plateau was a town they all knew. All of the

men but Arnie knew it, anyway, but first they had to buck headwinds, and Heber swore powerfully because if it wasn't snow four feet deep or catamounts killing the cattle, or black ice for the horses and men maybe to break their legs upon, why then, when they finally got out of that damned awful pass, it was wind coming straight off the eternal ice fields of the far north, blowing so hard that, if a man shoved a crowbar into a hole, by morning it would have been flat to the ground.

Walt said it was winter's dying gasp. Or else he said it was the first good wind of springtime. The men glowered, covered all their faces but the eyes with towels, for those who'd lost their neckerchiefs used string to tie down their hats, buttoned blanket coats to the chin, and hunched down in the saddle to present as small a target as possible. Still the wind battered them and howled around the herd, blew stinging particles of soil and flint into their eyes, and they couldn't even vent their feelings with rich profanity because they couldn't hear their own voices.

It lasted three days, and, when it stopped, they had to take time off to mend the rotting old soiled canvas across their wagon's ash bows. When they took care of that and were ready to push on again, and turned cautiously to look all around, there was no wind. They listened, and gradually stopped resembling bent-over gnomes in leather pants and spurred boots. They even lowered their face coverings and looked from swollen-lidded, bloodshot eyes at one another, and smiled.

One hour later the wind returned. They had it for a further twenty-four hours. Heber couldn't even tell them for the hundredth time that, if he thought he could get back down to the south desert, he'd quit first thing in the morning and turn back. The reason he couldn't tell them was because no one could have heard him; the wind tore words away before they'd been fully articulated and lost them in its force and howling cry.

II

The wind stopped on the fourth day after a lull, which caught them unprepared when it rose again, and that last time the lull arrived, no one was fooled. They bedded down under everything they owned including smelly saddle blankets, and in the morning they buckled on coats, tied down their hats with string, rigged up neckerchiefs or towels as face protectors, got the cattle out of their bedding ground, and rode steadily for two hours looking like a band of Canadian Indians, clawing their way out of a winter snow-in. The sun kept getting hotter, the air kept smelling sweeter; there were birds around them in the treetops, and even a few bold larks in the weak grass underfoot.

They encountered a horse trader named Jackson with his big stout riding mule and his tail-tied string of ponies, heading south, down through the pass they had recently come through, and he was pleased because they had churned up the trail for him. The last thing he said before riding on was: "Boys, no call to ride all bundled up like that, unless you all are coming down with the influenza."

He was right, but they only very gradually removed all their bad-weather attire, and, when they pitched it into Cookie Weston's camp wagon, they said they'd be close by just in case. They had no faith at all in Colorado's weather in the springtime. But it did hold. The days were magnificent. The nights were still as coldly unrelenting as original sin, but if a man rolled in fully clothed except for hat, boots, and gun belt, after sitting a half hour by the fire, he slept warm all night.

They paralleled a band of straggling Indians for ten miles, wary and watchful. Not that they would have begrudged them an old cow, but Indians were unpredictable at best and in this band there looked to be about ten bucks. There were only five range men including the drive boss, Walt Clanton. One of them, Blackjack Hodge, was older even than Walt. He was very dark and his beard, like his hair, was shot through with gray. He was burly and strong as an ox, and he despised Indians, any and all kinds of Indians. He had his reasons, but he never confided them to anyone. All he said, when the emboldened Indians sashayed forth now and then, two or three in a little group to look over the driven cattle, was: "They're not going to just leave us go along mindin' our own business. They'll try to stampede the herd, steal horses in the night, or maybe catch one of us off by himself and shove a knife in him."

Then the Indians made another of those little skirting rides and scouted up the herd as though selecting the fattest animal, and Blackjack Hodge growled for Arnie to come along and cover his back, while he rode down there without a word to Walt. There were three big bucks, lean and black-eyed and gaunt as snakes after their long hibernation in a secret camp somewhere. They watched Blackjack riding toward them. One of them raised his carbine and placed it lightly across his lap, one-handedly holding the breach, trigger finger in place.

Arnie was white in the face. Back at the head of the herd Walt and Heber saw, and were too distant to do anything, even yell for Blackjack and Arnie to leave the Indians alone. Junior Plunkett was closer. He was minding the drag so all Junior had to do was ease to one side and start upcountry to approach from the rear of the bucks. That made the odds better, but Blackjack did not even notice. He had selected the big buck with the menacing Winchester across his lap. He rode up to that Indian and let them all see what they could not have noticed before because Blackjack had kept his right side screened from them. He had his six-shooter in his lap, cocked. That bony buck with the Winchester did not have his weapon cocked. He might just as well not have owned the carbine.

Blackjack said: "You sons-of-bitches get back over yonder with your squaws and, if you so much as glance over your shoulders, I'll back-shoot each one of you!"

Arnie Wheaton had his right hand lightly resting upon his holstered Colt but the expression on Arnie's face showed just how rigid and useless he was. It was Junior Plunkett, halting behind them a dozen yards and leaning upon his saddle horn with his fisted Colt that may have influenced the bold Indians. They understood Blackjack to a man; even if they hadn't, his gun and his eyes would have told them all they had to know. The one with the carbine was a strong-heart, a fight-proven, scarred, and proud man-of-war. Walt and Heber were coming at a slow lope, but they still would be unable to get there in time.

Junior did not want Blackjack to kill the buck. Not because Junior liked bronco Indians any more than anyone else did, but there were soldiers and Indian agents all over the land nowadays. Riding out and killing a bronco Indian wouldn't really get a man into serious trouble, but, if Blackjack shot that buck and the Army or the agent found out about it, they would delay the entire drive for perhaps two or three days, and Walt would be fit to be tied.

Junior called to the other two, the lanky strong-hearts on either side of Blackjack's special Indian. "You fellers better do like you was told to do. Go on back over yonder to your band. If you got to have a critter, go talk . . . just your head man . . . to our drive boss, and maybe trade. You understand me? You'd better get your red butts away from here and take that feller with the carbine with you."

It was sound advice and it was offered in an almost friendly tone of voice. One of the Indians looked from Junior to the big warrior who was defiantly giving Blackjack glare for glare. He started to say something to the man-of-war.

Blackjack pulled the trigger. The reaction was instantaneous. None of those standing horses had expected anything like the thunderous explosion and only Blackjack had known he was going to fire, so only Blackjack Hodge was really prepared for the violent shying jump when his horse reacted. Both the more distant Indians had to fight with both hands not only to remain atop their animals but also to prevent their horses from stampeding.

Junior's shying horse did not even loosen Junior in the seat, but the look on Junior's face when that gun-bearing big Indian went over backward off his wrenching, twisting horse was a classical study in shock and disbelief. He did not even think of all the pandemonium. Arnie grabbed his horn and hung on hard to avoid being thrown. His mount was notorious among the range drivers for bucking; it would bog its head under the slightest pretext. The only reason Walt had not shot the horse long ago was because, despite his willingness, he really did not know how to buck. But Arnie was totally unprepared. He fought the horse one-handed, forcing it back around facing the other men. Some yards distant the nearest cattle had bolted, too, tails over their backs like scorpion tails, horned heads high with panic, but they only fled a short distance. None of the more distant cattle even raised their heads.

The Indian on the ground was spilling blood and trying to roll over and claw his way to his knees. He was stunned; he could not co-ordinate what he was doing well enough. Twice he fell back and rolled heavily to claw his way up onto all fours again. That was as far as he ever got. He hung there, legs and arms braced, head hanging, blood puddling below, gut-shot from a distance of only a few yards. He had caught the full power of that big lead slug without being really prepared for it.

Walt and Heber ran their horses the last hundred or so yards and hauled down to a dead stop to sit and watch the big Indian fight for his last breath. He would not collapse; he wobbled, sagged in the back, had both eyes closed and his mouth sucked flat in a white line. Then he fell.

From across the plain there was pandemonium in the Indian train, and Junior called to Walt with a quick warning. "They're coming, sure as hell, and they got us outnumbered. You better get your rifle from the wagon and tell Cookie to double load that god-damned shotgun of his."

Walt dismounted, stepped to the side of the dead Indian, then turned for a brief, black look at Hodge, and with his right hand on his Colt he looked last at the two remaining bronco Indians. They finally had their horses fought down to a standstill and were sitting up there, staring at the dead man in his great welter of congealing scarlet. They did not look as though they really believed what they saw.

Walt turned slightly, saw the Indians across the prairie running for horses, howling and acting mindless the way they usually did when they were taken by surprise, and spoke sharply to Junior: "Get the carbines from the wagon. Tell Cookie to get ready."

That was his preliminary tactic. His war-like tactic came next. "Arnie, you and Blackjack and Heber ride fast to get around behind the herd. Aim it straight at those Indians yonder."

The two remaining strong-hearts raised black eyes and watched all the cowboys but Walt Clanton ride away in a spurring rush. Walt faced the bucks, still with a hand on his holstered Colt. "Pick up your friend," he told them. "Take him over to your people."

One Indian pointed to the carbine on the ground. "He did not draw the hammer. We were not here to fight. Your man killed without reason."

Walt did not argue. "Haul him out of here and be quick about it." He did not take his eyes off the two Indians. "Tell your people that, if they bust out of their tracks over yonder, I'm going to stampede this whole god-damned herd of cattle right over the top of them. Men, women, and children. Now pick him up and get the hell back over there!"

Walt's last sentence had the snarl of an uncoiling whip. The strong-hearts slid to the ground, picked up their dead companion, flung him across one of their horses because the dead man's horse had fled, and they then started back across the long intervening distance. They did not look back.

Walt rolled a cigarette with cold hands, lit up, and watched as a swarm of wailing Indians boiled out to surround the two bucks with their dead man. That keening and barking and howling put Walt's nerves on edge. He and his men were outnumbered. They only had one weapon, but it was a very excellent one. He did not believe the lamenting Indians would jump on their war horses, grab their weapons, and come charging at him, but, if they attempted it, he meant to do exactly as he had said—wipe out the entire scraggly band no matter how many cattle it cost him.

Heber came back, leaned, and handed down a booted carbine, straightened up to look across where the wailing tribesmen were, then twisted in a different direction as he said: "For Christ's sake, that was stupid. You know what they'll do come darkness tonight?"

Walt knew. He turned to get back up into the saddle. "All right, let's get the damned herd out of here. There's a town about six miles yonder and we'd better be within sight of it come time to bed down." He looked upon the opposite side of the herd where Blackjack Hodge was sitting, slightly apart from the other range men, and pursed his lips in a bitter line and said nothing, but raised an arm to signal.

They could distinctly hear the wailing even when they had the herd moving again. They all rode with one eye cocked for trouble from across the plain where the Indians were not moving at all now, were acting as they usually acted when something had badly upset them. They were making noise and running back and forth, howling and wailing and paying no attention to the disordered line of travel of the drovers nor to their skinny, wormy-looking loose stock.

Walt hung back once to allow the camp wagon to come up. He held out a hand and the wizened, bowlegged little parchment-faced camp boss wordlessly passed up the bottle. As Walt took three swallows, the camp boss said: "What in the name of God happened out there? Did that blasted Indian try to draw on Blackjack?"

Walt passed back the bottle, pulled a hairy hand across his chapped mouth, then blew out a big breath of whiskey-scented breath, and shook his head. "The Indian's gun wasn't even cocked," he replied. "Blackjack just shot him."

"Like that? Just upped and shot him?"

Walt looked down: "Yeah. And if we're not within the lights of that cow town up ahead five or six miles come darkness, Cookie, we're not going to be in too good a position, are we?"

The old man tucked away the bottle, raised his lines to slap team horses' rumps, and concentrated upon picking up a little speed. He did not say a word. He did not look up again, either.

III

Walt sent Heber Jenks back to ride in the drag with Junior Plunkett, not because the herd was hanging back, but because he wanted someone back there to keep a sharp watch on the distant Indians. The drive was moving right along, and it also helped greatly that for a full hour those Indians ignored the trail drive and remained in place, perhaps holding some kind of wailing ceremony over their dead tribesman.

Walt had an idea that the man Blackjack had killed had either been the spokesman for the little band, or maybe had even been a chief of some kind. Two things he knew for facts—foremost was that the dead Indian hadn't had the chance of a snowball in hell, and the other thing he was sure about was that, even if they escaped the fury of the tribesmen, they were not going to be able to just break camp tomorrow on the outskirts of that cow town and ride away from this difficulty. Townsmen were no more keen about people arousing Indians on their outskirts than cattlemen were, and whether Walt's crew kept quiet about the killing or not, surely the Indians would not be quiet about it.

He twisted in the saddle and watched Blackjack on the east side of the drive, pushing the cattle along as though this were just another day and the things folks did during it were just ordinary things. He was so angry he was tempted to leave the point and ride back down where Hodge was. He couldn't leave, though, because there was no one to replace the point rider, and without someone up there, the lead critters would begin to fan out. As long as they had a rider on ahead to watch and concentrate on, they marched along just like soldiers and with a similar, or maybe even the same, blind ignorance.

Heber loped up when the sun was canting a little off center. He looped reins and rolled a smoke as he said: "They're breaking trail again, but they're sure demoralized, judging from the way they're straggling along. Hell, no Indian band I ever saw on the move was tidy, but these folks are downright disorganized."

"Strong-hearts?" said Walt, and got a head wag.

"No one's leaving the band at all. No strong-hearts and none of the others." Heber gazed a little critically over at Blackjack but he did not mention his name. None of them did. "Walt, they're going in the same direction we are. Sure as hell they know there's a town up yonder, and for all we know it could have a lousy soldier patrol in it or one of those Indian agents. Maybe what we'd ought to do . . . well, scatter those bastards."

Walt looked at the man riding stirrup with him. "You want to bust the cattle out over them?"

Heber fidgeted in the saddle. "What's worse, an accident or getting held up maybe a couple of weeks over someone accidentally shooting an Indian?"

"Accident my butt," snorted Walt. "And I'll tell you what's worse, having the Army and the federal marshals after us all the way up to Wyoming for wiping out a band of Indians. Heber. . . ."

"All right," grumbled the cowboy without meeting Clanton's look. "But we're going to be in trouble."

"Hell," growled Walt, "we've never been in anything else from the time we put the Cimarron behind us. Go on back and keep an eye on those Indians, and, if they start making little rushes, let me know."

But the Indians did not make any of those little defiant charges, their way of challenging other men to individual combat. In fact, the Indians did not even make an effort to catch up and parallel the trail drive, the way they had been traveling earlier.

Walt finally made his judgment by eyeing the sun's position, then loping ahead a mile and a half until he could make out the roof tops of the yonder town. On the return ride he was satisfied they could make it into camp within the protective perimeter of the cow town before darkness fell.

As he resumed his point position, he rode twisted from the waist, watching the distant Indians. Pity touched him, briefly, and exasperation. There were people by the hundreds who had personal reasons for killing Indians on sight. Walt drove cattle, and bought and sold horses, mules, anything that ate except sheep and buffalo, to make his living. He had never in his life had a serious brush with Indians. He was an exception and he knew it. Now, hours after the killing, he knew something about Blackjack Hodge he had never had much reason to consider before—Blackjack was an Indian hater.

That, too, was all right with Walt Clanton, but not if Blackjack's hatred got in the way of Walt's successful cattle drive. The important thing to Walt, to all his other men excepting Hodge, was the drive. They hadn't suffered like that back in the pass, nor during their first few days on the Colorado plateau, to have someone's itching trigger finger rob them of their head start toward Wyoming.

They were passing over a pale green carpet with flowers in it so small a rider had to dismount really to see them, when Arnie loped up to the lead, hauled down beside his employer, and said: "I swear it, Walt, I didn't know he was going to do that, was going to pull the trigger. I saw him ease out the gun as we was riding up onto them, but I never had no idea he'd do that."

Walt was sympathetic. "All right, Arnie, it's done and what we got to think about now is the consequences. The Army, or someone anyway, will likely catch up to us in a day or two and want to talk to you."

"But I didn't have anything to do with it, Walt. All I know was that we was riding along and he said for me to come with him and see that no one got behind him. I didn't have any idea under the sun."

"All you've got to do is tell them exactly how it happened, when they ask, Arnie, and don't try to help Blackjack or anyone else. Now get on back to your spot. We'll commence fanning out directly, as soon as we've got more roof tops in sight. Arnie, stay away from Blackjack."

Someone driving a battered old top buggy came down toward them from the direction of the town, then halted out a mile or so looking them over, and finally turned and whipped up his shaft horse to race back toward the town again.

Walt shook his head. If that had been a cattle buyer, fine, but Walt was beginning to think in terms of trouble, and, if that someone was identifying his drive so that other men might make up a posse and come down here, maybe to take Blackjack into custody, then that wasn't good at all. He finally gestured wide with both arms and his men eased back away from the herd, which was a sign the cattle understood very well as an excuse to spread out, to make a big drift far and wide in search of something to fill their paunches for the night.

Cookie Weston larruped his surprised harness horses and swept around the herd, heading up where Walt was before dropping his tailgate, freeing his horses, and starting the supper fire. Cookie was beginning to feel this was one night that the closer his rig was to roof tops the better. Normally he was typical of his generation; he considered towns sinks of iniquity and only visited them when he had sin in mind. Cookie was sixty-five. Except for a periodic great drunk he hadn't had much sin on his mind in several years and even those heroic drunks were becoming fewer and farther between because he was afterward ill sometimes for a full week, which made the cost exorbitant. Tonight he had in mind riding into town if the crew went. He belonged to that generation that had fought the Indians down to the bitter final shot; he knew something the other riders around him only had as hearsay, that fanatically enraged Indians were capable of cruelties most folks couldn't even imagine, and that old wives' tale about them not attacking in the night because they feared dying in darkness was a lot of hogwash. He'd seen the results of cow camps that had been attacked by stealth in the darkness.

When Walt finally rode over and stepped down near the tailgate, Cookie called over to him: "You goin' into town after supper?"

Walt considered the monkey-like, wrinkled, and weathered countenance before answering. He went back to his off-saddling as he said: "I don't figure we'd ought to, not tonight." He did not elaborate but he did not have to. Tonight would be when those mangy Indians finally got over their lamentations and began scheming meanness. Cookie shook his head and went back to work.

"God-damned fool," he muttered under his breath. The last person he had spoken to had been Walt Clanton but that was not who he meant.

The evening came with slightly less haste than previous evenings, which was a fine omen except that none of the range men noticed as they completed their big encirclement of the cattle to make the worst drifters think twice before pushing steadily outward. If the cattle were held loosely in place until dusk, there was not much chance of them drifting away, particularly the cows; steers would always drift; they were in fact inveterate walkers, but then they had no reason not to be, their primary function having been taken from them as small calves and now they only thought about finding plenty of feed and wandering aimlessly. The finest-looking bulling heifer in all creation did not mean a thing to a steer.

The men were uneasy. Somewhere behind them and westerly a fair distance was that straggling band of Indians. They did not expect to be ambushed and for as long as daylight lasted they were too wary for it to be successfully accomplished against them, but it was not what occurred during daylight that concerned them. They were thinking ahead to dusk, and later to full nightfall.

The town, which was visible several miles overland, was a comforting vision, even though it could be fairly well assumed that those townsmen over there would be indignant about a band of south-country range men bringing this kind of trouble to them. There was no doubt about it, that the law over in that town was not going to be pleased at either the arrival of dry-throated range men or at what one of them had done.

Walt and Cookie set up the rope corral for their saddle stock and during this process Cookie said: "You know, for thirty years I've known that town over yonder, and, when folks keep sayin' the same thing about a place, it's likely to be somethin' you can depend on. They been sayin' Caliente is a bad place for drovers, and although I've never personally noticed nothin' when I've rode in, for a fact I've heard some pretty good stories about what they done to outsiders who got into trouble in Caliente."

Walt worked in silence. He knew the town, had in fact at one time spent a couple of months there recuperating from a leg that a falling colt had broken for him. That had been fifteen, almost sixteen years ago, and he had no illusions about there being anyone around who remembered him from those days. Even if there had been, remembering a young buckaroo was one thing, looking favorably upon an outside drive boss who had brought this to their doorsteps was another thing.

The men began drifting in after the sooty early evening had arrived, wordlessly caring for their animals, then going along to fill the basin sparsely and take turns washing. There was no creek nearby so a lot of washing was postponed. Arnie, who was the first rider to come in and off-saddle, wordlessly went in search of faggots for Cookie, a chore riders did not ordinarily have to perform, but these men did it, had been doing it since they'd left the desert. There was no *prima donna* among them.

Cookie responded to this camaraderie by making it a point always to have hot coffee available as soon as camp was set up, and to place a big quart bottle of rye whiskey right beside the cups upon the tailgate. Arnie seldom laced his coffee, but he did tonight, under the understanding eyes of two older men, Cookie and Walt Clanton.

Walt strolled over for a second cup and rolled a smoke, too. The other men would be drifting in momentarily. He said—"Is it quiet out there?"—to Arnie, and the raw-boned tall young rider answered affirmatively, and added a little more along with a crooked rueful grin. "Too damned quiet. So quiet you can almost hear those broncos breathing down your neck."

"Naw!" exclaimed Cookie, speaking from long experience. "You never hear the ones that get you, son. If you can hear them devils, you're not too bad off."

Junior rode in shortly afterward, being followed by Heber. Junior grinned at the men by the cook's supper fire but Heber didn't; he said—"Blackjack ain't here?"—and looked all round as he swung to earth.

That was the first any of them had reason to suspect that they would never see Blackjack Hodge again.

Walt and Cookie exchanged a look, then Heber glanced in their direction, read their thoughts, and said: "God damn! And we're left here stuck with it!" Heber turned and angrily went to work caring for his horse. A short distance away Junior Plunkett continued to lean across the seat of his saddle, staring at them all, until it finally soaked in, then he, too, turned to caring for his horse, and he had nothing to say at all.

IV

Some things would take precedence over the end of the world and suppertime on a cold-country cattle drive was one of them. The men had been hungry; their inner resources had been depleted, for hours. Now, as Cookie and Walt stood by the tailgate quietly talking, the other riders were seated close to the fire, eating like horses.

Walt was going into Caliente. He had decided upon that before the last two riders came in and reported that Hodge had hightailed it, but it was a relief, in a way, that Blackjack would not be around, because what Walt had in mind was making a full admission of everything that had happened to the officials in Caliente, and that would have no doubt encouraged some angry officials to come back to the cow camp with him to arrest

Blackjack Hodge.

"Just keep 'em here," he told Cookie Weston. "Leave the bottle over there with 'em and keep their cups full of java. When they ask, tell 'em I went into town to pick up another couple of bottles."

Cookie sniffed. "That ain't a bunch of children over there, Walt. They'll know why you went to town."

"All right, then they'll know," stated Walt, and stood a moment longer, gazing into the wizened face of the older and shorter man. "God-damn' foolishness anyway," he snarled in a quiet tone. "It's not hard enough, trying to be the first to Wyoming."

"Not your fault," said Cookie. "How was you to know he'd shoot that damned Indian? Anyway, now that he's hightailed it, let the law go lookin' for him if it wants to, and leave us to our work."

"Yeah," stated Walt, "if that's what the law'll do." He turned. "I'll be back in a couple of hours, with any luck."

The ride overland was pleasant. The stars were bright, and, although the night was chilly, visibility was excellent and there was none of those threatening clouds aloft that Walt worriedly looked for every evening about this time. He wanted—he needed—a couple of weeks of decent weather with firm ground underfoot to get clear of Colorado. If he got that, he wouldn't complain about the rest of it.

Years ago there had been a family by the name of Everett living in Caliente. The man worked for a blacksmith in town and the daughter had had the bluest, nicest eyes Walt Clanton had ever seen. He rode the last mile into the southerly end of Caliente, remembering that girl.

It was a week night so the town was fairly quiet. There were no more than twelve or fourteen tied saddle animals at the racks out front, and upon both sides, of the saloon. Down at the jail house there was a lantern hanging out front, just below a weathered old sign that read *Caliente Township Jail,* and next to the jail house a general store had two lighted lanterns hanging inside although the place was closed for the day.

At the livery barn where Walt turned in, a disreputable older man, paunchy, whisker-stubbled, unwashed but shrewd-faced and ferret-eyed, came forth with a smile as false as a lead dollar to take Walt's reins and listen as he was instructed to curry the horse, grain him, stall him, and fork him a manger full of meadow hay. The liveryman nodded all through those instructions, and, as Walt was turning away, the man said: "You wouldn't be one of them drovers south and west o' town, would you?"

Walt turned back. "Yeah. Why, you want to buy cattle?"

The liveryman chuckled softly. "Not so you'd notice it, friend. I got enough mouths to feed right here in this barn. I rented a rig to a stranger this afternoon, though, and he drove down to sort of scout you up."

Walt remembered. "Cattle buyer?"

"Indian agent," said the liveryman. "Seems there's supposed to be a drive arrive around here directly, and he's worrying himself gray-headed because there's Indians converging from all over hell, to pick up their allotment for this time o' year. The agent's scairt the redskins'll arrive and set up camp hereabouts, then the herd won't arrive or it'll be late as hell, and his hungry redskins'll commence stealin' local cattle . . . and we'll have a big war or something."

Walt heard all of it, but the part that stood out in his awareness was what the liveryman had said about other bands of Indians converging. Sure as the good Lord had made green apples, those stragglers who had been paralleling his drive for the past few days were one of those converging bands, and for a blessed fact the moment they encountered another band, or another bunch of bands, they'd tell about the killing of their strong-heart. Whether the Indian agent's cattle arrived in time or not, they still might just damned well have that war.

Walt beat his hat upon his leg as he walked in the direction of the jail house. He had the headpiece looking almost presentable when he opened the door and looked in. The building was empty. He pulled back with a sigh and headed on a diagonal course across the roadway in the direction of the saloon.

The saloon had a big iron wood stove near the north wall, and there was a big boarded sandbox for the stove to sit in. This sandbox was also the nearest thing to a cuspidor so far from the bar, and, when Walt walked in, there were two burly, wool-shirted big freighters standing there, warming their backs, and, cow-like, chewing their tobacco while they impassively looked at everyone who entered the saloon. The place was only about half full. There were only two card games in progress among the tables, and up along the rather lengthy old bar there was room for twenty more men than were leaning along it, drinking and idly talking.

Walt went over, bought a drink to get settled, and, when the barman had a free moment, he also got him to fetch two quart bottles from his storeroom. That kind of a sale improved the barman's disposition sufficiently for him to lean over and say: "You figurin' on being snake bit a lot this summer, mister?" They both laughed.

Later, Walt saw the man he had been looking for earlier. There were five older men, hard-looking, seasoned, confident, and capable, talking together near the north end of the bar. They all looked like cowmen but a grizzled, thick-set, and graying man had a badge on his coat front,

Walt waited. He was in no great hurry and the delay before he met the lawman allowed him ample time to organize what he was going to say. Finally those five men broke up, two of them drifted toward one of the poker games, another one thumped the bar top for service, and the grizzled lawman came walking down the bar.

Walt turned, two bottles in his hand, nodded, and said: "I'd like to talk to you, if you've got a minute."

The lawman halted and ran a bold and speculative look over Walt, then he jerked his head, and still without a word led the way to one of the vacant tables near the front wall. As he sat down, he eyed the bottles and said: "You must have one hell of a thirst, mister."

Walt smiled, put the bottles aside, and pulled out a chair. "My name is Clanton," he said, "and I've got that herd southwest of your town, Marshal."

The grizzled lawman accepted this matter-of-factly. "All right. My name's Chad Reading, and, as you can see, I'm town marshal. I heard a herd was coming. It's a mite early, but that's your affair, isn't it?"

"I want to be the first one into Wyoming this year," Walt explained.

Marshal Reading had heavy features, a thick mane of graying, iron-colored hair, and the look of a man who had probably never taken a backward step in his life, but he was not a large man, at least he was not a tall man although he probably weighed close to two hundred pounds. He was compact, solid, and rough-looking. Walt made this assessment as the lawman went on speaking about cattle drives. They hadn't had one on the prairie since the previous summer, and he hadn't expected to see but one drive until the middle of this coming summer. The drive he'd expected to see was the one the liveryman had mentioned, and in fact the marshal said the same thing about the Indian agent hearing there was a herd on the move and had rushed out there in a rented buggy to see it.

Marshal Reading shrugged. "Wrong herd."

Walt waited patiently until all this had been said, then explained why he had wanted to talk to the lawman. "One of my riders killed an Indian about ten miles south of here, Marshal. There was this band of 'em paralleling us, but keeping maybe a mile and a half westerly, then some of their strong-hearts began making little scouts along the herd, and one of my men rode down when three of them came up, armed, and he shot one of them."

Chad Reading stared at Walt. "Just up and shot him, Mister Clanton?"

"The buck was armed. All three of those bucks were armed with Winchesters, but they didn't have them cocked when my rider rode up on them. There was another rider with this feller . . . young cowboy named Arnie Wheaton. You can talk to him."

"What about the feller who killed the Indian?"

"His name was Blackjack Hodge, and he didn't come to camp tonight."

Marshal Reading digested this slowly. "Didn't ride on in? You mean he hightailed it?"

"I mean haven't any of us seen him since before nightfall, Marshal."

Chad Reading loosened in his chair, clasped scarred large hands upon the edge of the table, and continued to sit and impassively regard Walt Clanton. Finally he said: "Did those redskins make any rushes on you boys after the killing?"

Walt shook his head. "No. In fact they didn't even follow along for an hour or so after they got their dead buck back. We could hear them doing a singsong for a while, then we got out of earshot."

Marshal Reading turned and glanced slowly around, then turned back to Walt again. "There's supposed to be a herd of government beef arrive here directly . . . within maybe the next four or five days. And along with them, there is supposed to be maybe three, four hundred Indians arrive out there, too, for a beef allotment. And you fellers had to go and shoot a goddamned Indian."

Walt had expected no other reaction, so Marshal Reading's slowly kindling anger did not upset him. "*We* didn't shoot an Indian," he stated. "The man who did shoot him left . . . at least there's no sign of him at our camp tonight. If I could have prevented that killing, you can count on it, Marshal, I sure as hell would have. Not because there was a band of 'em out there or because there might be more of 'em around, but because, if they'd come around and palavered, I'd have given them an old cow. There was nothing to get anyone shot over. Not a damned thing."

Chad Reading listened, studied Walt a moment or two afterward, then swore. "Damn it to hell, Mister Clanton."

Walt was sympathetic. "I understand. We'll pull out first thing in the morning, heading north."

Reading seemed to be pondering this when he said: "I don't know, Mister Clanton. You've got beef, and we've got a dead Indian, and somewhere there'll be a hell of a lot more of 'em arriving out upon the plain over the next week or so. If you leave, where does that leave us? Holding the sack, Mister Clanton."

This was the one thing Walt had feared. There was not enough grass in any case for him to hold the herd around Caliente more than a day or two, and the information he'd gleaned about more bands of Indians converging on the area had encouraged him to decide against lingering even for a day or two. But Marshal Reading had the power to keep the herd right where it was. He could get an impound order, if there was a circuit rider anywhere around, and make it illegal for Walt to move one mile from where his camp now was.

"If we stay," he told the lawman, "we'll destroy your feed, and sure as hell, if those redskins get troublesome over that dead buck, and we're still here, there is going to be trouble. The best thing would be for us to strike camp in the morning and. . . ."

"No," stated the lawman, rising from the table and looking soberly at Walt with no particular animosity now, but looking worried. "You stay where you are, Mister Clanton. I'll ride out in the morning and talk to your riders. Then maybe we can decide what's got to be done."

Walt did not argue. He sat and watched the lawman stroll back over to the bar where he immediately fell into conversation with one of those four ranchers he had been talking to earlier. Walt saw that cowman's head come up, then he watched as the cowman turned slowly and stared over in Walt's direction.

Walt picked up his two bottles and walked out of the saloon in the direction of the livery barn. That damned flappety-tongued lawman was going to have his entire damned countryside informed about Blackjack Hodge's stupid stunt by morning, so, along with a lot of irate Indians, Walt and his crew were also going to be under the glare of a lot of just as irate local townsmen and cattlemen. Maybe riding into town to make a clean admission had been the wrong thing to do; maybe he shouldn't have said a blessed word, and in the morning just trailed on northward as though nothing had happened. Maybe, but now it was too late.

V

No one was awake except Cookie Weston when Walt rode back to the camp and off-saddled, and Cookie was drowsing fully clothed with his evil-smelling little pipe ready to fall from his mouth. He had a carbine on one side of him and a meat cleaver on the other side. His old six-gun was lying upon the tailgate within easy reach. Walt smiled when he came back from turning out the horse. "You expecting to have to repel Sitting Bull?" he asked, and Cookie removed the pipe to expectorate healthily into the dying red coals of their fire before saying: "That's no damned joke. They're out there because I can smell 'em."

"Just to make you feel better," Walt said, leaning to stand the two quart bottles of whiskey beside Cookie's handgun, "that is only one of the redskin bands converging on Caliente where the Indian Bureau has decided to make the springtime beef allotment this year. Also, it seems that the cattle drive that is supposed to show up here with all that redskin beef might not get here when it's supposed to."

Cookie was now wide-awake. He knocked his little pipe empty and pocketed it, then watched Walt fill a cup with black coffee as he said: "Then by God we'd better dust it the hell away from here, Walt. How many of them Indians is there likely to be?"

Walt, hunkering beside the dying fire with his dented tin cup of black java, looked up wryly. "It'll be more than five, Cookie. That's how many of us there are, so, if it's only twenty or thirty Indians, it's still too many."

"I'll be ready to wheel out of here before sunup," stated the older man.

"The lawman from Caliente says we're not to move."

The cook stared. "Not to move?"

Walt dumped dregs into the coals and listened to them hiss, then he went over to sink the cup in Cookie's greasy bucket load of wash water, and finally he smiled at the older man. "See you in the morning," he said, and went off to his bedroll.

Ten minutes later Cookie Weston routed Junior Plunkett from his bedroll and handed him a cup of fresh coffee liberally laced with the whiskey that Walt had brought from Caliente, told Junior all that Walt had said, then Cookie went off to his own bedroll, directly beneath the old wagon, and left keeping the vigil up to Junior.

In the morning Walt told them around the breakfast fire what had occurred in Caliente the previous night. They were glum. "I suppose," growled Jenks, "that if some lousy strong-hearts come charging onto us, them nice folks over in their town'll just set back and cluck their tongues."

Cookie, hovering nearby wearing his cleanest flour-sack apron, had something to say on that score. "If they come chargin' at us, Heber, we'll have plenty of warnin' out on this flat prairie. My guess is that they won't get that brave, not until there's a hell of a lot of them. My guess is that they'll stampede the herd to hell and gone. That'd be their way to get even." Cookie looked over where his employer was eating. "Any sign of Blackjack in town last night, Walt?"

Clanton did not answer; he went right on eating but he shook his head.

"For how long," asked Junior, "is that damned lawman going to keep us setting here like ducks in a rain barrel for anyone to take a shot at that cares to?"

Walt had no answer. All he could say was that Marshal Reading would be along directly and they could ask him face to face.

Arnie looked apprehensively around, and groaned loudly enough for them all to hear and raise their heads.

Two horsemen were visible against the rising sun, coming toward the cow camp from the direction of Caliente. Cookie said: "Who'll the other be?"

Walt took a chance when he said: "The Indian agent, I'd guess."

He was correct. The agent was a younger man than Marshal Reading, and he was taller. His name was Casper Dunagan, and, although he was as tall as any of the other men at the breakfast fire, he habitually stooped so he did not seem as tall as he was. He was worried-looking, but that was not an unusual expression, even Junior and Heber and Cookie looked worried. Walt told the other men to saddle up and start circling to hold the herd from drifting, and kept Arnie there with him. Marshal Reading stolidly watched Heber Jenks and Junior Plunkett ride off, and shook his head as he sighed and faced back around to spear Arnie with his hard glare. "Tell me," he ordered. "You was with this feller when he killed the buck . . . tell me in your own words what happened."

Arnie accepted the cup of coffee from Cookie, and tasted it. Cookie had laced it. Neither Cookie nor Arnie so much as blinked an eye. Walt asked if the visitors would care for coffee and they both declined. Arnie then told his story exactly as he had told it to Walt and to the other drovers. When he had finished, the Indian agent said: "Maybe the warrior was cocking his Winchester."

Arnie shook his head. "No, sir, he wasn't doing no such thing. I could see all them Indians, and I was watching their gun hands you can darned well believe. None of 'em commenced to cock their guns."

Cookie rolled up his eyes. Arnie had just ruined the agent's attempt to provide Blackjack with an alibi, and, in ruining it, Arnie, the damned idiot, had also ruined the chances of the drovers to move on northward with their herd. No one even glanced over where Cookie was eavesdropping while pretending to be busy cleaning up around the fire.

"He had his six-gun drawed already," said Marshal Reading. "You saw him ease it from the holster while you two was approaching the redskins?"

"Yes, sir," stated Arnie, and finished the coffee.

"Why didn't you call him? Why didn't you say something about him sneaking out his gun like that?"

Walt broke in. "Say what?" he demanded. "Marshal, if I'd

been riding behind Hodge toward three armed, hostile bucks, I'd be hoping right hard someone would have a gun handy. I think you'd have done the same. Most men would have."

Arnie answered as though Walt hadn't spoken out indignantly. "Marshal, I was right scairt. I never thought Blackjack would really shoot at them, not unless one of them did something threatening. I saw Blackjack draw the gun on the blind side of those redskins, but after that I watched the Indians, not Blackjack. When he fired that gun, no one was any more damned surprised than I was." He looked from Reading to Agent Dunagan. "Right at the time it never crossed my mind, but since then I've thought about it a lot. Why didn't those other two bucks open up? They had their guns in their laps and had their hands on 'em. Sure, the horses all shied like the devil, but they were a good pair of riders, they still could have cocked their carbines and fired."

Agent Dunagan said: "I'll tell you why they did not fire. They did not have any bullets for their weapons."

Cookie straightened around, staring. Walt looked squarely at the Indian agent, too. It was Arnie who broke the silence.

"They were running a bluff," he said softly. "No one had ever ought to do that. That's the first thing Blackjack taught me when we first signed on with Walt Clanton. Do your work, don't lie, and don't run no bluffs."

Marshal Reading spoke swiftly. "You and Hodge was partners, then?"

"No," replied Arnie. "I just met him in Socorro one afternoon at a bar, and we got friendly, you know how that is, then he took me with him when we went out and braced Walt for work. He hired us both on."

Chad Reading did not give up that easily. "But he told you where he was from, didn't he? He mentioned his family, maybe, or some old friends, or some of the places he'd worked?"

Arnie shook his head. "I never asked no personal questions and he never volunteered nothing personal about himself . . . except once, and that was the night when we was drinking in Socorro and he said something about there not being anything in this world worse than Indians. That's all. He didn't say why that was and I didn't ask."

Marshal Reading turned on Walt. "You hired the man, Mister Clanton."

Walt gave the lawman look for look. "I hired Arnie here, too, Marshal, and Cookie over yonder, and those two fellers who rode out to the herd, and I only asked each one of them if they had worked cattle before, how much experience they had, and if they wanted to help me head up a drive north before the snow was off. I never even asked them if they had a middle name. Marshal, I only ask men I hire what they can do for me. What else they might have done or where they came from, I don't give a damn. All I can tell you about Blackjack Hodge is that he rode away on one of my horses. It's got a rising-sun brand on the left shoulder."

"A damned horse thief, too," stated the lawman. "All right, by God."

Walt faced the stooped agent. "Mister Dunagan, how did you know that buck didn't have any loads in his gun?"

"Because, Mister Clanton, I rode out to their camp before sunup this morning and got their side of the story. They haven't had bullets so they haven't been able to hunt for the past couple of weeks as they drifted over here for their beef allotment. They'd been killing a horse every few days."

"And they scouted up my cattle," said Walt.

The agent made no excuses. "They were almost out of horses they dared kill, Mister Clanton. They told me they had in mind trading you something for a couple of cows."

"So they came with guns," said Walt dryly. "Mister Dunagan,

when a man wants to palaver with me, he hadn't ought to do it with a gun in his hand. I wouldn't approach him that way."

The agent reddened. "Are you trying to defend your rider, Mister Clanton?"

"Nope. And he's not my rider. What I'm doing is suggesting to both you gents that, if your damned Indians hadn't come over to my herd looking and acting hostile . . . if they'd left those worthless Winchesters at their camp, no one would have been killed."

Marshal Reading was not ready to concede this. "How do you know that Blackjack Hodge wouldn't have shot that Indian even if he hadn't had no gun with him, Mister Clanton?"

Walt did not know, but he was pretty certain of it, so he said: "I was on the trail for quite a spell with Blackjack Hodge, Marshal. He wouldn't have shot that buck if the buck hadn't had a gun on him."

They stared steadily at one another, neither of them willing to budge an inch, and neither of them in a position to prove or even to verify what he believed. Then Cookie Weston strolled closer and looked squarely at the agent when he said: "Mister, while Blackjack was ridin' down where them hostiles was, one of them bucks hoisted his carbine and sort of flourished it. Mister, I seen that myself. Now I can tell you from forty years of bein' around your blessed Indians, mister, that no bronco buck makes that move unless he's tryin' to make a threat to someone."

Marshal Reading looked with distaste at old Cookie but he said nothing. Agent Dunagan, though, had one comment to make. "If that cowboy hadn't shot," he said, "there wouldn't have been any trouble. I told you, these men had no bullets for any of their weapons. So . . . the point is, gents, if your rider hadn't fired, there wouldn't have been any trouble. But he *did* fire. He killed a spokesman for that band he'd been leading up here, and now I've got to make my report to the government, and also to the Army post nearest Caliente."

Walt said: "Mister Dunagan, if I have to stay here with my cattle and my men, it's going to be on someone's head besides my own. Marshal Reading's head or yours, because the first damned hostile who comes around here all braved up for a coup is going to get shot all to hell."

"You'll stay," said the burly lawman, glaring at Walt. "I can hold you two days without an order, and meanwhile I'm going to try and find a circuit rider and get an impound order. Mister Clanton, you'd better not leave."

"Marshal," exclaimed Walt Clanton, "do you know what you're doing? If there is trouble, you're causing it. If a bunch of Indians gets all fired up over this killing and come chanting around here with their lousy coup sticks, none of us is going to just set here all contrite and guilty and all."

"Let me tell you something," snapped the grizzled lawman. "I don't care what you fellers do. I've got a whole town to look after, plus a bunch of cowmen all around here in the countryside, and we all been discussing this mess since last night, and, Mister Clanton, our decision was to keep you here so that, if there is trouble, the hostiles won't be mad at us, because we didn't do anything. They'll be mad at you, and we like that better'n having them start up a fight with the rest of us. In a case of you or us, Mister Clanton, we're looking after us!"

VI

Cookie made a remark at the noonday meal that no one disputed. He said: "I sweated all yesterday after Blackjack shot that redskin, and last night I sweated even harder, and by God there was not one incident, not even one bronco come ridin' over here to shake his fist at us. You know why? That Indian agent was tellin' the truth. Those bucks don't have any bullets.

If they had, take my word for it, gents, the hour after they had their spokesman shot off his horse, we'd have been up to our lousy gullets in Indians."

It was probably true. It certainly was reasonable, and, although none of them excepting Cookie Weston had ever been in a real fight with Indians, they could appreciate the validity of what he had just said.

But Heber had another thought. "Yeah, they was out of bullets, thank the Lord, but how long is that going to last? Just until they can barter around among some of the other bands, I'd guess, then they'll be armed again. And then what happens?"

Junior said: "Let the damned Indian agent keep 'em on a leash, that's what he gets paid for, isn't it?"

No one argued with Junior but no one really believed the Indian agent could control those Indians if they decided not to be amenable. One man with all the paper authority in the world was not going to prevent a band of grieving, terribly aggravated Indians from making a battle if they wanted to do that.

Walt said: "Cookie, there used to be an Army post about thirty miles northeast of Caliente. You reckon it's still up there?"

Cookie had no idea. "I ain't been around here in twenty-five years, so how would I know? You want someone to ride over there?"

"Not unless I'm damned sure he'll return with the Army," stated Walt. "If it's going to be a wasted trip, then I'd rather keep every man here."

Heber looked at all their glum faces and said: "I'd quit. Sure as hell I'd quit and go back down to the desert, except that they probably wouldn't let me get over as far as the pass."

Junior's hard, clear eyes clouded up with bleak humor and understanding as he surveyed Heber Jenks. "They wouldn't bother you," he said. "You look too mangy."

Cookie laughed and Arnie tried to work up a creditable smile. Heber arose, shook himself to get his gun and belt back where they should be, and slowly turned to look far out and around. "Walt, if they stampede the herd . . . what?"

"We'll go after them," said Clanton promptly. "You don't have to ask a thing like that."

"Except that if they scatter the cattle," mused Heber, still searching the sun-bright endless flat landscape for something he could not find, "they'll maybe do it with a plan in mind, and, when us fellers split up to commence the gather, they'll pick us off one at a time. Why else would they stampede the cattle?"

"To steal as many as they can," stated Cookie matter-of-factly. "They'll have their throats slit, their guts yanked out, the meat cut up, and the hides rolled and hidden in less time than you can find the blood."

Walt said—"Riders."—and pointed.

Because everyone had been talking about angry Indians, and also thinking about them, they whirled to look. It was not Indians. It looked to be range men like themselves, and that was a relief. Heber and Junior sprang to their feet and went to the coffee pot to make certain it had water enough in it. If these were sympathetic cowmen, they would certainly be lavishly welcomed.

They were indeed local range men, but when they rode on up and halted, making no move to dismount and each one of them looking stonily at the riders around the fire, Walt recognized them as the cowmen Marshal Reading had spoken to along the bar in town the previous night. Walt had no illusions as he nodded and gravely invited the strangers to light and set a spell.

The four hard-eyed older men wore blanket coats in spite of the sunshine. They did not look any cleaner or more reputable now than they had looked last night in town. One of them said:

"Gents, we just figured we'd ought to ride out and warn you against trying to sneak away."

Heber and Junior and Cookie looked incredulous. Arnie had ceased to believe anything good was going to happen while they were around the Caliente countryside so he was not at all surprised at this gruff warning.

Walt answered shortly. "How do you sneak anywhere, mister, when you've got about three thousand head of critters?"

Another of the local cowmen folded gloved hands across his saddle horn and looked balefully at Walt. "If I was in your boots, mister, I wouldn't stand near no lighted lamps from tonight on, and I wouldn't back up to no fire to warm my backside."

Heber turned on this man. "Thanks for the warning," he said, straightening fully around and glaring. "Who'd be most likely to bushwhack a man at his supper fire, mister . . . you or the damned Indians?"

A raw-boned older man growled at Heber, apparently in order to speak before the other, insulted cowman had a chance to speak. "Cowboy, you had to expect no one'd like what you fellers done. We don't make trouble with the Indians, and, if you fellers come into our country doing that, why you got to expect that decent law-abidin' folk aren't going to be on your side."

Heber's anger was fully up now, and Junior was not much cooler. Between them, and perhaps with old Cookie buying in out of plain loyalty, they were probably the match of the four cowmen, but Walt scowled them into silence, then nodded coolly at their visitors and said: "All right, gents, you've come out and warned us. If you've nothing else to say, you can head back. Just in case you'd like to know, though, it wasn't any of us standing here right now who killed that strong-heart, so why blame us?"

"You came here, didn't you?" demanded a cowman. "You brought them cattle up here, and you brought these fellers and that other feller, too, didn't you? Well, that's all we're concerned about. You brought the feller here who caused all this trouble, mister, and to us that makes you just as objectionable as he is." This man raised his rein hand to turn back. A couple of the other men had done the same, but one man waited a moment longer. He hadn't said a word thus far. He was short and thick and wore glasses. He was one of those individuals who could have been forty or sixty; it was almost impossible to make a decent guess just from looking at him. In a quieter, less antagonistic tone of voice than his companions had used, this man said: "I'd give it some thought, if I was you fellers. You got what the Indians need badly. Beef. I think it might help like hell if you fellers would ride over there and make your peace, and maybe hand over two or three hundred head."

Cookie acted like he'd been stung: "Two or three hundred head? Why you be damned!"

"Whoa," Walt bellowed at his fiery-eyed cook. "Hold off a little, Cookie."

The local cowmen did not linger after this; they turned without another word and headed in a slow lope back in the direction of town.

For a while the angry men were silent—disturbed, antagonistic toward just about everything, even each other, and silent. It took a while for the kind of fury those cowmen had stirred up to fade, but when it eventually did, an hour or so later, and Walt went over to the rope corral with Junior to rig out and make a sashay around the herd, Arnie called out that there were three riders approaching. Everyone stepped clear of whatever interfered with their visibility and watched, certain this was going to be either more troublesome cowmen, or perhaps this time troublesome townsmen. It was neither.

When the riders were close enough to be identified by their

attire, Cookie sniffed and said: "Grubline riders, sure as I'm a foot tall."

He could have been right. He wasn't, but he could have been. The three men were astride fair saddle stock, and, although their saddles were battered and scarred, they were good range rigs. The men themselves looked down-at-the-heel but each one was rawhide-tough in appearance, unshaven, and none too clean-looking, but resourceful and savvy. They looked like top hands, or at the very worst like the kind of range riders most cow outfits hired on sight because they were accustomed to nothing better than range-country hardship.

They had tight little bedrolls behind their saddles, saddlebags, and carbine butts sticking up just forward of the swells of their working saddles. It was the guns that interested Walt, and, when the men finally reached camp and sat, grinning, Walt began forming his private opinion. He was correct and Cookie was wrong.

One of the strangers leaned and wrinkled his nose in the direction of the stew pot Cookie was working over. "Gents," he said affably, "whenever I see a camp cook's got gray in his hair, I figure I'm in the presence of a feller who can cook rings around a woman."

They did not dismount. It was customary to wait to be invited to dismount. Walt leaned across his saddle seat with Junior nearby doing the same thing, and Walt said: "What's on your mind, gents?"

A raffish, shrewd-eyed man scratched vigorously as he smiled at Walt and said: "Well, sir, we been hearin' around town and elsewhere . . . out here on the range . . . that you boys are in some pretty damned hot water for shootin' a lousy Indian. Well now, gents, we seen how folks was gettin' all set against you fellers, and the three of us figured . . . for a price we'll just join your camp. And if them other folks get some idea of sendin' out a night-ridin' posse or the like . . . me and my partners here, we've had experience in this here kind of work. We can sure as hell make them townsfolk tuck their damned tails and run for shelter. For a price, gents."

Walt gently inclined his head. As he had thought, they were gunmen. So far they had been threatened by the law, by an Indian agent, by cowmen, and now he was being propositioned by hired killers. The only thing yet to come was a probable Indian attack, and perhaps a stampede. He said: "Sure appreciate the offer, gents, but we don't like to drag other fellers into something this bad. There's a big herd of Indians on the way to join the band of the one we shot. When they get here, it's going to be pretty damned hot around this camp."

The smiling, raffish man stopped smiling. "You been told this for a fact?" he asked. "I mean, about a big band of stronghearts on the way?"

Walt nodded gravely. "Yeah. By the local Indian agent himself."

"Well now, hell!" exclaimed the raffish man, raising a hand to scratch his whiskery jaw. "You see, we hadn't heard that. All we'd heard was that the cowmen and the folks over in Caliente was mad about you fellers shootin' that redskin almost in their front yard, then settin' out here with all these cattle big as life. But no one told us the Indians theirselves was fixin' to gang up on you." The raffish man jerked his head and both his friends joined him in giving a rough hand salute before they turned northward and loped away.

Cookie said—"God damn."—in a tone of such enormous disgust they all turned to face him. He was glaring after those three hired guns with an almost indelible look of contempt. "And they called themselves fightin' men. Why, hell's bells, when I was forty years younger'n I am now, a man could walk into any livery barn or any saloon and hire himself a whole danged army of real gunfighters, and not a blasted one of them would run from fifty-to-one odds." Cookie spat into the fire to show his supreme disgust, then he went back to work as Walt and Junior exchanged a wink, and headed out of camp.

The land was empty of horsemen. The cattle were scattered and seemed to be getting enough to eat because many of them were contentedly lying, chewing their cuds. The sunlight was blessedly warm, and a man could not have asked for a more peaceful, beautiful, and serene day. It was almost as though springtime was past and summer had finally arrived.

Walt separated from Junior to start his counter-clockwise ride out and around the herd, pushing inward any drifters. Junior did the same but in the opposite direction. They would meet somewhere over upon the westerly prairie, have a smoke, compare experiences, then continue on around and head back for camp.

For Walt, the ride should have been a pleasure. His cattle were on the Wyoming trail, were still managing to hold their own fairly well even on the new, short grass, and evidently the weather was going to hold. Normally he would not have had a genuine worry on his mind. Normally.

VII

Walt left the other men in camp the following morning and headed for Caliente alone. Even though normally he would have had a near rebellion on his hands over making the riding crew remain in camp within sight of a town, this time all he got was a few disgruntled looks. There was no pleasure to be derived in a town that was hostile. Even Heber and Junior, who were inveterate trail drovers with every vice that went with their kind of work including bracing every town, every saloon in every town along the way, simply saddled up to make a sashay around the cattle.

At breakfast they had discussed the uppermost thought among them: a stampede. It could be easily accomplished by vengeful Indians. The Indians sure as hell knew this, and they also knew something else—if the herd was stampeded in the direction of the cow camp in the darkness, three thousand cattle were going to charge right on and over the men in their bedrolls, and, when the last critter had gone on, all that would be left would be some pulpy, blood-soaked mud and shredded bedding. The loss of the herd if it were stampeded in any other direction worried them considerably, but if it were deliberately stampeded over the top of them. . . . Even Cookie, who was a tough, grumbly, fatalistic old man, had something to say about that prospect.

"If we was camped near some decent hills, I'd like it a heap better. Out here on this damned plain there's nothin' . . . not even no trees and no wagon that'd help. Seems to me the smart thing for us is to do it first."

Walt had growled that kind of talk into silence, then had decided to go to town and tell the marshal and the Indian agent whether they liked it or not that he was going to move northward.

When he got there, he had a small stroke of luck. Both Marshal Reading and Agent Dunagan were at the jail house office. Dunagan, who was younger and perhaps had never been through anything like this before, was friendlier than was Chad Reading, who was scarred and lined from all varieties of trouble. They were having coffee when Walt Clanton walked in, and Reading unsmilingly offered Walt a cup, which was declined on the grounds that Walt hadn't finished breakfast but a short while earlier. Then he made his statement, "We're going to pull out, Marshal."

"No you're not," returned the lawman. "I haven't been able to find that damned circuit rider yet, but I still got authority to hold you until tomorrow."

Walt acted as though he had not heard. "I'll tell you why. Not because we want to defy you or break the law or anything like that, but if anyone at all gets a notion to stampede my cattle . . . and you know damned well that's going to occur to someone sooner or later . . . my cow camp is squarely in the path if the herd's stampeded southeasterly. We wouldn't stand a chance. There's not even any trees out there. And there's something else, Marshal. My boys don't like being made to stay where they're likely to get killed any night. They've got an idea that the best way to keep from being ground to death beneath three thousand cattle is to turn the critters in some other direction and stampede them first." Walt looked with deliberate candor toward Casper Dunagan. "Right over the top of a big band of Indians, maybe."

The stooped, worried-looking younger man shot Marshal Reading a look of quick appeal. The lawman arose from his desk, holding the cup of coffee, and said: "Mister Clanton, I sent for the Army yesterday." He paused, stared coldly at Walt, then added a little more. "There is a band of Indians due on the prairie east of town this afternoon. They've just left the foothills fifteen miles northeast of here this morning. There is another band coming in from the west. Not as big, but they're a troublesome band. Folks over yonder have been having all kinds of trouble with this little band most of the winter and last autumn, too. They got a bunch of young strong-hearts among their people. Altogether, Mister Clanton, according to Agent Dunagan, we're fixing to have as many as four, five hundred Indians camped around Caliente in the next two days. Out of that many they're going to be able to put maybe two hundred, maybe two hundred and fifty broncos on horseback with guns."

Dunagan spoke up. "Mister Clanton, we've been keeping track of their approach for several days. They're all very hungry.

They've been raiding herds along the way and eating other people's saddle stock, too. I'm afraid they're not going to be in a very tractable mood."

Marshal Reading scowled at the stooped, younger man. "Why don't you just damned well spit it out," he snarled. "Clanton, the herd of cattle which is supposed to arrive here to be parceled out to those blasted Indians ain't going to make it for another ten days . . . if it makes it at all."

Walt was interested from a professional standpoint. "Why isn't it?" He had just come up across the mountains from the hot lowlands. He knew the passage could be navigated with a herd.

"Because," said Chad Reading in a sour voice, "the trail boss who is supposed to be making the damned drive has heard there is bad trouble up around here, and he's stopped thirty miles southeast of here. That's why." Reading went to the stove to refill his coffee cup. "That's what Dunagan and I were discussing before you walked in." Reading filled the cup and turned back toward his desk. "I wish to Christ both of you fellers had gone through on a different trail. I'm going to take it up with the town council that after this we don't allow no trail herds and no damned rendezvous to take place within five miles of Caliente."

Walt was not the least bit interested in this, so he turned his back on the lawman and spoke to Casper Dunagan. "I've trailed in allotment beef a few times, and, when there was the smell of trouble, the Army always furnished an armed escort. Why not now, Mister Dunagan?"

"There wasn't any trouble," explained the aggravated Indian agent, "until your man shot that Indian. There was no reason for anyone to think there might be trouble."

Walt thoughtfully went to work rolling a cigarette, not because he felt any need for a smoke but in order to have his hands occupied while he pondered the increasing dilemma caused by one gunshot from the Colt of a man called Blackjack. When he had lighted up, he faced Chad Reading again.

"It's not up to me to tell you your job, Marshal, but unless you know for a damned fact the Army can get over here within the next twenty-four hours, or unless you know those Indians aren't going to hold a big palaver and come out of it painted for war, you'd better round up one hell of a big posse to keep the lid on until the Army does get here. And like I said before, we're not going to sit out there like a bunch of sage hens squatting in the grass waiting for someone to stampede the cattle over the top of us."

Reading emptied his cup for the second time and said something he had evidently been thinking of during Walt's statement. "There'll be trouble. Some kind of trouble, sure as hell, if not over that buck your rider shot, then over the damned beef not being here. Mister Clanton, if you and Cas Dunagan could work something out on the beef, maybe the other thing could take care of itself."

Dunagan threw out his arms. "I can't do that," he said loudly, in an almost wailing tone of voice. "I can't up and buy a big herd of cattle. I don't have the money or the authority."

Reading looked caustically at the younger man. "God dammit, Cas, you been moaning and groaning around here for the past two, three days, and we don't need no lamentations."

Walt was inclined to agree with the lawman. As for the cattle . . . well, Colorado wasn't Wyoming, but then it didn't look like they were going to make Wyoming anyway, and, if he came right down to it, he had cattle to sell whether he sold them in Wyoming or Timbuktu. "Twenty-five dollars a head and they're yours," he told the Indian agent.

Dunagan looked stunned. "Do you know how much money that totals up to, Mister Clanton?"

Walt knew; he had plenty of reason to know. He did not even answer. Instead, still gazing at the agent, he said: "Yesterday three gunmen rode out and offered to hire on with us. Before that, some of the local cowmen came out to warn us not to try and run off. Gents, it just don't make a bit of difference what we do, it's going to be wrong according to someone, and that leaves us on our own . . . and like I already said, we're going to move out because we're sure as hell not going to set out there until someone kills the band of us and scatters the cattle from here to Kingdom Come." Walt leaned to crush out his smoke in a tin ashtray upon the lawman's desk, and his eyes met those of Chad Reading without one flicker of compromise. "You can damned well do what you think you got to do, Marshal, but you see . . . we're going to lose no matter what, so whatever you come out there to do, you'd damned well better come armed."

Walt leaned back, saw Dunagan's dismayed expression, and almost smiled at the younger, taller, but stooped man. "I hope the Army gets here in time to bail you out," he said, and started for the door.

Chad Reading spoke in a cold, hard tone of voice just as Walt was reaching for the door latch. "Mister Clanton, you try and move that herd and I'll be out there to stop you."

Walt looked around. "All right. And the best ones you can fetch along to try it would be those four cowmen you talked to at the bar night before last. They already came out and made a threat." Walt looked steadily at the seated man as he lifted the latch and opened the door a fraction. "But you'd better tell them we figure we're going to lose no matter what happens, so we're likely to give them as much trouble as they'll want,"

Reading arose red in the face. "Cas," he roared at the stooped man, "make some kind of a god-damned deal for his lousy cattle, will you?" And when Dunagan stood there, looking helpless, Reading turned toward Walt again. "Will you peddle them to him?"

Walt would. "Sure, that's what I've brought 'em up here for, to sell."

"On an IOU paper?" said Reading.

Walt eased the door closed gently and leaned upon it. "I don't know, Marshal. If it's guaranteed by the Indian Bureau or the Army or some government office, yes." He studied Chad Reading's dogged expression and his square-jawed, scarred face. Reading was an honest man; he wasn't tactful or very diplomatic, but then Walt understood men a lot better who were neither of those things, and right now he was beginning to like the lawman a little. At least Reading was trying. Walt said: "Mister Dunagan, do you have the bill of sale for that herd that's supposed to be on the way?"

"Well, no, Mister Clanton, not the bill of sale, but I've got a copy of the contract that was forwarded me from Washington, and it shows the herd has been paid for and all. Why do you ask?"

"How many head in that drive?" asked Walt.

"Twenty-five hundred," replied the Agent.

"By my reckoning, I've got about twenty-seven or twenty-eight hundred," stated Walt. "I'll trade you herds, and, providing your herd's as good as mine, we'll be even and you won't have to put up any money, and you'll have the critters for your redskins."

Chad Reading suddenly smiled from ear to ear. Normally a smile improved a man's look and his features. Chad Reading's hard features were only minimally improved, but there was no mistaking how he felt. He even included Walt Clanton in that smile. "Done!" he exclaimed, and pounded his desk top with a big balled fist. "Cas, there's your damned answer! Now get out there and talk to those Indians like a Dutch uncle. Explain why that buck got killed . . . that it was a bad mistake . . . tell them you'll allocate more beef to sort of patch things up. Tell them the law is going to find that son-of-a-bitch who killed that strong-heart and he'll get what's coming to him."

Walt stood waiting.

Agent Dunagan was a typical government man. He was afraid to take the initiative; he was timid in the face of acting by himself; he had very little actual intelligence and Chad Reading's loud voice instead of seeming to inspire Dunagan seemed rather to increase his timidity and confusion.

Reading straightened up staring in disbelief as Dunagan procrastinated. Reading's face reddened, he clenched his fists, and finally he said: "Cas, you're going to do it. God damn you, you're going to do it if I have to hold a gun to your lousy head." He turned. "Mister Clanton, we'll fetch out the papers for you to sign this afternoon. And I'm beholden to you for making that offer."

Walt was skeptical and stood a moment or two longer, eyeing Casper Dunagan. The agent still did not commit himself.

It was Chad Reading who came from behind his desk who finally jarred the Indian agent out of his tracks when he said: "Cas, you and I are going over to your office, and, if you weasel out of this, by God, I'm going to arrest you for . . . some goddamned thing and act for the Indian Bureau."

That made Dunagan say: "You can't do that, Chad. You don't even work for the government."

Walt left, got his horse, and headed back for the cow camp thinking that so far he'd found one man in the Caliente plateau country he understood. Chad Reading. But until today he hadn't thought he'd either understand Reading or like him. Maybe desperation makes men crawl out of themselves.

VIII

When Walt arrived back at the cow camp, Cookie was loading his wagon preparatory to pulling out. Arnie and Junior were heading in from out where the cattle were, and loping up from southward was Heber Jenks.

Walt off-saddled without haste, and, when he finally strolled to the tailgate for a cup of coffee, the others were drawing closer. All he said to Cookie was that he thought they just might come out of their trouble with whole hides after all. When everyone else came up, he explained about the trade, and Heber slapped his leg.

"Best damned idea anyone's come up with yet," he averred. "I figured, if anyone could bail us out, it'd be you, Walt."

When they were all standing around looking immensely pleased, he told them about the other two bands of Indians shortly to arrive, and what had been said in town about them. That wiped away several smiles and Junior wanted to know how quickly they could peddle the herd.

"When Dunagan and the law arrives out here this afternoon with the papers," explained Walt. "And if it was up to that Indian agent, I'd give you fair odds he wouldn't show up. But Marshal Reading's not going to allow trouble to arrive if he can help it."

Junior was not satisfied. "Walt, Arnie and me made the sashay this morning." Junior paused and looked at Arnie as though in need of support. "There was a hell of a lot of barefoot horse sign out there."

Cookie pursed his lips, then said: "How old was the sign?"

Junior turned on him irritably. "How in the hell would we know how long they scouted us up? Maybe last night, Cookie. It sure wasn't this morning after sunup or Arnie and I'd have seen them. But I'll tell you this much. It was more than three or four of them. More like maybe twenty." Junior returned his full attention to Walt. "Now you know why I asked how long it'd take to get shed of the herd." Junior raised a muscular arm to gesture. "They was yonder, behind the herd. If they busted it out from over there, they'd bring it right through here . . . right smack dab where we're standing."

Walt was worried, of course, but he was fairly certain the Indians would not try to stampede the herd in broad daylight. At least it would be very foolish of them to do it like that, but Walt also knew something else about Indians—they damned seldom did what folks thought they'd do, or wouldn't do. "Finish eating," he told Junior, "then you and Arnie go back out there and keep watch. Not on the cattle, Junior. You understand?"

Junior muttered something and went closer to the tailgate. Cookie had an iron kettle suspended from a steel tripod there. Stew was not usually the preference of range men, but when a camp cook was getting ready to strike camp he was likely to make stew, since it was very easy to cook, and woe to the complainer who approached the camp wagon's tailgate.

Heber Jenks rolled and lit a smoke, then suggested that maybe he'd ought to ride out and do a little scouting, or maybe ride farther out and around to make certain there were no skulkers hiding a mile or two away.

Walt simply said: "Take the outfit off your horse and turn him loose, Heber." Then Walt also went over to the tailgate.

Nothing much was said. Even after Arnie and Junior rode out and there was no reason not to talk, the men still in camp remained occupied with their personal thoughts until old Cookie cackled and gestured. There were several horsemen riding slowly overland from the direction of Caliente. Walt and Heber each counted eight and Cookie swore up and down there were ten of them.

There were eight. One was Dunagan, another was Chad Reading, four of the others were those bleak-faced cowmen who had ridden out earlier to make their threat, and two of the men were strangers to Walt, but they, too, were clearly range men, although they did not look like owners, so Walt tentatively assumed they might be someone's straw bosses or foremen. They were deputy town marshals and Chad Reading introduced them as such, but actually they were hired riders. No one said which outfit had hired them and no one acted as though it might be one of the cowmen with Reading and Dunagan.

Walt invited everyone to get down and sample Cookie's coffee. The men dismounted, and, as they started past, Walt stepped over to block Chad Reading's headway. He let everyone else sift on past before he said: "Did you bring the papers?"

"Yes," replied the lawman a trifle harshly, "but not like you might figure. Dunagan refuses to trade herds. He says, if your animals aren't as good as the other ones, he might lose his job."

Walt smiled to hide his rising anger. "Better to lose a job than a life, Marshal. As for the quality . . . if his are better quality, he's still picking up an extra two or three hundred head, isn't he? He said his allotment cattle number twenty-five hundred. My herd was originally three thousand head and I figure with losses and strayed I've still got between twenty-seven and twenty-eight hundred. We can make a gate count anywhere you gents care to drive them. I think Dunagan's coming out best."

Reading fished around inside his coat until he found a large folded paper that he extracted and held out to Walt. "Signing over the allotment herd to you. That's the top paper. The underneath paper is your bill of sale to us for your herd." As Walt accepted the papers and thumbed back his hat to let more light fall as he read them, someone over at the tailgate laughed, and that made everything seem as normal as it looked to be—until Heber quietly but insistently called from over near the rope corral, and, when Walt raised his eyes, while all those other men turned their heads, Heber rigidly pointed. There was a band of Indians strung out for about six or seven hundred yards coming toward the herd from the northwest. They were widening their front as they walked their horses ahead, in order to take in as much of the grazing, scattered herd of cattle as possible. What Walt particularly noted was not so much the Indians as the way they were riding. They would shortly be on the west side of his herd in position to stampede the herd right over the men who were presently watching from over by the wagon camp.

Reading said—"God damn it."—and two of the dismounted cowmen began sidling away from Cookie's tailgate even before they had got a cup of java. They knew, perhaps from experience, that a man on foot in front of a stampede did not have a chance, not even the prayer of a chance, but that a mounted man might get clear if he moved quickly enough. One of those younger riders who had been deputized to assist Chad Reading stood very straight for a moment, then turned toward the lawman and said: "Who said there was only eighteen or twenty strong-hearts with that band that got their head man shot? Count 'em, Marshal, it's more like fifty over there."

Someone else had already made that estimate. A cowman who was toeing into his stirrup to get back in his straddle said: "Chad, that's got to be some bucks from another band. We told you yesterday . . . we scouted up the band that lost their spokesman. They didn't come near to being able to mount this many."

Walt gestured for Heber to rig out three saddle animals, and, when he had done this, he faced the lawman. "If they hit that herd, we'll never get away in time. They're too close as it is. You'd better get out here damned fast, with Dunagan, and hold their attention."

Reading barked for the men who had arrived with him to get astride and he set the example by swinging up without touching a stirrup. He was not as angry as he was grim and purposeful. As he swung to lead off, he called back to Walt: "Don't stand around! Bring along the cook and turn your corral stock loose."

Heber worked, looked out there, then worked some more. Cookie reacted to the imminent danger like Walt had thought he might. He ducked inside the old wagon swearing and complaining at the top of his voice, and emerged just as Heber was readying a profane order for him to shag his tail feathers out to the corral, carrying a sack of personal things, plus a belt gun slung over one shoulder and a shotgun. He had a filthy, old, greasy hat atop his unshorn gray hair and his foul little pipe was clamped, cold, between his teeth, making whatever it was he was saying impossible for anyone to understand.

Walt dropped one side of the rope corral. The horses walked out, walked a little farther, looked around, looked at the men who were mounting up, then the loose stock suddenly threw up their heads and raced away.

Walt looked back at the camp. The old wagon looked more forlorn than it usually looked, standing alone with the tongue stuck out and the soiled old patched canvas top hanging slackly against the bows in raw sunshine.

Walt took them in the direction of Chad Reading and his party to beef up the lawman's support, if he needed any. He did not see Arnie and Junior until Cookie called his attention to a pair of riders heading on around to the northeast, aiming to intercept Walt about a mile closer to where Walt would eventually join up with Marshal Reading. They would all make it, and that was very reassuring. If the herd stampeded, there would be losses; there always were, but at least now they would not kill anyone in the drover's camp.

Marshal Reading and his strung-out companions were loping directly toward the center of that long line of mounted bronco Indians. They looked very business-like the way they were riding. Even the fact they were badly outnumbered did not impress itself upon the watchers at the moment, perhaps because the Indians were strung out even more, covering several hundred yards with lots of room between each individual Indian horseman. Walt had no idea how this might end; he did not really believe there would be a fight. It just did not seem reasonable. Everything that could possibly be done to placate the tribesmen would be done. All Chad Reading and Agent Dunagan needed was the time to explain, the time to implement what they wanted to do.

Cookie, with his effects bouncing along in his old war bag and with his scatter-gun held tightly in his free right hand, had somehow managed to pocket the little pipe. He was riding a strong, big, young horse and Cookie rode well as he leaned to call over to Walt: "That damned lawman ain't doin' it right! Right about now he's supposed to drop off all his men and go on to make the war talk by himself. Them other men is supposed to dismount, stand on the off-side of their horses, and lay their carbines over their saddle seats. That's how you get a redskin's attention and hold it. Not chargin' straight up to them like that lawman's doin'."

Walt, who had long ago developed the ability to hear Cookie without really heeding him, did that now. As he rode with Heber at his side, he watched the band of cowmen far ahead, heard what Cookie had to say, and did not even comment on it. Then he saw the distant puff of smoke. Instinctively he hauled back, sliding his horse to a halt. Heber did the same. So did Cookie.

Those bunched-up men riding with Chad Reading suddenly slammed down in wild confusion. Walt saw one riderless horse break clear and go wildly rushing back in the direction of Caliente. He couldn't believe it. The three of them sat without speaking, watching as the men with Marshal Reading began to whirl to run away. Cookie suddenly spoke with a shrill insistence: "God-damned idiots! If they run, they're done for, and most likely so'll we be. You can't tuck tail or, so help me

Hannah, they'll charge you."

This time, Walt heeded the older man's words, sank in his spurs, and raced straight at the withdrawing body of men. Heber and Cookie spurred right along. They met Reading and the others a quarter of a mile farther along and Walt raised an arm as he slid his horse to halt again. He bellowed at them: "Damn it, turn back! If you run, they're going to come down here loaded for bear!"

Marshal Reading was white to the hairline. He looked back, as did the men with him. One man swore and busted out his horse and fled in an arrow-straight line for Caliente. The others looked ready to follow, so Walt swore at them, then suddenly closed his mouth. Indian Agent Casper Dunagan was not with them.

It was Heber and Cookie who set the example. They piled off, swung their horses, and laid gun barrels across saddle leather, facing the Indians. Very gradually several of the older cowmen did this, too, and, finally, when the Indians looked to be converging upon one mounted head man, everyone dismounted to make their stand, but Walt and Chad Reading.

Cookie called curtly: "Wait, go back there! Don't give an inch. Let them come to meet you, but don't get beyond our gun range. Don't give a damned inch. Go on!"

IX

Walt and Chad Reading exchanged a look. Walt led off at a walk, and he reached down his right side to yank loose the little thong that prevented his six-gun from flying out of its holster when he was riding. Chad Reading had done that before, when he had led his posse men away from Caliente this morning. Reading said: "By God, there just wasn't any warning. Dunagan's head busted like a rotten pumpkin and down he went. I . . . didn't any of us expect it."

Walt understood what the lawman was doing, seeking to justify his abrupt flight when the other men turned and fled. "Dead?" he asked, and turned his head.

Reading nodded. "Right through the head. He never knew what hit him." Reading turned back to stare far out where the Indians were holding a conference. "That was no carbine," he said. "It had to be a rifle to carry that far. And that son-of-a-bitch is one hell of a fine shot."

Walt thought—*Or lucky.*—but let it pass as he, too, turned to face fully forward as their horses walked steadily closer.

The Indians were alternately talking and watching the pair of oncoming riders. It dawned on Walt that what the Indians were watching was how far the pair of white men would go before they halted. Walt twisted to see how far he had come, then he halted.

"Far enough," he muttered, and sat there, watching.

Two riders eventually rode away from the crowd of Indians and did a very creditable job of majestically walking their horses with vast dignity forward. One of them had plaited braids but the other rider was wearing an old coat and an old hat crushed low.

The dead Indian agent was well within sighting range and Walt wanted to ride a little closer. Not that he really had to; what Reading had said was obviously true; the agent was dead.

Chad Reading's color returned, and with it came his normal yeastiness. "They're going to say we killed one and now they killed one, and that makes things even."

Walt, who had never seriously palavered before, was mindful of one thing. "Don't get hostile," he cautioned. "If you're going to do that, Marshal, we'd do better to leave right now. They've still got the edge." Walt pointed. "Maybe we could outrun the buck and his friend in the old hat, but do you see those rifles? No one can outrun a bullet from one of those things, especially if that feller who shot Dunagan is a real sharpshooter."

The Indians were lining out farther back, spreading out then swinging to earth exactly as the posse men had done earlier. Cookie had been right, so far. The rest of it was something Walt and Chad Reading were going to have to discover for themselves, that part about not yielding an inch.

The approaching horsemen came at a steady walk. The buck with the braids had his carbine balanced upon a thigh, and rode with his head up and his body very erect. His companion had no carbine or rifle although his belted six-gun was visible under the flapping old filthy coat. This rider did not even raise his head, although he was clearly watching Walt and Marshal Reading every inch of the way. He halted, finally, a hundred yards distant, and turned to expectorate, then he turned back and lifted his head. He was a white man.

Walt was too surprised to speak at first, and Chad Reading's breath hissed out in astonishment. The Indian with his plaits said something from the corner of his mouth and the tobacco-chewing white man raised a hand to ease back his filthy old hat. He stared steadily at the two men opposite him across the distance and said: "What you fellers got in mind?"

Chad Reading's jaw was stone-set. Walt saw that. He also saw the dark blood beating upward into the lawman's face. Before Marshal Reading could speak, Walt answered. "The man who shot that strong-heart a couple of days ago isn't here. He left the same night he killed the buck. The law will find him and fetch him back, but meanwhile the rest of us didn't have a damned thing to do with that killing."

"Don't mean anythin'," growled the white man, leaning to spit amber again. "It was drovers with this herd who done it."

"One drover," stated Walt. "Just one man. Like I said, he pulled out."

"Yeah, and like I just told you, cowboy, it don't mean anythin' to the Injuns."

Marshal Reading pointed with a rigid arm. "That's the Indian agent. He came out here with me today to make sure there was no trouble."

The white man looked down at the corpse lying roughly midway, and spat again before saying: "I know who he was. I know who you are, mister, and that feller with you. And I know them are our cattle, our allotment cattle. But there's somethin' you fellers don't know. I'm just a feller who wants to see justice done, and by God we're goin' to see it done, too. We're goin' to gang up and clean them god-damned drovers out down to the last man. It would have happened sooner, yesterday or last night, except that the band who lost that head man didn't have no ammunition. Well, now, fellers, they sure got plenty of ammunition. Me and my band loaded up on it back a hundred or so miles at a trading post."

"What," Walt asked, "are you talking about?" He could not believe this renegade white was actually making a threat.

The slouched, tobacco-chewing man eyed Walt steadily from a weathered, unshaven, lined face while he chewed for a moment, then he finally said: "I'm talkin' about justice. These here are my people, and I'm goin' to see that they get justice. And you wait until the rest of the bands gather out here on this damned prairie, gents. Then you can take my word for it, you're goin' to see 'em get their justice." The white man gestured toward the cattle. "For now, we'll take what's our'n. That's for now, and we need the meat." He dropped his arm and stared. "The rest of it the chiefs got to decide. You fellers took away the Injuns' pride and decency. Me, I'm givin' it back to them. I'm showin' them how things is goin' to be if they'll stop back-trackin' to every son-of-a-bitch with a badge or a uniform on, or an Injun agent. I'll show 'em. Now take that dead carrion and get on back to your settlement, gents, and fort up, because you fellers haven't seen nothin' yet."

Chad Reading finally spoke, his voice thick with wrath. "Who the hell are you, anyway? There's laws against renegade whites living with the tribesmen."

The slouched man glared coldly at Reading. "Listen to me, lawman," he said very softly. "I'm married into the tribe. I'm a hunt leader and I been plenty adopted. I got the scars to prove it. You call me a name like that again. . . ."

Walt headed this off because he was genuinely afraid of what was going to happen if Chad Reading opened his mouth again. Lifting his rein hand, Walt interrupted: "You've got the cattle, and the tribesmen are evened up for the killing of their spokesman. Mister, don't make it any worse, don't stir them up or you'll be damned awful sorry."

"No," drawled the white man, "*you* might be sorry, but I sure as hell won't be." He spat again, turned his horse, spoke gutturally to the Indian riding with him, and started back toward the distant dismounted, waiting Indians without seeming even to consider it as a possibility that Chad Reading or Walt Clanton might shoot him. His companion with the braids, though, seemed unable to resist and he twisted to glance back, still holding his Winchester upright on his thigh as though it were his coup stick.

Walt said—"Come along."—and turned back. Now, finally, he believed something serious was going to happen. It still seemed incredible, this late in the history of the Indian troubles, that any tribesmen would actually consider returning to the war trail—except that, after looking at that squawman, and listening to him, it came over Walt that serious trouble not only could come, but in all probability was going to come.

By the time they had returned to the others, the tribesmen were fanning out again, but this time Walt viewed this tactic differently. They genuinely believed his herd was their allotment;

they were moving in to cut out and drive off a few head to take care of immediate needs.

The moment he reined up, Heber pointed and bitterly said: "Those bastards are fixing to drive off some of the cattle."

Walt shrugged. "Let 'em." Then he looked at the stone-faced cattlemen to whom Chad Reading was wrathfully explaining things, and, when they were all evidently ignoring him and his riders, he said: "Come along. We'll pick up the agent."

The five of them rode back out there. Reading and his companions came along only belatedly after they had the dead man hoisted behind Cookie's saddle and lashed into place, then one of the cowmen said: "You don't have to do that, Mister Clanton. Us fellers from town can haul him back with us."

Cookie sniffed. "Maybe something'd spook you boys and you'd hightail it again, and he might fall off. I don't mind haulin' him into your lousy town."

The rebuked cowmen reddened and glared but Cookie was not intimidated.

Reading rode up beside Walt on the return trip to say he'd like to borrow a horse at the cow camp, if he could, to haul Dunagan back to town. Walt's answer was to point far eastward where a small band of horses was indifferently grazing. "Turned 'em all loose when it looked like we might get a stampede headed our way." He dropped the arm and looked at Reading. "Who signs those papers now that Dunagan is dead?"

The lawman sighed. "Damned if I know. His replacement, I suppose."

Walt rode along in silence after this. His immediate problem was his herd. If Dunagan's replacement did not choose to sign the agreement to trade herds, Walt was going to be out a big band of cattle, and all his money because he had invested every dime he could borrow and save to buy up this gather and gamble on the Wyoming drive with it. He still had the papers he had been looking at when the trouble had broken out, but without signatures that's exactly what they were—just papers.

The others were not justifiably thinking in terms of Walt's cattle. One cowman said they should all band together and attack those strong-hearts, take that white renegade away from them and lynch him, then hunt down the man who had assassinated Dunagan. There was considerable strong talk. Walt heard it and listened to it, and took no part in it. Neither did his riders, but when they got back to their forlorn old camp wagon and the men from Caliente wanted to take the dead man off Cookie's animal, the old cook offered no objection, but he had another pithy comment to make as they were untying the corpse. "If you boys'd cut loose on 'em instead of turnin' to run, you likely could have nailed that lousy renegade, and, if he's their spokesman, you'd have ended the trouble then and there."

A craggy old rancher glared at Cookie. "Yeah? And where was you when the shootin' was goin' on? I didn't see you runnin' out there to make no war with 'em."

Marshal Reading snarled at them to stop arguing. Then he told Walt it might be a good thing for him to move his wagon and his men into town. Walt had already come to this conclusion, so all he did was nod his head and watch the humiliated posse men get back astride to head for town.

After they had gone and the range men were again alone with their wagon, Walt looked over past his herd to where those Indians had been. They were no longer there, but distant dust indicated the route they had taken with their appropriated cattle.

Arnie walked over to say: "Is this the end of the drive, Walt?"

This was the end of it all right, but Walt answered differently because he knew what was in the cowboy's mind. "Yeah, until that other herd gets here, Arnie, then we'll go right on, and trail up to Wyoming. Anyway, I don't think the law'd look kindly on you drawing your pay and pulling out."

Walt smiled, slapped the tall, younger man on the back, and turned. They walked back to where Cookie had let down the tailgate and was handing around a bottle. It was too early in the day for serious drinking and there was no hot coffee to go with it, but that dead man with half his head shot away was a pretty fair incentive.

X

By the time Walt and his crew reached the outskirts of Caliente, it was midafternoon and there was a surprising degree of heat for so early in the season. No one complained; they had survived all the bad weather one riding crew needed. Also, they were concerned with something that had nothing to do with the weather. The town by now knew everything that had happened at the meeting between the law and the Indians, and it required no lengthy explanation for the range men to guess Caliente's mood.

They drove around to the northwest area above town to set up camp because that was the only place where there was a creek full of running water. There was no shade, but they had not expected to need any this early in the year. Nevertheless, Cookie unfurled the rolled length of canvas that, when staked out along the far side of the wagon, provided both shelter and shade. Here, Cookie flung everybody's bedroll with a look of distaste over this chore, and, when Walt returned from helping erect their rope corral, Cookie was polishing a piece of broken mirror he treasured before he undertook to shave and do what he could with his matting of grizzly hair.

They could almost walk over to town. If the creek had been a hundred and fifty yards closer, they could have, but none of them was strong on walking. They subscribed to the range man's edict about the good Lord giving a horse four legs and a tiny brain, while he gave man only two legs but a much larger brain, and consequently horses had to pack men around on their backs.

When Heber returned to the vicinity of the wagon, he put a puzzled look upon Walt and said: "Where was that band the old renegade come here with? Only bunch of 'em I saw was that herd Blackjack shot the head man of." Heber waved an arm. "Don't see another band anywhere around here, do you?"

Walt didn't, but before he could mention the possibilities old Cookie snorted disdainfully at Heber Jenks. "What do you expect . . . they're going to ride right up onto us here in camp and shake their medicine bundles in our faces?"

Heber was not sure what a medicine bundle was, either, but he'd have died before he'd have allowed Cookie to know this. "All I know," he growled at the cook, "is that there's supposed to be three bunches of the bastards, one big bunch and two not-so-big bunches. Well, do you see any Indians?"

Cookie stopped polishing the mirror, looked into it a trifle anxiously, and recoiled from what he saw, then he spoke again. "You don't *see* Indians, Heber. Sometimes I marvel fellers of your generation managed to live this long."

"Why shouldn't we?" snapped the cowboy, fully annoyed now by Cookie's attitude as well as his tone of scorn. "You old-timers got the Army to run off all the Indians before we younger fellers came around."

Cookie reacted like a scorpion. "Damn you anyway, I never in my whole blessed life asked no lousy bluebelly to do so much as pass the molasses. Never! And I never got no help in an Injun fight from no bluebellies, neither. What do you know?" He turned in towering wrath to Walt. "What do *they* know?"

Walt avoided a direct answer. "If you two can stop snapping at each other long enough to round up Arnie and Junior, I'll take you all to the café yonder and buy a dinner with genuine pie and milk."

Arnie whistled from over at the rope corral, then pointed. A rider was loping casually from the direction of town. By now they had all become sufficiently familiar with Marshal Reading to recognize him a mile out astride his horse.

Heber said—"Hell, there goes our town supper."—and dourly watched the lawman's approach.

When Reading got close enough to walk his mount the last few yards he called ahead to say: "You got the best camp ground around Caliente!"

Walt had no answer, but, when the marshal rode on in and swung off, Walt had a question. "I hope you didn't ride out to tell us not to show up in town . . . did you?"

Reading glanced at angry-eyed Heber Jenks and at old Cookie Weston, who always, or at least nearly always, looked antagonistic. "Nope, you can ride into town any time you're a mind to," he said, "and it never was anything real personal, you got to understand. It was just that folks were not in a mood to see range riders walking around town who'd brought us trouble."

"We're still the same range men," stated Walt, but the burly lawman dissented.

"Not since you handed over your herd to keep the peace. I saw to it that story got plenty of talking around. And not since you fellers backed our play at the shooting."

Walt studied the lawman's face. Chad Reading was neither a very complicated individual nor a man whose open, candid features did not mirror every mood he felt. "What's on your mind?" asked Walt. "You didn't just ride out here to welcome us to town."

"No sir, I sure didn't," conceded the marshal, and eyed the half-empty bottle of whiskey standing upon the tailgate. "I come out to tell you what I found out since we were on the west range. To start with, that band of Indians arrived last night sometime, and got right into the camp of the fellers who had lost their chief. That's how come we ran onto so many bucks out there this morning. Another thing. That big band is skirting around Caliente to join the other two bands."

Cookie nodded his head. "What did you expect? Them other Indians sent a messenger. That's how they do. When you figure they won't know something . . . hell, they already knew it for a couple of days. They picked it up from the moccasin telegraph."

Reading gazed steadily at Cookie and spoke to him in a slightly hostile tone when he said: "All right, old man, you know so damned much . . . what will they do next?"

Cookie peered frostily back at the lawman. "Not a damned thing, if you'll find a feller with a long-barreled rifle who'll go lie out in the grass and, when that renegade rides out, kill the son-of-a-bitch, and, mister, if you *don't* kill him, I'll tell you what else they'll do . . . commence skirmishin' out around the damned countryside stealin' horses and raidin' ranch houses, and maybe, when some scairt feller fires at 'em, they'll commence a massacre." Cookie pointed. "You want a glass of rye whiskey, Marshal?"

Chad Reading continued to regard the raffish old man without acknowledging Cookie's offer. And after a while this steady staring bothered the old man so he took his mirror and went around to the tailgate of the wagon, leaving Reading and Walt Clanton standing up near the offside front wheel.

Marshal Reading said: "I never could abide those old devils. No matter what anyone else does, it's always wrong according to them."

Walt defended his cook. "He was right this morning, Marshal. We didn't handle that thing right or maybe Dunagan would still be here."

"*Humph!* And if he was still here, we wouldn't be one damned bit better . . . well, never mind Cas. He's done for and they'll hold the burying in the morning. The other thing I come out to tell you is that the renegade is a man by the name of Joe Murray. There's folks around town who remember him from thirty, forty years ago. He was a hell-roarer back then, and the Army tried to kill him a dozen times. He's a squawman like he told us, but he's a lot worse. This is the first folks have known about him in years. They told me around town they had figured he'd died long ago."

Walt said: "Maybe Cookie is right,"

Marshal Reading stared at Walt. "We don't bushwhack around here."

"Too bad," said Walt. "Too bad someone didn't do it thirty years ago, too. Well, what about Murray and the Indians? Most important to me . . . what about my cattle?"

"I sent three fellers down to find the allotment herd and help drive it up here. One of them is a man I've rode with years back. I told him to get those damned cattle up here whether those other drovers like the idea or not. He'll do it. Now, I want to ask you one question. Your riders won't be pulling out, will they?"

Walt hung fire a moment before answering. Arnie would pull out in a minute. Maybe Junior and Heber might but Walt doubted that. They would grumble a lot and threaten to leave but he knew their type; they'd stay. As for Cookie, he wouldn't leave, not as long as there was some kind of trouble for him to supervise, or at least for him to try and supervise. "They'll likely stay," he told the lawman. "Why, couldn't I hire a fresh crew around Caliente when the other herd gets up here?"

"Oh, sure," stated the lawman. "We got plenty of men around Caliente willing to sign on for a Wyoming drive. I was thinking . . . if your men rode off, those damned redskins would catch them sure as hell. This afternoon I must have listened to a dozen tales of how old Joe Murray runs his band . . . like it was a real army and he was a real general, spies and scouts and squads of bloody-hand bucks, and all. Your boys are number one on Joe Murray's list. *You* and your boys." Reading glanced over where the rope corral was. "Post a watch every night, Mister Clanton." He turned toward his horse to swing up across the saddle. "Come on into town when you're ready. I'll stand the first round."

Walt watched Reading lope back toward the nearby roof tops, then he called his men together to relate everything Reading had said.

The first reaction, almost predictably, came from Cookie: "God damn!" he exclaimed. "Joe Murray? Why I heard twenty-five, thirty years ago him and a bunch of his Crows got tangled into a battle with some Big-Belly Sioux and got cleaned out down to the last man."

Walt made a dry comment on that. "Maybe the others got cleaned out, but Murray didn't. I'll tell you what I think, after listening to Murray this morning and hearing about him this afternoon. He's likely to get a lot more of those Indians killed before he's finished, and I think he'll do it deliberately so that he can collect whatever is left behind, including loot and horses and whatever else they had. Otherwise, why would he deliberately make that kind of genuine war talk nowadays when those Indians could not possibly win?"

Cookie laughed. "That's Murray's way, sure as the devil."

Junior Plunkett said: "What's worth laughing about, Cookie? We're talking about cold-blooded killing. That's not funny."

Cookie was unabashed. "Murray, that's who's funny. He's alive and he's still workin' hard at being the most notorious son-of-a-bitch this side of Fallen Timber." Cookie laughed again and waggled his head in an expression that could very easily have been interpreted as admiration for the renegade Joe Murray.

Junior got the bottle from the tailgate and passed it around.

When it got back to him, he drank, then stoppered the bottle, and gazed northward into the settling late-day shadows. "How long does it take the damned Army to show up?" he asked of no one, but he got an answer right back, and another burst of cold laughter from Cookie.

"After the last patch of hair's been lifted and the last victim's been stripped and his tendons cut so he can't chase no Indian spirit in the Sand Hills." Cookie turned to walk back up where his mirror was propped so he could finish trimming his hair. He hummed a little rollicking tune as he walked away.

Arnie shook his head but said nothing. It was Walt who made a comment. "It's a hell of a lot different world now than it was when he was our age. They grew up thinking different."

Heber made a thoughtful comment about that. "Maybe, and maybe tonight or tomorrow, when all those redskins get together and that bloody-minded old Murray fires them up on whiskey and lies, we'll have to learn to figure things old Cookie Weston's way."

They went to rig up their horses for the short ride to town. When Cookie finally walked over to join them, he smelled of something that could have been compounded of musk and some kind of French toilet water. All the way over to Caliente the men tried to make up their minds about that scent; sometimes it wasn't too bad and at other times it was pretty bad. But no one commented until they were on the outskirts of town and the usual town dogs ran out to try and startle the horses into running or bucking, then Heber controlled his horse with one hand and steadied himself by the other hand upon the cantle as he looked around and said: "Cookie, you got all those darned male dogs in a frenzy with that female wolf scent all over you. Do the rest of us a favor and ride on ahead and draw off them dogs, will you?"

Cookie answered in a blistering array of epithets that doubled them all over laughing. They were still laughing when they crossed the road to tie up at the hitch rack in front of the saddle and harness works because the tie rack out front of the saloon was full.

XI

All the hostility had not atrophied in Caliente toward the south-desert riders whose departed member had wantonly killed the Indian buck that had started all the trouble, but there were a large number of other range men in town this evening, and they decided to defend the men from the Cimarron country. As things turned out, though, after everyone had stood a round and the range men had all become acquainted, there was no threat of trouble. As one local rider said: "Who's goin' to get up on his hind legs when there's all of us to drag him back down again?"

Walt encountered two of those older cowmen he'd had occasion to see twice before, the most recent sighting being out where Dunagan had died. The ranchers bleakly nodded; evidently their animosity took longer to die out. Walt did not even nod; he walked past, walked on down where Chad Reading had just settled against the bar, and bought the first round. Reading bought the second round, then they talked.

Reading needed men to mind the south-desert cattle bearing the lightning-strike brand until someone from the Indian Bureau arrived to take over the allocation chore. He asked if Walt and his riders would do it since they knew the herd. Walt was remembering that big party of strung-out Indians as he leaned to peer into his whiskey glass when he answered.

"Who pays our wages? And if we do it, Marshal, we're going to want some other riders to be along. That was a hell of a big crowd of bronco bucks out there this morning."

Reading was agreeable. "I'll send you over four or five fellers in the morning. As for pay . . . damned if I know what to say. Like Cas told you one time, I don't work for his bureau nor even for any other agency of the government. Of course the Indian Bureau will owe you fellers. We can't just leave the cattle out yonder for the Indians to run off and make meat out of a few head at a time. Even the Indian Bureau's got to realize that." He looked up at Walt a trifle quizzically. "They'll pay you fellers, I'm sure of it."

Walt shrugged. "We'll wait for the reinforcements in the morning, then lope out and look around. Marshal, if there's a big band of hostiles out there, I'll turn right around and bring the boys back. You understand?"

Reading understood. "Yeah. I don't blame you. Me, I've got to ride over and talk to them tomorrow. I got a couple of complaints already from the outlying ranches."

Walt thought of Joe Murray's shaggy, weathered, and unclean face as he said—"Good luck."—and flagged for the barman to bring them a bottle. Then he turned toward the lawman and studied Reading's granite jaw and tough-set features. He already knew that Chad Reading could become furious at the drop of a hat. As he stood there now, it occurred to Walt that almost anyone but old Cookie and Chad Reading would be preferable as emissaries to the Indians. "When will the soldiers arrive?" he asked, and got an ironic glance and a grunt from the town marshal.

"Tomorrow or the next day, or maybe the day after that, Mister Clanton. My experience is that they don't set no records getting somewhere even when there's a war taking place. I just hope they get here. I don't have no word that they'll even come."

Reading refilled his shot glass from the bottle the barman brought, then shoved it toward Walt. He was not as opinionated or as briskly efficient and knowledgeable this evening as he had been earlier. He really had no immediate reason to worry; at least Walt did not believe he had, providing he were very careful in the palaver tomorrow. On the other hand there was at least one strong-heart who would not hesitate to shoot. Perhaps there were a dozen or two dozen more.

The longer he stood there, thinking, unmindful of the noise and smoke and jostling going on around him, the less he thought of the idea of Marshal Reading going out there as a representative of the townsmen and the cowmen. But it was not his affair. What he wanted was full recompense for the herd; beyond that he simply wanted to resume his drive toward Wyoming.

A large old pale-eyed cowman in baggy trousers and run-over boots walked along the bar and settled against wood on Chad Reading's far side. He did not raise his voice but he was one of those individuals with a voice that carried even in a noisy room. "The night stage just come in, Chad. The whip and shotgun and two passengers seen a hell of a straggle of tomahawks this afternoon coming out of the hills to the northwest. They said it looked like maybe four, five hundred of 'em."

Walt was unimpressed. He had already heard that the big band of Indians had arrived in the vicinity. He was sure these were the Indians the stage passengers had seen. It was Chad Reading's reaction that made Walt wonder.

"Afternoon?" the lawman exclaimed. "Coming from the northwest?"

The cowman nodded, watching Reading's face undergo a complete change.

"That's got to be a fourth band," the town marshal said. "The big band we were expecting already got down here, and they have already gone out and around the town. . . . From the northwest?"

The cowman nodded his head, and without another word Chad Reading turned from the bar and strode briskly in the direction of the roadside doorway.

The old cowman watched, then glanced at Walt and made a guess. "He'll go over to the corral yard to verify it. Maybe he'll also go to the rooming house and hunt up them passengers."

Walt had also decided this had to be another band, not the big one Agent Dunagan and Marshal Reading had been expecting. He did not require verification; all he wondered about was the reaction a fourth band of Indians would have upon the current antagonisms.

The cowman, mindful of Walt's pensive expression and silence, heaved back off the bar and went elsewhere to spread his news. Later, when a pair of range riders stepped to the bar next to him, one said: "Hell, don't matter how many comes around as long as you feed 'em plenty and leave a few bottles of whiskey around, they won't make no trouble." Walt turned. They were youthful men, both of them, about Arnie Wheaton's age, which was good under most circumstances, but not this time.

Cookie came straggling along and a couple of times Walt saw his other riders. It was very easy to strike up friendships in a cow-town saloon. Junior and Heber were already the center of a small group along the north curving of the bar. They were unique among all those other range riders in that they had been out there this morning when Dunagan had been killed.

Walt had one more glass of whiskey and was finishing it when Chad Reading returned, walked up, and without a word thumped the bar. When his drink arrived, though, he turned and said: "Now we got better'n twelve hundred Indians out there. The guess around town is that they can mount four hundred, maybe five hundred warriors." He shoved the shot glass away and glanced along the bar. "There's a bunch of stockmen here tonight that had ought to be out at their ranches."

A black-looking man with a full beard and jet-colored eyes came up and said: "Chad, there's some fellers rode out down at the livery barn after tellin' the night hawk they was goin' out to join the Indians."

Reading frowned. "White men?"

"Yeah."

Walt turned slowly and surveyed the burly, very dark individual. "Three of them, by any chance," he asked, "who look like down-at-the-heel riders?"

The swarthy man gazed boldly at Walt and said: "Who are you?"

Marshal Reading growled: "Just answer the damned question, Mike."

"Yeah, mister, there was three of them. All the night hawk told me was that they was strangers hereabout and they looked like grubliners."

Walt turned toward Reading. "Remember me saying we had three gunmen ride out to the camp and offer to hire on?"

Chad remembered. "Those three?"

"Sure sounds like them." Walt turned to look around the room and, when he finally located Cookie, for whom he had been searching, the older man was only about twenty feet distant in conversation with another grizzled older rider like himself. Walt called and beckoned. When Cookie walked up, Walt put his question to the older man.

"Those three gunmen who offered to hire on this morning, Cookie, likely just rode out of town, heading for the big rendezvous to hire on with the Indians."

Cookie stared. "Well, what about it?"

"What are their chances of riding alone into a band of maybe a thousand fired-up redskins?"

Cookie shrugged about that. "Depends on who they know out there." Cookie turned speculative. "If they know Murray, or even if they'd heard there was a renegade white skin callin' the shots over there, they'd make it all right. Only way they could get hurt before they got to see the spokesmen would be if them Indians was all smoked up." Cookie looked searchingly at Chad Reading. "Anyone taken a wagonload of pop skull out there that you know of?"

"Not that I know of," stated the lawman. "I doubt it like the devil. Maybe by tomorrow they can get some whiskey, but they've only just set up their camps. The last straggling band won't even be that far along. Anyway, no one around here's going to peddle them whiskey. Everyone hereabouts is already worried enough."

Cookie looked cynically at the lawman. "Mister, Walt just said them three other worthless bastards went and rode out there. How do you know they didn't have their bedrolls and their saddlebags chock-full of liquor bottles? Let me tell you something, Marshal, there's usually someone around who'll sneak a few gallons of whiskey to Indians. It's a right quick way to make a big profit."

Cookie turned on his heel and went up in the direction of the other range men he had come up from the south desert with, leaving Marshal Reading stonily staring after him.

Walt took some of the sting out of it for the lawman by saying: "I'd never use Cookie as a peace negotiator, Marshal, but he's been through his share of Indian troubles over the past forty years or so. I'd sort of figure he was right about two-thirds of the time."

Reading faced back to the bar and leaned there for a while without speaking. In the end, shortly before Walt left him, he said: "The damned Army'll never make it in time. None of the merchants around town want to do it, but it's got to be done."

Walt waited.

"Someone's got to organize a defense of some kind, Mister Clanton. I got less and less faith that riding out there to palaver tomorrow is going to help things. If it don't help, then we are sure as the devil going to need an army . . . sort of . . . all our own."

It made sense to Walt, but he still thought of this approaching crisis as an Indian disaster. There just was no way under the sun for the Indians to achieve anything more than a very fleeting triumph, if they managed to accomplish that much. What most certainly was going to happen, if the Indians let Joe Murray set them on a war trail, was arouse a lot of newspaper interest, and after the Army and the volunteers finished up and departed, there would be dead Indians, burned-out camps, orphans and widows by the dozen. "When are you going to ride out there?" he asked.

Chad Reading looked around. "Early. Why, you want to ride along?"

Walt answered frankly. "Marshal, you get mad too easy. Riding out there while you face Murray and maybe those other renegades would be about like walking into a den of bears with a fly swatter. No thanks."

"There won't be any trouble," stated Reading. "At least if there is, it won't originate with me. Be glad to have you along. Only other feller who'll go with me is Harold Hatfield. He's from here in town. Owns some of the buildings here and runs the rooming house. He was at Fort Laramie a few years back when they had that big powwow there between the Indians and the government. He's not very young any more, but there's no one else around I'd ask to go with me, nor anyone else around who's ever been through anything like this before. Hasn't been any Indian trouble in Colorado in fifteen or maybe even twenty years."

Walt smiled. "You'll make out just fine without me," he said. "I've never sat in on one of those powwows, either, Marshal. All I'm waiting for is that other herd of cattle to arrive, then I'll be trailing out of Caliente for Wyoming. There is one suggestion

I'd make, though . . . next time don't let any people from the Indian Bureau talk you into using the range around here for distribution of the beef allotment."

XII

The men left town and rode slowly out to their wagon camp when the moon was still high. Elsewhere around the community there were armed men making patrols and not all of them were townsmen; the livestock men had finally decided to react seriously, and the news of that fourth big band arriving at the rendezvous five or six miles west of town caused that.

Cookie was off-saddling at the rope corral when he said: "I'll fire up the coffee pot, if anyone's interested."

No one was. On the other hand, no one was prepared to turn in quite yet, either, so they went over by the dead fire and hunkered down for their last smoke of the day. That was when Heber said: "Someone in the saloon told me you'd agreed to ride out tomorrow and mind the cattle, Walt. Is that right?"

It was certainly no secret so Walt confirmed this. But he also explained what else he had told Marshal Reading. If there were hostiles out there in any kind of numbers, he would bring his men right back to town, or to their wagon camp.

Heber blew on the scarlet tip of his brown-paper cigarette and spoke in a soft drawl when he said: "I run into the local gunsmith tonight at the saloon. Him and me took a bottle to a corner table and set talking for a spell. He's a right nice feller. And very sensible."

The other men gazed expectantly at Heber, awaiting his culmination of this barroom meeting. Heber took his own sweet time, and that was what began to make Walt have a bad feeling even before Heber finally said: "That old feller's got some of the finest long-barreled guns in his shop a man ever saw. Sighted up to a half mile and even farther." Heber paused to see the reaction of his companions thus far. He smiled and continued. "He'll loan each one of us a rifle."

Junior's eyes widened, but he said nothing. Walt had already guessed what was coming and sat there smoking. Arnie and Cookie patiently, almost stoically, stood waiting.

"We can lay in behind where the strong-hearts got their camp, according to the gunsmith, with plenty of shelter, providing we're right cautious about sneaking up there. And we can bushwhack Joe Murray and anyone else we're of a mind to from one hell of a long ways off. Then we can hightail it back out of there and be halfway to Kingdom Come before the tomahawks even know which way we went." Heber lowered his hand with the cigarette in it and slowly ranged a tough look around the stone ring with its dead fire. "You know what folks call doing something like that?"

Arnie spoke up. "Murder, Heber?"

The older cowboy snorted. "Not murder, damn it. It's called extermination, Arnie. Justifiable extermination."

Cookie had no fault to find, but he had a question to ask. "Does your friend, the gunsmith, know how many damned Indians are likely to be at that rendezvous? Heber, you might get close enough . . . although I doubt it like hell, none of you havin' any notion how to do something like that . . . nevertheless you might get close enough and you might drygulch those renegades, but, son, you'd no more escape with a whole hide than you could take to the air and fly back here to camp. Take my word for it."

Heber scowled. "That gunsmith knows the country as well as he knows the inside of his paw, Cookie, and he says, if we're downright cautious in retreating, we can make it because by the time those Indians figure out where the gunshots come from, and rode back there to look for us, we'd be miles away heading over in this direction."

Heber looked triumphantly at old Cookie, after having got all this explained. But Cookie simply stood there, cigarette drooping, patiently listening and wearing a sardonic little crooked grin. "I don't know the gunsmith," he told Heber Jenks, "and I don't have to know him because, son, I know Indians, and, if you and that damned gunsmith think all them strong-hearts is going to do is ride back west lookin' for you, that is your first mistake. Your second mistake will be when you fellers go charging over in this direction and ride smack dab into the second party of redskin manhunters. Heber, they just aren't nowhere nearly as stupid as your gunsmith made them out to be."

Junior had a question for Cookie. "Are you telling us that no one could get up there and bushwhack those lousy renegades?"

Cookie flipped his cigarette stub into the dead ash when he replied. "No, I never told you any such a thing. What I said was that you boys couldn't begin to pull that off . . . you don't know how."

Junior pressed for a direct answer. "But it could be done?"

Cookie smiled. "Neat as a greased pig, it could be done."

Walt looked sardonic. "With you organizing and leading it?" he asked.

Cookie nodded. "Yes, but if you figure I want to do anything like that, Walt, you better guess again. At my age I'm only figurin' on maybe another year or two of trailin' upcountry, then I'm goin' to quit and go spend my last years settin' in some nice little drowsy Mexican town down in New Mexico Territory where a man can marry himself a nice big fat *señora* with a million-dollar smile who can cook *chili con carne* until the cows come home."

Walt laughed. "Cookie, you could no more stand that kind of a life for more than one month than I could."

The older man snorted. "Try me, son, just you try me. I could stand it."

Arnie went over to his bedroll, then turned to call back over to Walt: "You want someone on night watch? I'll take the first watch."

"Go to bed," stated Clanton, and included Junior Plunkett and Heber Jenks in this with a nod in their direction. "I'll take the first watch. Cookie and I'll brew us a pan of coffee."

The three riders drifted away, and Cookie, eyeing his employer shrewdly, finally went to draw water for the pot and to pitch in a double fistful of ground coffee while Walt slowly and methodically set to work creating a small hot little fire that would not spread much beyond the outer rim of the old pot. On a dark late night, a man sitting in front of a fire was a perfect target.

When they had the stones arranged for the pot, and banked their small fire so that all its flame and heat was directed upward beneath the big old pot, Walt said: "Cookie, tell me the truth . . . did you ever do that?"

The older man did not ask what Walt was referring to. He simply said: "Truthfully? Yeah, I've done it, Walt. And if you are now fixin' to ask me if I'd do it again . . . ?"

"Well?"

"You thinkin' about maybe just the two of us sneaking away from here to do it, then?"

Walt stared into the stingy little fire. "Yes. If it fails, no sense in getting a kid like Arnie wiped out, too, is there?"

"No sense at all," confirmed the old man in a voice so soft it did not carry ten feet from the stone ring. "My eyes and ears aren't as good as they once was. And where would we get those long-barreled rifles?"

"In town," said Walt, and finally gazed at his cook. "You've got the savvy and I've got the eyes and ears."

Cookie was quite willing to accept this, but he had a question about something else. "How's your conscience these days, son?"

Walt said: "What do you expect the chances are if those Indians start raiding out over the countryside, and maybe even raiding around town?"

"Oh, they'll raid," stated the old man, vigorously bobbing his head. "They're fired up to that, no question about it. How much of it they'll do before they're stopped is anyone's guess."

"But they'll kill and be killed."

"For a plumb fact," confirmed the old man.

"But if we broke it up before it got started, Cookie, maybe a lot of women and kids on both sides wouldn't end up dead or worse . . . homeless and under some kind of damned banishment because they didn't have paws and husbands to make their way for them. Hell, Cookie, my conscience don't bother me at all."

Cookie smiled, scratched his middle vigorously, and looked at Clanton differently than he had ever looked at him before. "All right, then. And what's the sense in squattin' around here the rest of the night when we can damned well use the darkness for better things? Anyway, I just as soon do things and not be forever talkin' about doin' them." Cookie's hard, sly smile got pegged upon each uplifted corner of his wide, lipless mouth. "You ready?"

Walt arose, stretched, looked over in the vicinity of the old wagon where the lumpy shapes were scattered in slumber, and wondered how to handle the matter of wakening the next man to take over the vigil without that man also guessing what he and Cookie Weston were up to.

Cookie had the answer. "I'll go saddle us a couple of horses and fetch along a little jerky in the saddlebags. I'll lead them horses a mile or so out, and, when you hear a coyote wail, you keep the wagon 'atween you and the sentry, and sneak down through the darkness, headin' for the sound. All right?"

Walt almost smiled. Cookie Weston was probably just as devious as was old Joe Murray, the difference being that one had chosen a special road to travel and the other one had chosen a more commonplace and logical trail, even though it was certainly a lot less spectacular. He nodded and allowed Cookie ten minutes to dump leather upon two of their horses and go walking soundlessly to the wagon with them, where Walt held the reins until Cookie returned with a pair of saddlebags and took both sets of reins as he turned and went westerly out across the range in the direction of town, but northward of it, still not making a sound.

Walt rolled a smoke and enjoyed it halfway down before he went over and routed out young Arnie Wheaton. He thought either of the older riders might be more susceptible to wonderment or downright suspicion. He was correct, for even after Arnie had his hat and boots on, and arose to buckle the gun and bullet belt around his middle, he was still only half awake.

He went to the tiny fire, stirred it a little, and poked some small twigs into it, then looked around for Walt, and, when he did not see him because Walt was on the far side of the wagon, Arnie yawned mightily and turned his attention elsewhere. He did not look like the best of all sentries, but then there was not a very big chance that the riders would be attacked anyway. Each hour that passed uneventfully increased the possibility of a serene night passing.

Walt's only feeling of guilt was when he paused out a couple of hundred yards to glance back. All he could make out very well was the ghostly outline of the wagon. It troubled him a little that what he and Cookie were doing implied a lack of trust in Junior, Heber, and Arnie. Of course that was not the case at all, but he was sure by morning one of those three would think of this, and would be upset by it. The alternative would be to take them into his confidence, and that would entail an absolute and total refusal by those three to stand apart from what he and

Cookie were going to attempt, and that was precisely what he did not care to go through with them.

When the coyote howled and Walt fixed its location as being somewhere south and west, then turned to go heading off in that direction, he momentarily forgot about the men back at the wagon camp. For one thing, unless they could find that gunsmith in town, and, after locating him talk him into going to his shop and opening up for them, all this was going to be for nothing, anyway, and they'd just have to return to camp. The second time the coyote sounded and Walt corrected his course to head directly toward the sound, he almost wished the gunsmith would refuse.

Cookie's dry voice suddenly said: "Hey, damn it, don't walk right on past. Who'd you leave on watch?"

"Arnie," replied Walt, stepping around through some underbrush to accept the reins to a horse.

Cookie approved. "Best one, under the circumstances."

They got astride and headed at a brisk walk down in the direction of town through a night that was not warm, but that certainly lacked by quite a bit being as chilly as most of the previous nights had been. Of course they had a long ride ahead of them, and a lot of night hours to live through; it always got coldest just before dawn, so they would be chilled sooner or later, and they certainly would be chilled before they got back over in the vicinity of either Caliente or their wagon camp again. *If* they got back.

XIII

There were two aspects of the darkness that Walt noticed as soon they were upon the outskirts of Caliente in the utter hush of late night. One of them was that in the darkness old Cookie Weston looked twenty years younger. Of course this was due to the weak light but nevertheless he still looked that much younger. The second observation had to do with a stealthiness, a deviousness Walt had never before seen in the older man. In fact before Walt had begun to give serious consideration to finding the gunsmith, Cookie resolved the problem by following an instinct; he led Walt down through town into the west-side back alley without saying a word, and, when they were directly behind one of the small stores, he pointed to what was obviously living quarters. Then he slid to the ground and looped his reins to a sagging old fence and approached the alley-side door of the gun shop and waited for Walt.

After that, the bizarre relationship that was to prevail between them for the balance of a very long night became noticeably manifest. It was not at all the same relationship that otherwise had characterized their acquaintanceship up until this time when Weston had been just another cattle-drive cook and Walt Clanton had been the *jefe*. When Walt knocked lightly upon the rear door and waited, Cookie innocently strolled around to the front of the shop and stood out there in layers of shadowed darkness effectively sealing off the gunsmith's withdrawal in this direction, if the gunsmith thought of such a thing.

He didn't. In fact when Walt had his fist raised to knock again, harder this time, the old door opened as soundlessly as though its hinges had recently been oiled—which they had—and an old-time hogleg .44 pistol with a foot-long barrel came out of the interior darkness to stare with its one eyeless socket straight into the chest of Walt Clanton. The man behind the gun was dimly visible; he was not even average in height, and his face was marred and lined by age and a look of having achieved this eminence of years in an environment that had never been mild. "What do you want?" he enquired softly, and in a voice that was neither hostile nor frightened, but which was coldly matter-of-fact.

Walt said his name and mentioned Heber's name as well,

then he recalled Heber's sitting with this man at the saloon, and, when he got that far along, the gunsmith slowly lowered the old hogleg and stepped closer for a better look. Then he said: "Yes, I recognize you now. Mister Clanton, it's awful damned late."

Walt said: "Mind if I step inside for a moment or two? This won't take very long."

Cookie suddenly materialized without a sound and the gunsmith's right arm began to swing. Walt said: "It's all right. He's with me. His name is Cookie Weston. Could we come inside for just a few minutes?"

The gunsmith, who had been upon the verge of allowing Walt to enter, now looked suspiciously at two armed men in the night and said: "Give me an idea what it is you want?"

"You told Heber you had some of the finest sighted rifles around, and you also mentioned to him how they could maybe be used to prevent serious trouble between us and the Indians."

The older man stepped aside and jerked his head for them to enter. He herded them on through his stuffy living quarters to the front of the shop, and there he went to the roadway window to draw the blanket hanging there, serving as a drapery, before he fumbled in the Stygian darkness that ensued and finally lit a small lamp. He put down the old hogleg and said: "There now, gents. That's better." He looked more closely at Cookie. "You fellers want two precision rifles, is that it?"

Walt nodded. "That's it. And some information."

"What kind of information?"

"You told Heber you know this country right well. We want to know where the Indians have their rendezvous, and we'd like you to tell us how you figure a couple of men could get over there and get off a couple of shots, and get away again."

The old gunsmith pursed his lips and very slowly studied first Walt, then Cookie. He seemed more impressed by Cookie because, when he finally spoke, he drew Cookie's attention to a pair of re-made Springfield rifles that looked as though they had at one time been two of those special weapons used by marksmen—called Sharpshooters—during the War Between the States. "Those'll do it," he announced. "I've worked on them two guns as a sort of hobby for most likely a year, off and on." He dropped his arm. "But no matter how good a gun is, it can't do nothing by itself. If you boys ain't right fine shots, then it'd be a waste to let you have those two weapons, and it'd be a waste to let you go out there to the rendezvous, wouldn't it?"

Walt answered a little harshly. "The choice then is to do nothing at all, isn't it?"

The gunsmith thought a moment, then grudgingly agreed. "Yes, I expect that's the size of it." He looked back at Cookie. "All right, one thing's a blessed fact, if someone don't yank the tail feathers out of those devils and their renegade leader, there's going to be a lot of useless burials around and about. All right." He crossed to where the glistening old weapons stood, lifted the oiled rag from over the top of the muzzles, and brought the guns to his worktable to place them gently there. "They don't shoot high nor low, left nor right. They're dead on. Only thing you'll have to do is allow for drift and drop, and that'll depend on how far you'll be from the snakes when you draw a bead." He looked enquiringly at Walt. "You know what I'm talking about?"

Cookie enjoyed this and broadly smiled, but Walt got a little red in the face; he had not been treated as a child or an idiot in a long time. "I understand," he told the old man. "Bullets?"

The gunsmith went to a heavy wooden box and delved there briefly, then turned and brought back two oily-looking small boxes. "Bring back what you don't use," he told them, handing each man one of the boxes. "It's a little hard getting them kind of shells nowadays." He looked at Cookie and sighed, then went over to a smaller table and returned with a large rough piece of brown paper and a pencil that was half gnawed through. "Pay attention," he said, and began laboriously drawing a rough map. "Right here is Caliente. Now then, you see where this pencil is heading? Almost due west. Well, that'd be the quickest way to get out there, but you'd never make it, not even in the dark. They'd catch you sure as hell . . . so you go north. Not south, like some folks would tell you, but north. And you go 'way up here, like this, and keep heading upcountry for maybe four, five miles before you commence dropping down again, and, when you commence coming downcountry, do it right gradual, and, if you're lucky, that should put you into some breaks and upended country a fair distance behind the rendezvous. You should smell the smoke and maybe see a few fires by then." The gunsmith handed Cookie the map. "Keep it. You can't see it in the dark, but keep it anyway." He turned to Walt. "Mister, they got very good ears, and they probably got those damned half-wild dogs with them they usually travel around with. I'll tell you right now I wouldn't bet a lead cartwheel on your chances of ever getting away from out there."

Walt said: "Mister, you've already bet two good Sharpshooter rifles."

The gunsmith nodded. "Yeah, have, haven't I? Well, in that case I might as well give you boys something else." He went to a drawer and removed four round black iron balls. Neither Cookie nor Walt had any idea what the objects were even after the gunsmith had silently handed each one of them two of those heavy little things. He pointed. "That's a wick. You light that wick and fling them things like they was stones if there's a mess of Indians about to close in on you . . . then drop flat because them little things is what they used in the Mexican War. They're called grenades. Some folks call 'em hand bombs. They'll explode all over the countryside and fling chunks of steel worse'n bullets."

Cookie stepped up, scowling. "No thanks," he muttered. "I'm not goin' to blow myself up."

The gunsmith picked up Cookie's two grenades and shoved them into Cookie's coat pockets. "They won't blow you up. They won't do anything at all unless you light them fuses." He stepped back. "It's up to you," he said, and waited for either Walt or Cookie to speak, and, when neither of them did, the gunsmith turned and led the way back down through his living quarters and out into the silent, star-washed night.

"Shed your spurs before you try to sneak in close," he admonished. "Mister Weston, you'd better keep an eye on this young feller. They don't even begin to know how these things are done. A bad one can get a good man killed." The gunsmith stepped into his doorway. "Good luck. I'll be waiting when you return the guns."

They were riding back northward up the alleyway before the gunsmith finally closed his door. He did not wave to them and they did not wave to him.

When they were clear of town and heading on a westerly course, Cookie said: "Well, that's how us older fellers feel, Walt, and it don't mean you fellers . . . you and Junior and Heber . . . can't do things, it's just that we don't figure you know how because you've never *had* to do them."

Walt lit a smoke and looked over at his companion with a slightly skeptical expression, but he made no comment, although he felt confident that he and perhaps Heber and Junior as well, and perhaps even young Arnie, could learn what to do awfully fast. He exhaled, gazed at the high stars, and decided that since this might be the last time old Cookie would ever have to exert his hoary capabilities since it was probably the last time there would be a serious threat of Indian trouble, he would allow Weston to be head honcho. Cookie was capable enough, Walt was satisfied about that, so allowing his camp cook temporarily to be boss and war leader wasn't much of a sacrifice in any event.

There was a thin-sliced little lop-sided moon that gave practically no light at all, and a million brilliant stars that made up for the lack, while the full curved panoply of a purple heaven made Walt feel infinitesimal. They had a lot of miles to cover and for as long as the darkness lasted they were relatively safe, as long as they were also very prudent. The Indians, too, would have sentries on duty, and they even more than the townsmen and cowmen back around Caliente would have reason to be extremely wary.

He said: "Cookie, I can't really understand a man like Joe Murray."

Weston's reply was blunt. "Sure you can. He'd sacrifice anyone . . . you, me, all his blood brothers, all the folks livin' in the outlyin' ranches and camps, just to be able to get his hands on all the loot, mostly the gold and the cash, the strong-hearts would bring back. His kind of a man don't have a conscience and he's never had any feelin'. You can understand him the same way you can understand a weasel or any other wanton, cold-blooded killer." Cookie smiled without a shred of humor. "You maybe haven't known too many like Murray. Maybe there aren't very many like that, but by God I've known 'em back a few years. They'd raid and kill and plunder and say they was doin' it to protect folks and all. Every word of it was a lousy lie. They killed and plundered for wealth, pure and simple."

"Then why haven't the Indians seen through Murray?" asked Walt.

"Likely, Walt, most of the responsible Indians have seen through him, but it's not them people who make the laws, is it? It's the war leaders and their followers. You can't buck a whole damned army, can you? And those strong-hearts hate us worse'n they hate death itself. Murray uses them. You know how they'll finally figure that out? I'll tell you. When they're as old as I am, and by then there won't be a blessed one of 'em left above ground."

Walt stubbed out his smoke atop the saddle horn, hefted his heavy Springfield, and held it up for a close examination. It was a beautiful example of a good gunsmith's pride and capability.

Cookie chuckled. "We'll nail 'em, Walt, you wait and see. We'll bust old Murray's head like a rotten pumpkin like he done with that Dunagan feller."

Walt turned. Old Cookie was happy; he was actually enjoying every moment of this, and, when it came time to take long aim and deliberately murder a man, he was going to do that happily, too. Not that Walt wouldn't also do it, but the difference was that Walt did not look forward to it with pleasure; he *had* to do it, so he intended to do it, but it was nothing he would ever afterward take pleasure in recalling, or even discussing.

XIV

They did not discuss why they were riding through the cooling night, primarily because their objective was more critically important to them than was their purpose; they had no illusions about the outcome, if they should stumble onto some sentries. The night seemed totally empty. When they got far enough away from Caliente to take fresh interest in what lay onward, Walt thought they had to be roughly five miles northward on their big curving ride. It was time for them to start the gradual descent that was supposed to bring them down behind the rendezvous in some broken country.

Neither of them had any idea where they were nor where they were going, except in a very general way. They both possessed an expert sense of direction, and that was what they had to rely upon from this point onward as they entered country they had never seen before, even in broad daylight. Cookie occasionally tilted his head to wrinkle his nose for a scent, but they did not detect anything like that for almost two hours, and finally, when they did detect it, the aroma made them both aware of something neither of them had considered lately—hunger. What they smelled was the remnant scents of cooking meat. Probably the Indians had flung fat into their cooking fires and, after having eaten, had also flung in the bones and other residue of their meal. Whatever made the aroma was beef, and, whether it was an edible part or not, it smelled to Walt like steak or roast. He made a little groan and grinned at Cookie. The older man fished in a saddlebag and held forth a slab of tough, cold beef. Walt took it and chewed almost endlessly on it as they finally entered some slightly uneven country, and, after reining atop a low little hillock, they saw what they had thought might be out there, and halted in a little awe, to look at it.

There were hundreds of dying little individual fires scattered southward, northward, and eastward. The rendezvous camp looked to Walt in the darkness as though it probably encompassed a mile or more. The camps were divided noticeably, even though in general it was one huge rendezvous. Each separate band seemed to have its own marked-off area, but the difference that separated each of the four bands was actually only a matter of a hundred yards or so. Except that it was very dark out there, and those little dying fires tended to show up against the blackness as four separate camps, the Indian encampment would probably look fairly well integrated in daylight. They heard horses, many of them, wandering in the night, and they also saw several mounted warriors passing at a sedate walk back and forth through the camp and upon its farthest outskirts.

Cookie said—"That's one hell of a big camp."—and made it sound as though, finally, he was sobered at the prospect of what they were out here to do. "One hell of a lot of Indians."

Walt nodded, an action Cookie did not notice because he was concentrating on the huge camp. It seemed almost ridiculous for just two riflemen to be out here, thinking they might be able to upset the plans of all those people down there. It *was* ridiculous.

Cookie sighed, looked off into the broken country behind them, and grunted at Walt to follow as he led off on a short ride of exploration. What Cookie sought was difficult to find—an ideal hiding place for two saddled horses. There was plenty of upended countryside back there, in fact there seemed to be an endless amount of it before they finally reached some higher slopes that would, in daylight, appear as mountainsides, but what they specifically sought were trees, and, although there were plenty of trees several miles westerly, Cookie had no intention of going that far back to conceal their mounts, and for the best of all reasons. After they had their horses hidden back there, and had concluded their undertaking, Cookie would never be able to lope that far on foot and he had no illusions about it. He finally settled for a little blind cañon with a huge boulder directly in front of it, and after they had dismounted back there, Walt came up with evidence that they were not the first men to utilize this spot. There was a very dark old skull lacking the lower jaw, sitting almost jauntily where someone had placed it upon the ledge at the back of the enormous, blockading boulder. Cookie looked and said—"Yeah, just the kind of an omen we need."—and refused to look again. They cared for the animals, lifted down the rifles, and went back around the huge rock on foot, to halt out there and study the horizon. There was no hint of dawn yet.

Cookie took over the lead and to his credit did not rattle a bush or dislodge a single rock as they made their way back down to the low hillock where they had first viewed the Indian encampment. There, he squatted, holding the gun barrel upright and leaning upon it while he made a long, thoughtful examination of the winking little fires on three sides of them. Finally he pointed and said: "We got a choice. You see that fairly big bunch of coals a half mile out there? Well, that'll be where they powwowed last night . . . Joe Murray, his war leaders, and the heads of the clans. Now my guess is that Murray and those other three sons-of-bitches, if he took them into camp with him which I expect he did, is sleepin' right around that big set of coals somewhere." Cookie made a death's-head grin at Walt. "We can shed our boots and try threadin' our way half through the whole bloody camp and come onto them fellers, and kill 'em where they lie, or we can do like we originally figured to do, set out here until daylight, and, when they stand up to head out from camp a ways to tend their mornin' business, we can sharp-shoot 'em from here." Cookie continued to squat there, leaning upon the Springfield and eyeing Walt Clanton.

The idea of trying to make their way through dozens of sleeping Indians, most of whom were light sleepers from training, did not appeal to Walt at all. He said: "We'll wait. Dawn's not far off anyway."

Cookie accepted this decision without a blink, but he got more comfortable and tightened his old coat around his sinewy, scrawny body, crossed both legs, and carefully placed the Springfield across his lap. "If we get away afterward," he said in a brisk and business-like tone, "our best bet is to head straight back into them mountains before we try to turn northward and work our way back around until we're headin' for Caliente."

Walt nodded absently. He was not thinking of escape; he was thinking of their chances of success at what they were waiting for. "Lead off afterward," he told Cookie, and lifted his Springfield to snug it back for a practice sighting. He grunted and lowered the gun, then threw it to his shoulder again. "Ivory bead," he muttered, lowering the gun to examine the front sight up close. They both had tiny ivory beads fixed into the front sights. Cookie was pleased. He also practiced sighting, but Cookie got belly down and used his elbows as a brace. He held that position for a long time, moving the rifle a little from one side to the other, before rearing back to sit up cross-legged again, and pull the old coat closer because, as dawn approached, the cold was becoming more marked.

"Can't miss," he crowed.

Walt had no comment to make about that. Having a smoke would have helped time pass but it also would have added an alien scent to the clearing cold air.

A mounted Indian passed majestically in front of them a hundred yards eastward, and halted once to glance in their direction. They turned to stone until the Indian gutturally growled and his horse moved off, continuing the long ride this sentry had yet to make before he reached this spot again.

Cookie sighed and watched the mounted man disappear. "He'll never come closer to losin' the top plate off his skull."

Walt had plenty of time to consider their position, their purpose, and the possibilities that would ensue the moment after those Indians out there got over being stunned when two riflemen opened up from back here.

He turned to Cookie. "Who the hell's idea was this, anyway?"

Cookie chuckled. "Don't matter now. We are here, they are out there, and it's going to be light enough to see by in another thirty minutes, which means we couldn't get to the horses and get back up and around this camp headin' for home without a thousand redskins seein' us, and maybe half of 'em takin' after us."

Walt softly scowled. "You felt this way from the beginning?"

Cookie turned away to gaze out where a thin rind of pale light was firming up the full, uneven length of the eastern horizon, and said: "I'm old, Walt, and I've lived through a hell of a lot, and if today is the day I been ridin' toward all those years, well hell, then I finally got here, didn't I?" Cookie turned slowly. He wasn't smiling but he looked as though he were almost ready to smile.

There was a stir of movement down among the little dying fires. Here and there sparks flew as someone stirred coals and punched in fresh faggots. The sentries came in, driving horses, and there were a number of indignant outcries as the loose stock wandered through, and over, private camps. Dogs barked for the first time, and far off a man's keening voice was raised in something like a prayer chant.

Cookie resettled himself atop the low hillock and shoved the rifle ahead to rest upon rock. Beside him, Walt also got prone. He opened the breach and fed a slug into his Springfield, then he said: "If we get more than one of them, I'll be surprised. It'll take too long to reload."

Cookie was silent. He gently lowered his head and hunched up a bony shoulder, settling into a curve that seemed to become part of the motionless rifle. It almost seemed that Cookie was merely an extenuation of the Springfield rifle.

Walt studied the older man. Clearly Cookie Weston was not assuming this position for the first time in his life. Walt, too, settled to the ground for a sighting, but, as he did so, he thought how interesting it would be to loosen old Weston up sometime when they had nothing to interrupt, and encourage Cookie to recite the story of his life. It would never happen, of course. Those things never did happen, desirable though they were.

The light came almost imperceptibly, but it came, and as visibility gradually increased Walt could see the entire huge camp. It was a very awesome sight. There were hundreds of Indians, horses, dogs, children, squabbling squaws, and strong-hearts with tethered war horses nearby, leaning upon lances with saddle guns slung carelessly across their backs, conversing in groups here and there. Cookie was interested in the bucks: "We might be too late at that. See all them daubed young devils? That's fight paint on 'em, and they ain't goin' near a breakfast fire, because warriors aren't supposed to ride off on a full gut. You know what I'm sayin'? They are goin' on raids and they're goin' darned soon, maybe within an hour or such." Cookie swung the Springfield and beaded in on a big strong-heart with a white ermine tail in his roach. "Hunt leader," he muttered with his head nestled to the cold wood stock. "Hunt leader and big war leader."

"And big damned fool," muttered Walt, shifting his attention to the near center of the closest camp where several Indian women hovered, speaking nervously, it seemed to Walt, as they hurriedly fed that big council fire and got ready to do some cooking there.

"Mind now," whispered Cookie. "Mind those women." He did not explain why but a moment or two after he had spoken it became clear why he had wanted Walt not to take his eyes off that particular camp. Several white men rolled out, pulled on boots, bundled up in filthy old coats, and crammed equally soiled old hats upon heads of awry hair. One of them stood up and stamped cold feet, then spat into the fire where the women were working, and slowly turned to look in all directions while vigorously scratching his middle.

Cookie said: "Damn my eyes, I didn't figure I'd be able to recognize the old devil from this far off. That's Joe. That's Joe Murray!"

Walt accepted Cookie's judgment. One thing he was certain of was that the unkempt man over there had been at the palaver right after Dunagan had been killed. Walt hadn't known him then and he only had Cookie's identification now, and Cookie by his own admission did not have eyesight as good as he once had had, but of one fact Walt was entirely sure—whoever that renegade white skin was out there, he was in that camp for just one purpose. To Walt, that was all the justification he needed.

He dropped low, swung the rifle gently, and said: "Cookie, I'll nail him. You hold off until I miss. If that happens, you nail him. If I don't miss, someone else is sure as hell going to jump up when I fire. You get that one."

Cookie's answer was muted. "Just shoot, damn it all, just shoot."

XV

Walt's heart was pounding and despite the cold his palms were damp. He watched that distant man slowly turn until his back was to Walt and Cookie, and for as long as the man stood that way Walt hesitated. Cookie muttered angrily at him: "God dammit, shoot." But Walt held off, and the unkempt distant man began slowly to turn again, coming almost fully around as he surveyed another sector of the huge camp. Walt said—"Now."—and three seconds later gently tightened his grip on the trigger. The Springfield roared and kicked hard.

Cookie said: "You missed. . . . By God, no you didn't."

Walt raised his head a trifle. The man out there had remained staring for a long time, at least it seemed like a long time, then without any warning he dropped. Instantly Walt grabbed the gate and wrenched it upward to eject his spent casing and to push in a second casing. For no reason he was immediately aware of, he retrieved the shot-out casing and pocketed it as Cookie suddenly swore, then went completely silent for a moment, and also fired. This time, when the second rising man down there raised a rifle, he almost had it to his shoulder before the bullet struck him. He fired into the air and went over backward, knocked that way by the recoil of his weapon. The squaws screamed and scattered like quail as the man fell backward into their breakfast fire.

From a dozen camps men appeared, carrying weapons and acting unsure, as though they did not know precisely where the gunshots had come from. It helped this difficulty, at least as far as Walt and Cookie were concerned, when several of those painted broncos who had been standing around earlier, awaiting the signal to ride, suddenly began howling and firing their saddle guns in different directions. Another of those renegades arose, this time holding his silhouette low in a crouch while he glared back in the direction Walt and Cookie were lying. Walt ducked his head to get a bead but Cookie reached over and rapped his shoulder. "Leave that one," Cookie commanded. "We got more than we deserved to get, and they aren't even sure where we fired from. Now come along, and hurry at it."

Cookie pulled back until he was on the downhill side of their low hillock, then he got stiffly to his feet, and turned to run. He did not look back to make certain Walt was following along or not. Walt was.

They did not say a word all the way back to the horses or even then, when they were untying the animals and springing up across leather. Their entire efforts from this point on were dedicated to flight. They left tracks, inevitably, but old Cookie was no novice in this business, either; whenever it was possible, he led the way across rock fields and stone ledges, and once he made Walt follow up a narrow little swirling creek for more than half a mile, which could only be done at a slow walk and this worried Walt who was certain that by now, back along the lower foothills, there was pursuit. The Indians would not be very long finding where they had been lying and where their horses had been tethered.

Cookie did not go directly into the westerly mountains. He started out as though this were his intention, but, when they left the creek, he picked up a game trail that angled circuitously around through the tall pines and followed the curve and sweep of northeasterly slopes. He apparently wanted to maintain their course where there was ample protective cover while at the same time hurrying to get on around so that, as they rode, they would be heading in the direction from which they had come. Walt followed. They halted once, on the far side of a hill to allow their horses a moment of respite, and walked back to the crown and squatted up there, rifles in their arms, looking and listening.

They saw nothing and heard nothing, which might ordinarily have been a good omen except that, as Cookie said, an Indian was never more to be feared than when he was silent and invisible. Then, to explain, Cookie waved with one arm.

"You see all that country eastward along the foothills? If they figure we come from around Caliente, they ain't going to send more'n a few bucks to try and catch up. They'll spread most of their force all along them foothills, and when we figure we're safe and drop down to the plain. . . ." Cookie drew a rigid finger across his throat.

They went onward from this place and never once lost the altitude they had initially gained. It was not the most pleasant or comfortable horseback riding Walt had ever done, but when he reflected upon the alternative to it, there was reason to think it was not too bad after all. They even climbed a little, as the sun appeared and also began climbing. They passed across a number of inviting secluded meadows and little lush grass parks. Occasionally they halted, always to favor the horses, but the last time, just before they decided they were far enough eastward, Cookie brought forth the greasy remains of that meat he'd brought along, and they ate the last of it, then watered at a little ice-water creek, had a smoke, and struck out again.

Cookie halted upon a broad eminence from where he could see hundreds of miles of the southerly and easterly open range. There was not a sign of Indians. They could see the distant roof tops of Caliente, and down there they could also see some kind of activity; at least there was dust, and that signified activity, but they were actually far too distant to make out any details even of the town itself. If they did not leave their succoring mountains at this point, they were going to be carried farther northward and farther eastward because that was the way the curving high mountains turned.

Cookie led, still, when they finally made a concerted downslope effort to get out upon the flat range, and he was still chary even though they had covered many miles without seeing Indians. Walt was the one who saw the Indian, though, not Cookie. They were only a couple of hundred yards from the open range when movement caught Walt's notice. He hissed and hauled down to an abrupt halt. The Indian was just within the final tree fringe at the border of the slope and the grassland, and he was walking his horse very quietly eastward. Obviously he was one of the searchers, perhaps the easternmost one of them because he was alone and there were no other visible Indians back the way he had come. His interest was less in the trees on his left than it was upon that dust down in the vicinity on his right, and maybe he was justified in showing more curiosity in that direction since he had not seen either of the escaping white skins up to this point, but he did see some kind of excitement out across the prairie.

Walt leaned and softly said: "Let him pass."

Cookie nodded. He had never had any other intention. They could have shot the buck, and the moment one of them fired his gun all the other Indians would know about where the white skins were. But the strong-heart pulled over into some tall trees, dismounted, tied his horse to a low limb, and, cradling a saddle gun in the bend of one arm, he walked ahead a few yards and intently watched that dust down around Caliente. Walt and Cookie exchanged an exasperated look. They were safe only as long as neither of them made a sound. If they turned, now, and tried going back up the slope, the Indian was going to hear them.

Walt sighed, handed Cookie his Springfield and the reins to his horse, slid off, kicked out of his boots, yanked free the tie-down holding his Colt in its hip holster, and soundlessly began his stalk. The Indian was a man of medium height, but he was sinewy, muscular without an ounce of spare flesh on him, and he had the litheness of a cougar. Walt had no qualms; if he could get close enough before the Indian heard or saw him, he was confident of what the outcome would be. The trick, then, was to get that close.

It helped immeasurably that the activity in Caliente interested the Indian very much. Walt was able to stalk within a hundred yards of the buck, then he stepped on some hidden gravel, which immediately grated underfoot, and, when the Indian turned, Walt was flat behind a large old bull-pine, holding his breath. The Indian was motionless for a long while, studying everything behind him, the trees, the underbrush, the little clearings here and there among some stumps where town woodcutters had been in years past, and he finally turned his attention back to the dust cloud southward, and Walt breathed a silent short prayer of gratitude, and from here on, when he moved ahead, one foot advancing ahead of the other foot, he held the Colt in his fist.

The Indian would not be able to kill Walt. Cookie was back there intently watching; he would shoot the moment he saw the Indian turn and face Walt. But the idea was to neutralize the Indian without having to fire a gun. Walt came up almost within rifle-barrel reach—and a twig snapped. This time the Indian whirled, fully alerted. He was throwing the saddle gun over into both hands as he came around, and Walt launched himself like a battering-ram, head low and long arms outstretched. They went down in a heap, an astonished Indian and a straining white man.

Walt tried just once to wrench the carbine away, then abandoned that effort because the Indian clung with both hands. Walt reared back, aimed and fired his coiled right arm. The fist struck alongside the buck's head with stunning force. The Indian relinquished his hold on the carbine and tried dazedly to twist his body, to turn his head and face away. He also raised a powerful arm to shove hard, and this made Walt miss with his second stunning strike. The Indian brought up his other hand. For one second Walt had a glimpse of gray steel, then he hurled himself sideward as the descending knife ripped the air where he had been. He kicked hard, shoving up to his feet.

The Indian rolled, swung fully around, crab-like, and glared upward from deadly black eyes. He still had that big knife in his right fist. Walt jumped ahead, aimed, and kicked out. The Indian rolled backward but could not quite regain his feet before Walt came in desperately and aimed another kick. This time, Walt felt the shock and heard the Indian gasp as his knife wrist was caught flush by a hard boot toe. The Indian rolled twice and came up onto his feet.

He had a broken right wrist; the hand hung and the man's arm was useless, but he faced Walt with a crouch and a snarl. He made his final mistake when he sprang like a catamount, one hand reaching with bent, talon-like fingers. Walt knocked aside the outstretched arm with his left hand, stepped forward one foot to be inside the Indian's guard, and he fired that cocked right fist again. This time the Indian took the strike flush on the chin. His head snapped violently backward even as his knees folded. He fell against Walt, and slid past, struck the ground, and rolled once.

Cookie came down, leading both horses and carrying both

carbines. He hardly more than glanced at the unconscious buck but pushed reins and rifle into Walt's hands and said: "Hurry up and get astride. I swear I heard some more of them coming on around up high, likely following out our sign."

As he said this, Cookie raised a fearful face and looked over one shoulder, then he swung up, settled into his saddle, got the Springfield in place, and started to rein onward. Again he did not look back, but Walt was mounting, too. He was a few yards back but he was not loitering, even though he did pause beside the tree where the senseless strong-heart was lying full out, and studied the man a moment, then turned and hurried onward.

They reached the last of the trees without hesitating, pushed southward through the final pine-needle bed and came forth into full sunshine and upon hard ground covered with early summer short grass.

At once, someone let go with a triumphant shout westerly, and, when they looked back, there was a single-file band of hastening Indians urging their horses down off the slope toward the open range.

Cookie was startled. "God damn, an' I never heard a sound. Damned hearin' just ain't no good any more." His hearing might have been impaired but his instinctive reaction to peril was certainly not impaired. He lifted his reins, sank in his spurs, and, when the surprised horse sprang ahead and lit down in a race for life, Cookie was reacting in the only reasonable way he could react. Walt sank in his heels, too, but since he had neither his boots nor his spurs, when the horse responded, it did so more because it had the example of Cookie up ahead to inspire it, than because what its rider had done meant much.

XVI

They were within sight of succor, but they were riding at a distinct disadvantage. Their horses were tired. They had been using these same animals since the previous early evening. They had covered considerable ground upon them, then they had skirted around through the mountains, which was always difficult going for horses, and now, eight or ten hours later they were urging the animals to give them speed. For a mile or so the horses gallantly responded, then Walt felt his animal hanging in the bit a little, and turned to look back. There were eight Indians back there on fresher horses. They were closing the distance a little at a time, but there was no question about it, they definitely were catching up.

Up ahead all the way to town there was open country without a tree, a decent erosion gully, or even a jumble of rocks, and the grass was far too short yet to be any help to men desperately in need of some kind of protection from their pursuers. The only hope, it appeared to Walt, was cruelly to force their worn-out mounts to get them close enough to Caliente for someone down there to see their plight and rush forth to help them. Then that option winked out when Cookie's heavy-legged horse stepped through the ceiling of a prairie dog's residence and went down to his knees. It was not normally a bad fall. In fact, the horse did not go all the way down, but when his chin struck the ground and his body dropped abruptly in front while remaining high in back, Cookie, who had been in the act of glancing over his shoulder and was therefore not expecting anything, went over the horse's head as though he had been shot from a catapult. For him the fall was not serious, either. A moment after striking the ground and rolling, Cookie bounded back to his feet still clutching the Springfield rifle.

His horse also regained its feet, but it veered away and went flinging tiredly on a southeasterly course far out of Cookie's reach, and, although normally Walt would have been able to rope the animal and bring it back, this time he had both hands full, so he ignored the fleeing horse and swept in low to help

Cookie. He even kicked a foot free of the near side stirrup for Cookie to use in making his vault to the area behind the cantle of Walt's saddle. But Cookie had already made his decision. He dropped to one knee and raised the Springfield as he yelled at Walt: "Get the hell on your way! That horse couldn't begin to make it carryin' us both!" He drew a long bead and fired, and Walt's horse shied from the thunderous explosion. Walt hauled his animal down to a walk and turned to look. Cookie was methodically opening the gate, extracting the spent casing and plugging in a fresh load. Farther back, several hundred yards farther back in fact, an Indian swerved his horse violently and drummed on its ribs with slick heels. He did not appear to be injured but apparently Cookie's bullet had come so close it had frightened and unnerved him.

The other Indians yelled back and forth and slackened speed. Cookie fired again, and this time a horse dropped like a stone. The Indians abruptly turned back and rode a few yards farther away, but reluctantly, then faced around again and sat out there, staring. Cookie cackled and reloaded. Walt stepped to the ground with the second Springfield, looped his reins to check the horse so it could not graze along the way, and slapped it on the rump after aiming it in the direction of Caliente. Then he, too, dropped to one knee and took a long rifle rest to fire.

The Indians had one chance. They obviously could not get in close enough to kill either Walt or Cookie Weston even though they, too, had rifles, without being in danger of being killed first. The one advantage was their numbers; if they could surround the pair of embattled executioners, then work their way in a few yards at a time perhaps using their mounts as shields, they could win. But whatever they did had to be done soon because the sounds of this little furious battle would carry easily as far as Caliente and eventually someone was certain to come out and investigate.

Cookie was not concerned with tactics. Each time he had his Springfield loaded, he would select a target and fire at it. This kept the Indians beyond rifle range, which was a considerable distance, even when they made their plan and started riding out and around, slowly and cautiously. They acted like hunters who had found their game and had discovered that it was a lot more than they had thought it would be. They never once dismounted to fire and they never once made one of those customary little skirmishing charges Indians usually made in the face of enemies. Cookie discouraged that, and so did Walt, although he fired less, and eventually, when he saw the depleted condition of Cookie's box of bullets, he growled at the cook for firing so often. Cookie promptly put his gun upon the ground, squatted there, and rolled a cigarette as though he were at his own wagon camp without a tomahawk anywhere near. He lit up and exhaled smoke and pointed to a particular Indian. "Mind that one, now. He's young enough to make one of those reckless charges."

Walt looked critically at the older man, but he had already said enough to irritate Cookie so he said no more, and he watched that particular buck. Even from that great distance it was easy to tell that this particular Indian was young, and that Cookie was correct; he was a genuine strong-heart. He made several sashays, brandishing his rifle in the air and screaming something unintelligible at the pair of embattled cowmen, and each time he did this, he seemed to Walt to be advancing a little closer, made bolder perhaps by the fact that the white men did not fire at him. Walt settled his rifle upon the ground, leaning upon it to watch as that young buck went through his bloody hand routine again. He said: "That damned fool's going to keep it up until he gets killed."

Cookie smoked and squatted and watched the surround gradually close. He ignored the young buck to say: "I'll tell you what I figure about this, Walt. Their rifles won't carry quite as far as our rifles will and they aren't nowhere nearly as accurate, but the moment they finish that damned surround and get off those horses and commence walkin' toward us with their horses in front of them, we're goners. They don't have to do much more than pump enough lead into this little spot where we're bottled up. Sooner or later they're goin' to hit us."

Walt did not need this dissertation to be aware of the Indian plan and its probable effect if it were allowed to be put into execution, but the surround was still a long way from being completed and meanwhile that young strong-heart out there was pushing his luck by making more and bolder little rushes, then riding slowly at a walk, his back to his enemies in great scorn. It was a very foolish enactment. Among the Indians it denoted great bravery. It also denoted among them great tragedy and Walt, who had never seen this before, could appreciate how courageous it had looked once, back in the days of bows and arrows, and how, now, in these later days of long-range firearms, it had resulted in so many pointless, futile deaths. He knew they could kill that young buck. Each time the Indian came closer, Walt, Cookie, and the other Indians were motionless. Once, an older warrior turned his horse to ride back but a couple of his companions growled at him and gestured until he went on back to his place in the surround.

Finally the young buck rode directly toward the squatting stockmen, rifle raised high, his head flung back in pride and challenge. He did not halt until he was so close, Walt could have shot him with a saddle gun, then he brought the carbine down one-handed to fire in the general direction of the squatting white men, and Cookie rolled flat out and took aim. Walt arose and deliberately put his Springfield upon the ground and faced the strong-heart with only his Colt, then he started walking forward. Cookie called sharply, and cocked his rifle. Walt walked a hundred or so feet, then called to the Indian.

"Get off your horse, put down your gun, and meet me hand to hand!"

The young buck was clearly startled. He had evidently believed his two enemies out there were quaking with fear of him. That only lasted a moment, then he slid off the horse, dropped his Winchester in the grass, and came forward. He was taller up close than he had looked to be in the distance; also, he was sinewy and had a spring to his step that only went with youth.

Walt was relying on something different; Indians were not good hand fighters. They never were and never had been. They were good warriors with weapons in their hands, but not without them. This buck finally reached to the outside of a legging and pulled a big knife as he advanced. Walt had a very effective counter to that. He pulled his six-gun and aimed it without pulling back the hammer. "Drop the knife," he commanded. "No knives, no guns." To prove he meant it, he dropped his six-gun.

The Indian halted, studied the gun in the grass, studied Walt, then flung down the knife, and came on, walking with a slightly toed-in, quick, panther-like stride. Walt had no illusions; experienced at hand fighting or not, this Indian was ten years younger, taller, and certainly more sinewy and snake-like. The Indian halted thirty feet away, made a careful, deliberate study of his cowman adversary, then gave a great shout of defiance and charged straight at Walt, but at the very last moment, when Walt cocked his right fist to fire, the Indian stopped, dropped down, and shot forward low, both arms extended.

Walt barely was able to side-step in time, and he had no chance to retaliate because the Indian came around ready for another of those bear charges with incredible speed. The Indian exuded confidence. He straightened up a little, this time, and wove back and forth to avoid that cocked fist. He went past in a blur and the last step he took was accompanied by a fast turn and a light slap that caught Walt across the face. The Indian came around again, and now he was fiercely smiling at the redness appearing across Walt's face where his stinging fingers had connected. He danced sideways, then dropped low, and charged again. It seemed the only way he knew to close with an adversary.

Walt made no attempt to strike the blurred silhouette this time; instead, he shoved out a booted foot. The Indian's moccasin struck that boot, the Indian lost his balance, and the moment he threw both arms ahead to break his fall, Walt went after him. The buck whirled even as he struck the ground. He had the agility of a snake, but what he needed was something more than lightning speed because Walt caught him coming off the ground with a jolting right fist, then crossed over with his left, and half tore the buck's jaw loose. As the Indian fell back, Walt stepped astraddle of him, caught hold, and hauled him up to his feet, then balanced him there, took his measure, and sank down one shoulder and let the Indian limply fall forward. With the strong-heart upon his shoulder, Walt turned and carried his senseless adversary out to his horse, pitched the body belly-down across the animal, then turned the horse, and led it out a fair distance and gestured for the nearest Indian to come get it.

The Indian rode slowly, warily, in close, his gun barrel never off Walt's chest. When he accepted the single rein of the strong-heart's war bridle, he said: "Dead?"

Walt looked at the blood dripping from the young buck's mouth when he answered. "No. No point in killing him. All he needed was a lesson. Take him away from here."

The buck looked around, then said: "He is the son of the war leader who started to ride over here."

Walt shrugged. "Just get him the hell away from here." He waited until the warrior turned to retreat slowly with the lead horse, then Walt turned and saw Cookie gesturing with both arms. Some of the Indians were withdrawing in the direction of the distant hills; some of them were sitting like stone statues watching as a big cloud of dust came toward them from the direction of Caliente. Walt saw all those mounted riders coming, and felt like breathing a prayer of thanks, but that was not what Cookie was gesturing about. There was a larger skiff of thin, sun-lighted dust coming from the northwest. A long double file of cavalrymen was coming down along the foothills.

Walt stopped to watch this second column. It looked to be arriving from the direction of the Indian encampment, and yet there had been no sign of soldiers earlier when he and Cookie had been there. He finally walked on back, picked up his Springfield, took the reins of his mount from Cookie, and leaned upon the rifle, watching and waiting. The Indians were finally withdrawing altogether. It would have been utterly senseless not to. There were not enough Indians to make a squad of the oncoming soldiers, nor a third of the number of whites coming upcountry from the direction of Caliente. Oddly enough, the soldiers made no move to interfere with the withdrawal of the hostiles. They, like the men from town, were riding directly toward Walt and old Cookie.

XVII

Walt's guess was correct. Those soldiers were coming from the direction of the Indian encampment, but neither Walt nor Cookie learned that until the townsmen arrived, one of them leading Cookie's horse. The gunsmith was with the town posse. He looked a little apologetic when he explained that, as soon as Walt and Cookie had departed from his building the previous night, he had gone at once in search of Town Marshal Reading with the story of what the pair of south-desert cattlemen were going to attempt, and at roughly the same time the column of cavalrymen had arrived in town, so Reading had passed all this information along to the captain in command, with the result that the soldiers had not even rested, but had struck out with a civilian guide from town to find the rendezvous. They had found it, this morning after sunup, and they had found the Indians in great confusion with their war leader, Joe Murray, dead, and one other white man dead beside him. The soldiers had then wasted about an hour rounding up all the clan leaders and laying down the law to them before they struck out on the trail of Cookie and Walt.

There would be no additional difficulty with the Indians, the captain reported to Walt and Cookie on the ride to town, and he did not seem willing to discuss either the killing of Dunagan, the Indian agent, or the other killings out at the encampment, but, when they finally reached town, both armed groups, soldiers and posse men intermingling, the officer, a red-faced, red-haired Irishman, looked steadily at Walt and said: "Your herd of cattle will be on the plain around Caliente by day after tomorrow, Mister Clanton. I suppose you'll be wanting to move right on to Wyoming?"

Walt nodded, understanding exactly that he was being told not to tarry around Caliente. "The day after they arrive and I get the bill of sale to 'em, I'll be on my way."

He and Cookie left the others and went along to Chad Reading's office at the jail house where the lawman stared balefully at Walt as he said: "I know why you did that. You didn't figure I could palaver with them, did you?"

Walt was tired and hungry and dirty, but he smiled now when he said: "Marshal, it's over. As soon as I get my cattle, I'll be on my way, you and your town'll settle back to normal, the Indians'll have their beef, and, if you're smart, when the replacement for Dunagan shows up out here, you'll meet the stage and tell him even before he sets foot on the ground that there won't ever be another beef allocation made within fifty miles of your town. And that'll pretty well end it, won't it?"

Reading motioned to chairs, and without answering leaned to rummage in a lower desk drawer. When he straightened up, he had a bottle of rye whiskey in his fist. He pried the cap off and handed the first drink to Cookie Weston. He seemed disinclined to speak for a while, as though perhaps Walt's side-stepping of his earlier comment had not set too well with him, but then Chad Reading was a somewhat complicated personality. One thing was clear. There would be no Indian uprising, no Indian raid or fight, and the reason for this change was that the renegade white man, who had fired up the Indians, had met with what Cookie refused to classify any other way than as an "accident."

That was the essential factor. Even the Army officer willingly accepted this, and after he heard Cookie classify Joe Murray's demise that way, the captain told a number of local people that his report would state that the renowned renegade and squaw-man, Joe Murray, had met with an accidental death.

By the time Walt and Cookie got out of Reading's office and went across the road in search of a meal at the hole-in-the-wall café both of them were beginning to have difficulty remembering where they had left their horses. As a matter of fact Arnie and Heber and Junior were at the livery barn when some soldiers led in their two mounts, and the cowboys immediately went uptown in their search.

They found Walt and Cookie at the café, dropped down at the counter on either side of them, and began bitterly denouncing them for having left Arnie, Junior, and Heber out of it. Heber was especially bitter. He said the whole thing had been his idea; they had not only left him out of it, had not only stolen his idea, but they had done it in the night like a pair of skulking darned redskins!

Walt listened, winked at Cookie who winked back, and, when the café man came with their meal, Walt told him to take the order of the other three range men, and this at least ameliorated the indignation a little. In fact, by the time the second load of food arrived, Heber was intrigued by the details; he had to be told exactly how Walt and Cookie had killed Joe Murray,

No one then or later, including the Army officer, the town marshal of Caliente, any of the troopers or the town posse men, or even Walt's own riders, ever called what had happened at the rendezvous murder. It *was* murder, but it was never categorized by that appellation until several generations had passed and those distant generations, residing in safety, security, and abundance thanks to men like Walt Clanton and his south-desert riders who tamed their land and made it productive, came along and condemned the killing of Joe Murray as a clear case of murder. In the day of Walt Clanton they knew better; they called it simply and more precisely what it was—justifiable extermination.

ABOUT THE AUTHOR

Lauran Paine who, under his own name and various pseudonyms has written over a thousand books, was born in Duluth, Minnesota. His family moved to California when he was at a young age and his apprenticeship as a Western writer came about through the years he spent in the livestock trade, rodeos, and even motion pictures where he served as an extra because of his expert horsemanship in several films starring movie cowboy Johnny Mack Brown. In the late 1930s, Paine trapped wild horses in northern Arizona and even, for a time, worked as a professional farrier. Paine came to know the Old West through the eyes of many who had been born in the previous century, and he learned that Western life had been very different from the way it was portrayed on the screen. "I knew men who had killed other men," he later recalled. "But they were the exceptions. Prior to and during the Depression, people were just too busy eking out an existence to indulge in Saturday-night brawls." He served in the U.S. Navy in the Second World War and began writing for Western pulp magazines following his discharge. It is interesting to note that all of his earliest novels (written under his own name and the pseudonym Mark Carrel) were published in the British market and he soon had as strong a following in that country as in the United States. Paine's Western fiction is characterized by strong plots, authenticity, an apparently effortless ability to construct situation and character, and a preference for building his stories upon a solid foundation of historical fact. *Adobe Empire* (1956), one of his best novels, is a fictionalized account of the last twenty years in the life of trader William Bent and, in an off-trail way, has a melancholy, bittersweet texture that is not easily forgotten. In later novels like *Cache Cañon* (Five Star Westerns, 1998) and *Halfmoon Ranch* (Five Star Westerns, 2007), he showed that the special magic and power of his stories and characters had only matured along with his basic themes of changing times, changing attitudes, learning from experience, respecting Nature, and the yearning for a simpler, more moderate way of life. His next Five Star Western will be *The Drifter.*